# THE ROCK OF KIEVER

Here are three classic short novels: *Range Jester*, *Slow Bill*, and *The Rock of Kiever*.

In *Range Jester*, Barry Home, once a spirited cowboy, now an ex-convict, returns to the small town of Loomis. His return is scarcely a welcome one, least of all by the rancher whose testimony secured Barry's conviction.

*Slow Bill* tells the story of Jim Legrange, who feels he can never live up to the success of his father, a millionaire rancher. He leaves home for an abandoned gold rush town, where he runs into Jack Rooney, an old prospector and a man claiming to have been the partner of Jim's father.

In *The Rock of Kiever*, the best friend of Charlie Stayn, a Texas Ranger, is killed during a raid. Charlie swears vengeance and defies the Ranger code, heading into the Kiever Mountains to track them down.

# THE ROCK OF KIEVER

## Max Brand®

**GUNSMOKE**

This hardback edition 2004
by BBC Audiobooks Ltd
by arrangement with
Golden West Literary Agency

ISBN 0 7540 8254 7

**British Library Cataloguing in Publication Data available.**

Printed and bound in Great Britain by
Antony Rowe Ltd., Chippenham, Wiltshire

# CONTENTS

# THE ROCK OF KIEVER

# *Range Jester*

"Range Jester" by Max Brand originally appeared in Street & Smith's *Western Story Magazine* (5/28/32). This story marks the second appearance of Frederick Faust's hero, Barry Home. The first story about him was "The Three Crosses" under the byline George Owen Baxter in *Western Story Magazine* (1/23/32) which has been collected in THE ABANDONED OUTLAW: A WESTERN TRIO (Circle Ⓥ Westerns, 1997) by Max Brand. In the short novel that follows, after three long years in prison that nearly made him crazy, Home returns to Loomis, having vowed to find the real perpetrator of the crime for which he was convicted—the robbing of a stagecoach.

# Chapter One
## "Horizon Trails"

Three men came over the horizon. The first came through the pass, the second, up the valley, and the third walked in over the flats from the direction of the railroad. All three were headed for Loomis, and one of them was to die before morning.

The man in the pass was Rance Tucker, flogging a pair of little mustangs in front of his buckboard that jumped and danced over the stones and the icy ruts of that trail. As he drove, he leaned forward in his seat a little, as though even that slight inclination of the body got him a vital degree closer to his necessary goal. He was a big man in his early forties, rawboned, with a weather-beaten face and a great crag of a jaw. As he came out of the mouth of the pass, he first looked apprehensively behind him, for he thought that he had heard the pattering hoofs of a horse galloping through the ravine. But that might well be in his mind; for days a dread had been gathering in him.

When he saw the iron-colored walls of the ravine behind him and nothing living between them, he flogged the mustangs again, until they bumped their hindquarters, switched their tails, and shook their heads in protest. But, according to the ways of their kind, they only lurched for an instant into a rapid lope, and then fell back to the dog-trot which was all they knew about a road gait.

Tucker forgot to whip them for a moment and stared down through the gloom of the winter evening into Loomis Valley. It was a heavy dusk, for the sky was sheeted across with gray, and long arms of shadow reached out of the heavens toward the earth, covering the mountains, obscuring utterly the level reaches of the desert, thronging over the lower end of the valley itself. There was the brittle chill of frost in the air, and before morning probably the ground would be covered with white. But the darkness only served

11

to make the lights of Loomis shine more clearly, a little bright cluster in the middle of the valley.

Rance Tucker sighed and nodded with reassurance as he made out the spot. He could remember when this had been Parker Valley, and yonder stood the town of Parkerville. But Parkerville had burned to the ground, and, when the ashes were hardly cold, before they had had a chance to blow away, in fact, Dave Loomis came along and bought up the entire site for next to nothing. It was only a crossroads little town, at the best, but Loomis built his hotel there, installing a blacksmith shop in a wing of it. He also found room for a post office and a general merchandise store. What more does a town need, except a barroom, which the hotel offered, and some sort of a dining room, which the same hotel possessed? So the hotel stood in place of the vanished town of Parkerville, and everybody was satisfied, particularly Dave Loomis.

That hotel was the goal of Rance Tucker. He had barely settled himself back in his seat and commenced clucking again to his horses, however, when he heard the sound of hoofs again behind him, and this time unmistakably. He looked back with eyes that started from his head. Like a ghost appeared the rider in the gloaming, but Rance Tucker, with a groan of fear, jerked the horse to a stand, pulled a double-barreled shotgun loaded with buckshot from beneath the seat, and, dropping low down, leveled his weapon, blinking rapidly to clear his eyes of the tears that the wind had brought there.

The rider came swiftly on, saw the gleam of the leveled gun, and jumped his horse far to the side with a yell: "Hey, Dad!"

Rance Tucker got up from his knees with a groan of relief. His big body began to tremble with weakness, now that the strain upon him was relaxed.

"Hey, you, Lew," he answered, rather feebly. "Whatcha mean by coming out like this? Your place is back there at home."

Lew Tucker reined his horse in beside the buckboard and scowled at his father. He was a huge man, only twenty-two, but already seasoned and hard; his strength was in full maturity as often happens when boys lead a life of constant activity.

"Lookit here, Dad," he said. "It's all right, you telling me to stay at home, but Ma wouldn't have me there."

"Whatcha mean? Wouldn't have you there?" shouted the father, relieving himself by falling into a rage.

"That's what I mean," said the young man. "You don't think that you been pulling the wool over the eyes of anybody, do you, the way you been acting for a couple weeks, do you?"

"Acting how?" asked Rance Tucker, with a little less vehemence.

"Acting," said Lew Tucker, "as though there was Injuns lyin' in wait in the next room at home or over the hill, when you're out riding. And staying up all last night, walking up and down . . . that's not deceivin' anybody, is it? There's certainly something on your mind, and you're drivin' to Loomis to get it off."

This assemblage of facts broke down the self-assurance of the older man. He said: "Look, Lew, you know that Barry Home is comin' back tonight, don't you? Tonight or tomorrow, he's sure gonna turn up, and who would wanta be alone on a ranch when that murdering devil comes back?"

"How d'you mean, alone?" asked the son. "Ain't you got me as well as yourself? Ain't there two hired men? Ain't four men enough to handle even Barry Home?"

"You think so, do you?" the father asked gravely.

"Four to one?" repeated Lew Tucker, as though the phrase was a sufficient answer.

"I got a wife and a son, and I got a ranch that I've made out of nothing with my own hands," began Tucker.

"Aw, wait. Don't go through all that again," pleaded Tucker insolently. "I know all you done, and how poor you and Ma were when you started the climb. Now, you tell me what you're gonna do in Loomis. Go and lie under a bed and shake for a coupla days, waiting for Barry Home to show up? Is that it?"

"Don't sass me back like that," commanded the father. "You think that you're a big, bold, rough feller, you do. But you don't know what Barry Home can do when he gets started."

"Well, and what could he do?" asked Lew Tucker. "He ain't more'n half my size, scarcely, and he ain't much older than me, only three or four years. And he's a damned jailbird, besides!"

"He's a jailbird," said the father. "And that means that he's gonna try to work out his grudge ag'in' me. He swore that he would be even with me, when the jury found him guilty. The judge and the jury, they all heard him."

"What I mean," said the son, "did you do dirt to Barry Home that time? Did you hide the stuff in his room, like he swears that you done? Did you plant it there to get him pinched, instead of you?"

"Lew, Lew, what you talkin' about?" exclaimed Rance Tucker.

"I'm askin' you a question."

"And you a son of mine!"

"I ain't saying that I'll let you down. No matter what you've done, you're my father, I reckon, and I'm behind you as long as there's any blood in me. Only, I'd like to know the truth."

"Was you in the courtroom when I give my evidence?" asked the father.

"It was three years back," said the son, "but I reckon that I could say every word over. Was it true?"

"Did I take an oath on a book before I talked that day?" asked the rancher.

"I reckon that you did."

"Is that enough for you?"

"Yeah, I guess that's gotta be enough, if you put it that way."

"Then go on home with you."

"I won't go home," insisted the son. "I wouldn't dare to. Ma sent me out to have an eye on you, and I'm gonna keep with you till hell freezes over."

Rance Tucker made a sound of vague discomfort and annoyance deep in his throat and struck his horses with the long whip. They jerked away into the dusk, with a clattering of the iron-shod wheels, and young Lew Tucker rode rapidly behind.

Up the lower part of the valley, that was still called Parker, as distinguished from Loomis, came another rider at this same time, as tall a man as either of the Tuckers, but with an air about him that suggested a foreign gentility. He was mounted on a horse of such obvious value that all the Tucker mustangs, their saddles, buckboard, harness, and guns together, would not have made half the value of that magnificent stallion.

The rider, taking the wind in his face as he came to the junction of Loomis and Parker Valleys, paused to adjust the silken scarf that he wore in place of a bandanna about his throat. As he paused, the wind turned up the wide brim of his sombrero, though it was stiffened and weighted with Mexican gold work, and showed for a moment a thin, sallow, handsome face, puckered a bit about the lips as though in great weariness, but with a reserve of fire gleaming in the eyes.

That was Tom London, known far and wide throughout the country, suspected of being a little light in his fingers and lighter still in his conscience. For he was a gentleman without visible means of support, but one, nevertheless, who was constantly able to do as he pleased. Moreover, nothing but the most expensive ever satisfied him. Some said that he was able to make all his expenses out of gambling, but others shook their heads. Though Tom London was a gentleman who gambled for high stakes, he seemed to lose even more than he won. There must be other sources of his revenue, and what could they be?

However, the question went no further than surmises, for Tom London was the very last person in the world of whom one would wish to ask questions, at least questions about himself. At the same time, his manner was the most amiable in the world, unless one crossed him suddenly, unexpectedly, and then danger peered out from beneath the straight, black brows.

He finished adjusting his neckcloth and rode on, just as Barry Home, walking through the desert sand, came within sight of the distant glitter of the lights of Loomis and paused in his turn to make a cigarette, light it with his back to the wind, and smoke it out while he remained thinking things over.

# Chapter Two
## "Jester of the Range"

It is not the easiest thing in the world to make a cigarette in the semi-dark; it is nearly impossible when a strong wind is blowing. Yet, Barry Home managed the thing with the most consummate ease, never glancing down at what his fingers were accomplishing. Neither did he have any difficulty in lighting the match, holding it for a moment in the secure round cup of his hands, and then opening the thumbs to get the cigarette in contact with the flame.

In this flash one could see his face. It was not the face that Loomis would expect to see. He had gone away as the buffoon, the good-natured jester of the entire range, and he was coming back with the roundness chipped away from his face. In fact, he seemed to be carved in a very different sort of stone.

He was the sort of man who would be described with difficulty. He had blue-gray, sometimes greenish, eyes; his hair was ordinary brown; his height was only a shade above average; there were no marks or scars on his face or on his body. In fact, the whole man could be summed up as average.

However, though Loomis would have been willing to admit that Barry Home was average in appearance, the community, of which town the hotel was the center, would have been the first to declare that there was nothing average about his mental equipment.

For that matter, when had there been a Home who was simply average? The grandfather of Barry had been one of those fellows who play the real Indian game. That is to say, you tag the Indians while the Indians are trying to tag you. You do the tagging with the point of a knife, or an ounce of lead placed in a vital spot. And Grandfather Home had done a great deal of tagging before the Indians finally put an end to the game and him. His three sons scattered to different parts of the West. One of them became a booster

16

of small towns and was wiped out in the fire that removed one of these towns from the map. Another started a gambling palace in Tucson and was said to have run it fairly and squarely. Nevertheless, an irate customer, whose roulette luck had been worse than his fortune in the mines, pulled a sawed-off shotgun from under his coat on a day, and emptied both barrels of it into Home. That left Barry Home, the third, the sole heir of the family name and the family fortune. The name was a wild one, and the fortune was nil.

Barry Home himself seemed to care nothing for the past and nothing for the future. He was content to ride the range, working here and there, a very good hand with cows, a better hand with horses. He was never offensive. His spirits were always high. Some people continually waited for him to show a spark of the old Home fire, but it never appeared, except in his jovial moments. The result was that half the range said that the old blood was burned out at last; the other half said that Barry Home, the third, was the best of the whole wild family.

Then came the day when the Crystal River stage was robbed of sixty-odd thousand dollars in hard cash and jewels, following which the trail of a rider from the point of the hold-up was traced back to the Tucker Ranch. The print of that horse was oddly like that of one belonging to Tom London. Tom was actually arrested, when suddenly Rance Tucker appeared and reluctantly confessed that he had seen his hired man, Barry Home, returning late on the guilty night, riding a horse whose shoes, in fact, were ringers for those worn by Tom London's Thoroughbred.

The sheriff jogged out to the Tucker place and searched Barry Home's room. He did not find much, only three gold watches and a single batch of currency. But what does a cowpuncher need with three gold watches, when he's working for fifty a month, or less, according to the season?

No one could tell, particularly the judge and the jury that heard the case, and Barry Home was sent to prison, but for only five years, though that state was hard on stage robbers. However, the boy was young; it was a first offense and, though he was threatened with a much longer term unless he would confess where the rest of the loot was hidden, it was a matter of record that he would not budge from his first story of innocence and complete ignorance of how the loot could have appeared in his bedroom at the Tucker ranch house. Nevertheless, he was given only five years by the judge, in spite of a furiously ranting district attorney. Good behavior in the prison, the special intercession of the warden, commuted the five years to three. And now he was out in the world again, a free man.

He had the clothes he stood up in. He had a dollar and sixty-five cents in his pocket. Otherwise, he had one handkerchief, and that was all. The young man, however, was optimistic. After he had stood there for some time, smoking out the cigarette and considering the distant gleam of the lights of Loomis, he dropped the butt on the ground, stepped on it, watched the little red shower of sparks blow away, and then stepped forward again, singing.

The angry wind tore the music from his lips and scattered it abroad, as it were, but Barry Home, undaunted, continued to sing. And his step was as light as a dancer's. As he came closer to the long double row of trees that led up to Loomis, he stopped and looked curiously up at their nakedness, barely visible in the rapidly gathering night. He was, like them, stripped of everything. They had lived for twenty-five years in the world, and so had he. Now they had come to a cold, naked winter. So had he. They were regarded by the world in the time of their need. And thus it was with him.

When he had come to the conclusion of these somber thoughts, he broke out into contented laughter and walked on again. It was plain that he was as good-natured as ever, and yet it was also plain that cheerful nature had changed a little during the three years he had spent away from Loomis and the range around it.

He reached the hotel. First, he stepped onto the front verandah, walked down the length of it, looked at the darkened windows of the store and post office, at the lighted ones of the lobby and sitting room, then turned back and regarded the pale gleam of the water in the troughs that hospitably bordered the whole length of the porch. Something made him dip a finger in that water. The cold of it bit his finger to the bone. He stepped from the verandah, rounded the hotel, and a great mongrel dog came running toward him, barking furiously out of the night.

"Hello, Tiger, you old bluff," said the young man pleasantly.

Tiger began to whine and sniff at the shoes of the stranger. He did not know the voice, to be sure, but he understood the familiar tone of one who feels that he is at home. Tiger was in a quandary. He began to growl again, when he saw this man walk up to the kitchen door and pull it open.

A thin drift of smoke and of fragrant steam blew out into the night. The young man stepped inside.

He saw Mrs. Dave Loomis, Gertie to the entire range, standing over the big stove in the corner, just now lifting the iron lid of a pot and, with a dripping spoon in one hand, peering through clouds of steam at the contents.

"Hello, Missus Loomis," he said with a smile.

"Hey! Hullo, there, Barry!" she cried.

She gave the metal spoon a fling into the sink, where it arrived with a great clattering. Then she bore down hugely upon the other and held out both hands, red and wet as they were.

"Barry Home!" she cried. "Now, I'm mighty glad to be seeing you, and since when have you started in calling me Missus Loomis, I'm asking you? Maybe I'm that old, but I don't want to feel it."

"Old?" he said, taking the moist hands with a hearty grip. "You're not old. You're just the right age, I think. But I've been taking lessons in politeness for three years, you know. I've learned to use names with a lot of care, I can tell you."

He laughed, his eyes shining with wonderful brightness and merriment. Mrs. Loomis sighed with relief, and nodded and smiled in return.

"Barry," she said, "I was thinking that maybe they'd put the iron into you, like they often do. There was that poor fellow Phil Dunlop, you knew him?"

"The killer?"

"Oh, he wasn't no killer in the beginning," said Mrs. Loomis. "All he did was to pick up a cow, now and then, just a wanderin' cow or a calf that didn't know where to go, and how could you be blaming a poor fellow with not much of a home, except of his own making? He never touched another man's horse! But they got hold of him, and they shipped him away to jail. When he came out, the spirit inside of him had changed, and he was mean. He was a nice boy, when he went away, but he was a gunman when he come back home. But you, Barry, they didn't do nothing to you. Not a thing! Except you're three years older. That's all. And I'm glad. I'm

19

mighty glad. Hey, Patty, come here and look at Barry Home come back to us! And just the same as ever he was in the old days."

The girl came out of the pantry with a bread knife in her hand. "Hey, Barry!" she cried, waving the knife.

"Dry your hands on my apron, Barry," said the cook. "I been and dripped all over 'em. Come along, Barry. Take a look at my girl, Patricia, will you? I'm a proud woman. Look what I've been and done with that niece of mine. You remember the skinny sixteen-year-old bit of nothing that she was when you went away? And now will you look at her? Just like Texas beef, after it's been fattened up all summer on our good grass. She's pretty, Barry, ain't she? Her eyes get bluer and bluer every year. The boys are dyin' for her, Barry, is what they are. And won't she be making the grand wife for somebody? She's a good girl and a handy girl, Barry . . . but she ain't quite settled down yet. She don't know whether she's a boy or a girl, or whether her place is in the kitchen or in the saddle. But my old man used to say many a time that a hoss that didn't need some breaking wasn't no hoss at all!"

# Chapter Three
## "Pantry Confidences"

Patricia had shaken hands firmly with the returned man and given him her best smile, but her eyes waited and dwelt on his face.

"Come here in the pantry and talk to me while I cut the bread and do something," she said. "Aunt Gertie, he wants some news, and that's why he's come in the kitchen way. Let me have him, and I'll fill him full."

"How should he be wanting news, when you've wrote him every week for three years, Patty?" asked Mrs. Loomis.

"Written news," said the girl, "is no good, because you can't make any faces in a letter. Come along, Barry."

He went into the big pantry and hoisted himself to the top of the cracker bin. There he sat with legs dangling, watching her swift hands at work. She looked at him rarely, giving him only her attention and her voice, and he was able to examine her with a tender curiosity and to nod with approval.

"I won't ask if you're glad to be back," said the girl. "I know how you feel . . . hard outside and hollow inside. Is that it?"

"Oh, no," he said. "I got over all the funny business in prison."

"You got all over it? You got all over what?"

"Foolish feelings."

"Ah?" she said. She lifted her head and looked not at him, but straight before her at her own thoughts.

"You were a good girl to write me once a week."

"And a whole year before the first answer came," she replied. She smiled a little ruefully.

"I told you why. Solitary."

"Solitary? Yes, but you never told me why they kept you in solitary confinement for a whole year. Isn't that a frightful lot?"

21

"It's a lot," he admitted. "They have a whole lot of hell there, besides. Rivers of it. You can get all you want there."

"Did you want it?" she asked.

"I confess that I was a little restless," he explained.

"Oh, was that it? Prying around? Did that get you into trouble?"

"Punching a few fellows on the chin started the trouble. Then I got the name of being a bad actor, and I was proud of that name."

"Ah, hum," said Patricia Loomis. She added: "Go on, Barry, talk, will you? You never told me about this. What happened? How did you get out of solitary?"

"They changed wardens, and the second warden didn't believe in solitary as a punishment."

"What did he believe in?"

"Double hours of work, heavier irons, a heavier sledge hammer, and plenty of beatings."

"Beatings?" said the girl, in a very quiet voice.

"Yes. They toughened me up quite a bit. I had a year of double work and short rations and plenty of beatings. It makes you thin, but it keeps you in wonderful shape. You sleep without any dreams, good or bad, when you're living that sort of a life."

"Ah, hum," she said. "But I thought that you had got out on good behavior, Barry."

"Well," he said, "they'd lengthened my term four times for me under the first two wardens. They had it up to about ten years. You never heard of the trials, because I didn't write about 'em. Then the second warden was changed, when the new party was elected . . . and a little over a year ago, the third warden came along. He was a different cut. He wasn't holding down an easy job. He was trying to do some good. He took the bad characters out of chains. He said they simply had excess energy, and they could use it to entertain the boys every evening with boxing bouts in the prison yard. He split us up into our weights. I was a middleweight, Patty, but I got the heavyweight championship finally. I took some whalings on the way up, but I got there." He laughed.

"Good old Barry," said the girl. But she frowned as she continued to cut the bread. "Go on," she commanded.

"Well, when I won the championship . . . that was six months ago . . . the warden made me his personal trusty, his bodyguard, d'you see? There was a terrible howl from the old trusties and all the old prison officials. They said it was rewarding crime and bad behavior. But the warden stuck to me."

"Ah, there was one white man, eh?" murmured the girl.

"White man? He was more than a white man . . . he was good luck to me. Then, one day, a crazy Swede tried to smash the warden's head with a crowbar . . . that was in the blacksmith shop. But he happened to hit my head, instead. So I went to bed and, when I got out of bed, the warden was at work getting all the sentences reversed, except the first one. He couldn't manage that. But he got me out inside the smallest limit of my sentence."

"God bless him!" said the girl. "But tell me this, Barry, isn't it true, when you were hit, that it wasn't by accident? You just chucked yourself into the crowbar's way, wasn't that the fact of the matter?"

"My job was to take care of the chief," said Barry, frowning a little, for the first time. "Now tell me about things around here in town. And tell me first what started you writing letters to me, Patty? We'd never known each other very well when I was here."

"It was like this," explained the girl. "Everybody always had a good word for you till you went away. After that, they began to shake their heads and say they always had . . . well, anyway, I thought that I'd write to you. And I did."

"You did," he said soberly. "You saved my life, Patty."

"No, I didn't do that much for you," she insisted.

"I would have gone crazy that second year," said Barry Home. "I was crazy, part of the time. But your letters kept coming every week. When I got out of solitary, imagine what a heap was waiting for me . . . fifty letters from you to read through! I used to read 'em over and over. I could see that you were growing into a sweet youngster and getting finer all the time. About the end of the second year, they took all your letters away from me. They did that!"

His voice had not changed greatly, there was simply a new, faint ring in it. But it made Patty Loomis turn sharply upon him and catch his wrists with her strong brown hands. He was still smiling about the mouth, but his eyes were sober and very bright.

"Don't, Barry," said the girl. "Don't act that way!"

"I'm not acting any way," he assured. "I said they took your letters away from me, that was all. There were almost a hundred of 'em. I knew 'em by heart, but I used to keep on reading 'em.

Nobody else wrote me any letters. Not a soul. But I could tell your letters one from another by the outside of the envelopes. Then they took 'em all away." Barry laughed a little. "That was not so good," he said.

She kept her hold on his wrists. "Good old Barry," she said. "I'll tell you one thing."

"What?"

"You've got to watch yourself."

"Have I?"

"Yes."

"How should I watch myself, Patty?"

"You know what I mean. You just keep a tight hold on yourself, will you?"

"You think I might do something violent. Is that the idea?" he asked.

"That's the idea," she admitted.

"Ah, but you're wrong, Patty," he said. "I'll never do anything violent that I can be checked up for. I'll never do anything more violent than to defend myself from danger. Oh, no, I've become the most careful man in the world. Believe that?"

She kept her straight, steady glance upon him. Then she shook her head. "Oh, Barry," she said, "they've hurt you right to the heart, haven't they?"

"Not that deep. They've just toughened my skin a little. I have a good, tough skin, now, believe me."

"I believe it," she murmured.

"Now, tell me what the picture's like here at home," he said.

"It's just the same," she answered. "I'd like to ask you a question that I never dared to put into my letters."

"You want to ask me if I robbed the stage?"

"Yes. I want to ask you that."

"I won't answer."

"It wouldn't harm you to answer."

He laughed cheerfully, again. "You see," he said, "I said under oath, at the trial, and I said it a good many times, that I was innocent, that I didn't rob the stage, that I didn't know where the loot was. But they chucked me into prison for three years. Two years of hell and one year of hoping. That was all. Now I talk no more about the robbing of the stage. And people won't wonder if I have money, even when I'm doing no work. There was over sixty thousand dollars in that job. I'm supposed to have it cached away, somewhere."

"Barry, what d'you mean?"

"I mean that I'm not going to work for a while. I've worked for three years hard, and now the world can work for me a while."

"There's only one way to get money without working," she said.

"No," he answered, "there are a whole lot of ways, and they're all honest, unless you're found out in the middle of the job."

She turned away from him, not answering.

"That's the way of it," he said grimly. "Does it make you despise me, Pat?"

"No," she said, her voice trembling. "I don't despise you, but I feel pretty sick. You go and talk to Aunt Gertie for a while. I'm going to cry, or something, and be a fool."

# Chapter Four
## "The First Run-In"

Barry left the pantry and went down the short hall toward the dining room and lobby just as the farther door opened and young Lew Tucker strode in, facing him. It was a narrow hall with a low ceiling.

Young Lew bowed his head a trifle to keep the lofty crown of his sombrero from touching the ceiling. When he saw Home, he stopped short and stared.

Barry Home walked straight on, pausing just in front of Lew and looking up to him with that faint smile about the lips and that gravity of the eyes that was now his habitual expression.

"Hello, Lew," he said.

"Why, Barry Home!" exclaimed Lew.

"That's me," nodded Home.

"Home," said Lew Tucker, "I gotta ask you something."

"Here I am for the asking," said Home.

"I don't mean no damn' joking."

"No, you don't mean any damn' joking, I suppose," said Home.

Calmly he looked the big fellow up and down. A red flag in front of a bull could not have been more infuriating than this attitude of detached indifference.

Lew Tucker raised his right hand. All of it was fist except the forefinger, that protruded, and that he now shook at the smaller man.

"Because," said Lew Tucker, "trouble is something that you might start around here, and that other folks would do the finishing of."

"Other folks are always apt to finish the trouble," nodded Barry Home, his smile unaltered.

"Are you tryin' to make a fool out of me?" asked Lew Tucker, his voice rising and turning as harsh as a rasp on metal.

"Oh, I couldn't do that," declared Barry Home. "Easy, there,

26

Lew. It looks as though you're trying to back me out of the hall. You mustn't do that. There's room for me to squeeze by even a great big man like you."

"I've got a mind . . . ," said Lew. And he turned his right hand into a complete fist by curling back the forefinger.

"You have a mind to what, Lew?" asked Barry Home, in the same amused manner.

"I gotta mind to sock you on the chin," said Lew Tucker. "I would, if you was my size. You're tryin' to make a fool out of me?"

"Now, Lew," said Barry Home, "you're a good fellow and a big fellow, but don't you think that you're making a mistake?"

"What kind of a mistake?"

"Taking a bite, when you don't know whether you can swallow it or not?"

"Oh, I dunno what you mean, except you mean that you need a licking," said Lew Tucker, "and I've a mind to give it to you. You damn', sneakin', mockin' jailbird."

"That's all right," said Barry Home, shrugging his shoulders. "You can't irritate me, Lew. I've had men talk to me, real men with vocabularies."

It was the final insult for Lew Tucker. Besides, he was on edge for just such a scene as this. He knew that his father was frightfully worried. He knew that the cause of the worry was this ex-convict, and he felt that any gesture he could make against Home would be against the common enemy of all his family.

So he made a half-step forward with his left foot, feinting with his left hand at the same instant, and then leaning his ponderous weight forward so that all of it came behind the whip of his right shoulder as he drove a long, straight right for the mouth of Barry Home. These were the tactics that had won for Lew Tucker many a stiffly contested school-yard fight. Over and over again, that feint had fooled the other fellow, and the heavy right had gone to the point. The mouth was the best target, he felt. For one thing, the lips were easily cut, and the taste of one's own blood and the sting in the numbness of the lips are disheartening. In addition, the punch is likely to stun the other fellow, so that a second and far heavier blow can often be landed with ease.

But it was not for nothing that Barry Home had fought his way up among the tough fellows of the prison yard, not for nothing had he fought thrice with Tiger Humphries, the ex-prizefighter, for the heavyweight championship of the jail. Twice they had fought out twenty desperate rounds to a draw. The third time, he knew the Tiger's tricks by heart, and a merciful umpire stopped the slaughter in the fifth round.

A fellow like Lew Tucker, big as he was, was merely a much easier target. Barry Home let the feint go. The serious purpose, he knew, was in the following right. When that punch came, he flattened himself against the wall and let it shoot past his face.

Lew Tucker bumped into a short right jab which was as solid as the projecting fork of a tree. It hurt his ribs and took his breath. He twitched to the side and, clubbing his big left fist, smashed it downward at the restless head of Barry Home. The smaller man stepped inside that punch and heaved all his weight into a flying uppercut that landed just under the chin of the big fellow.

Lew Tucker did not pitch back. His head jerked convulsively with the impact, then he fell on his face as though a trip hammer had fallen on the back of his brain. He lay still, with his arms stretched out before him and the fingers twitching. Otherwise, there was no movement.

Barry opened the door into the lobby. Straight before him he saw the sheriff, Bert Wayland, in earnest conversation with Rance Tucker.

"Hello, Tucker! Hello, Sheriff Wayland!" he said. "Won't you come and take a look at poor Lew, here? He's had an accident. He must have slipped and fallen on his chin. He's knocked out!"

Rance Tucker went back a full stride, as he heard that voice. His eyes opened and let Barry Home look deep into his soul, to see all that he had suspected that he might find there—stark, staring guilt.

However, Tucker ran forward into the hall, and Barry Home heard him exclaiming over the fallen body of his son. Then Lew Tucker began to groan and make feeble, kicking motions with his legs.

The other men in the lobby hurried forward to enjoy the scene, waving and nodding greeting askance to Barry Home as they went by him.

Only the sheriff remained where he had been before, and he said tersely: "Kind of like an entrance in a play, ain't it, Barry?"

"The villain's entrance, d'you mean?" said Barry Home.

The sheriff glanced quickly at him. "How d'you mean that?" he asked.

"Why, I always mean what's right. I never mean any offense," said the other.

Wayland thrust out his jaw. "I wanta talk to you, my friend," he said. "And I guess there's no better time for talkin' than right now."

"I can't think of a better time," said Barry Home, "except over a glass of whiskey. Step into the bar and have one with me?"

Wayland thrust out his chin still farther. "You've got yourself all polished up smooth and smart while you been away these three years, ain't you?" he asked.

"I've had a good deal of grooming and dressing down. I ought to be polished enough to shine, Sheriff," he said.

He smiled, as though expecting sympathetic comment from the other, but Wayland was only angrier than before.

"You wanta watch yourself and your step, now that you're back here," he said.

"In a rough country, a man always has to watch the ground under him," agreed Barry Home gently.

"What I mean," said the sheriff, "you wanta look out for yourself. Right now you been slugging Lew Tucker, have you? You're gonna try and ride the Tuckers, are you, because old man Rance told the truth about you and landed you in stripes?"

"My dear Sheriff," said the other. "I never pick a fight. I really never do. I've had enough fighting to last me the rest of my life. But I don't mind taking on the trouble that's brought to me by others. I dare say you know what I mean."

"You dare say that I do, eh?" said the sheriff, snarling and growing angrier as he listened. "You been and worked up your language a lot while you was away, did you?"

"I read a few books, if you don't mind," said Barry Home. "They had an excellent library at the prison. It wasn't a bad place at all, as a matter of fact."

Sheriff Wayland grunted.

"Perhaps you'll see it, some day," suggested Barry Home.

"Meaning that I'll be sent up, eh?" exclaimed Wayland. "Now, looka here, young feller, if you think you can start badgering me, I'll tell you this . . . I'm here to keep Loomis peaceful tonight. And peaceful is what it's gonna be. You hear me talk?"

29

"I hear you talk," agreed the other.

"Well, you keep right on hearing, then!"

"Thank you," said Barry Home, "I'll keep right on hearing, Sheriff."

"Mocking me, are you?" shouted the sheriff suddenly.

"Why, who am I to mock the sheriff of the county?" asked Barry Home, opening his eyes as though in smiling and polite surprise.

"I see your line," said the sheriff, crimson with anger. "And maybe . . . hey, Lew Tucker!"

Lew Tucker was on his feet, at last, looking around and settling his hat on his head with one hand, while with the other he fumbled at a small, bleeding place on his chin.

"Well?" muttered young Tucker.

"Did this gent jump you, Lew?" asked the sheriff. "Go on and tell us what happened. Breaking the peace is enough to slam folks in jail in this here neck of the woods."

But Lew Tucker, making no answer, his eyes darkly fixed before him, simply strode across the lobby. A minute later his footfall sounded heavily on the verandah outside, and he was gone.

# Chapter Five
## " 'Drink It Down!' "

Rance followed his son to the door which he jerked open, and, leaning out, bawled loudly: "Hey, Lew, Lew! Come back in here, will you?"

There was no answer from Lew Tucker, but from the night came the whistle of the storm, hooting like an owl in the distance and then whistling high and small, near at hand. A gust of icy wind entered and caught a paper from the floor, sending it hurrying in tatters until it flattened against the glowing body of the big stove. There the paper began to smoke, and Dave Loomis caught it up and folded it against his fat stomach, saying: "Now, Rance, just close that door, will you? It looks like Lew had had a kind of a fall, and he ain't likely to come back inside here and face all the folks for a while. I'm sorry about that, too, because Lew is a good scout. But you know how it is, when you're kind of proud. A young gent, he don't like to stumble over nothing and get a fall, not even over Barry Home."

Rance Tucker closed the door and turned about. His face was pale. Even in that instant the strength of the rising wind had blown a film across his eyes. Now, looking down, he brushed from his knees a few glistening flakes of snow. They turned to water at the touch of his hand. He flicked the drops away and shook his head, with the air of one who is striving vainly to solve a problem of immense depth and importance. When he looked up at last, his glance fell upon Barry Home and hastily jerked away from him, again.

The sheriff lifted his voice.

"What I wanta know," he said, "is did Barry Home jump Lew Tucker out there in the hall. If he did, I'm gonna do something about it!"

31

No one answered.

Wayland, with a shrug of his shoulders, growled out: "You've gone and turned yourself into a fox, have you, Barry Home? But foxes can't last long in a place like Loomis!"

"Of course not," agreed Barry Home. He made the gesture of one deprecating all hard feeling and withdrawing all opposition. "I told you what happened," he said. "Poor Lew just stumbled and fell on his chin. That's hard luck, and I'm sorry."

Dave Loomis went up to him and laid a fat, brown, red-backed hand upon his shoulder. "You go and be a good scout, will you, Barry?"

"Why, of course, I'll be a good scout," said Barry Home. "I've learned how you're punished when you're bad in this world, and now I'm going to be good. I'm going to work night and day to be good, of course. You would, too, if you'd had three years of the strict teaching that I've been through."

The whole crowd was listening to these words, as it gathered more and more closely to the stove. This was the first of the really cold weather. In the morning, they might awake in a white world, one that would stay white for five long months. Later on, they would grow acclimated to the cold, but now the drafts worked up sleeves and trouser legs and down inside neck bands like little fingers of ice. It was a moment when women could stop regretting that their work was over a hot stove; it was a moment when the hotel keeper seemed the luckiest man in the world. Some of those men would be out riding range in the dusk of the next morning, their horses slipping through slush or sliding on well-iced surfaces. They were down-hearted now, thinking about what lay before them, wondering why they had chosen this country to live in and how the summer could fly away so fast. So they gathered near the stove, edging toward it, turning their shoulders to the heat, stretching out furtive hands to it, as though it were a solid thing of value that could be stolen and kept in one's possession.

In the meantime, they listened to Barry Home's pleasant and excited voice, as he spoke to Dave Loomis and pronounced the values of a life in prison.

"Now, Barry," said Dave, "don't you go and laugh behind my back."

"He ain't laughin' behind your back . . . he's laughin' in your face," said the sheriff. "I dunno what I oughta do about him. I dunno but what I oughta lock him up, right now, and by the jumpin' Jiminy, I think that I'm gonna do it!"

"Why, I wouldn't do that," said the voice of one who had just stepped into the lobby from the barroom. That was the tall, elegant form of Tom London, his silken scarf adjusted neatly now, his clothes well brushed, his boots polished, his whole manner alert, genial, gentlemanly. He was smoking a cigarette, and the very way in which he flicked off the ash pronounced him to be a man of taste and of understanding.

The sheriff turned sharply on this man of strange and suspicious character.

"Are you turnin' yourself into a judge, Tom?" he asked. But his words were spoken in a complaining, rather than an insulting, tone.

"I'm not a judge," said Tom London. "But I remember that they always used to say in this part of the country, in the old days, that one never should kick a dog when he's down."

"That's good. That's right," said Dave Loomis. "Now, mix around, everybody. Step into the bar and everybody's gonna have a drink on the house, in honor of Barry Home getting back to us. Come on, Barry, and we'll lead the way."

With that, he took the arm of Barry Home, and so violently interrupted the argument and the wrath of the sheriff. The latter followed thoughtfully toward the end of the line. He found Tom London beside him, and muttered: "What would you be takin' his part for, Tom? You think that it ain't too late to make a friend out of him?"

"Oh, I'm not thinking about that," answered Tom London. "I don't so much care whether he's friendly or not. He's not apt to be so friendly, because he tried to put the blame for the Crystal Creek robbery on my shoulders. You know how it is, Sheriff. Men always hate the people that they've wronged. So I suppose he hates me. But that's all right. I can take care of myself, I hope, even when there's Barry Home about."

The sheriff looked curiously at his companion. He, in common with the rest of the community, had his doubts about London's source of income. Nevertheless, he was interested in the truth of the last remarks.

"He's changed," he said.

"Of course, he's changed," said London. "Prison changes men."

"Yeah, it changes every one of 'em."

"It doesn't often improve them, to be sure," said London.

"No, it don't," admitted the sheriff. "That's the bad part of it. You'd say that prison is a thing that had oughta improve a gent. If it takes him when he's bad and makes him worse, then what good is it?"

"Prison," said Tom London, "is like hammering in a blacksmith shop. You put the hot iron on the anvil, and then you beat it. Sometimes you beat too hard, and you crystallize it. Then it's brittle, and won't hold any edge. It breaks when it's most needed. But sometimes the hammering works up a perfect temper. I'd say that Barry has more of a cutting edge, right now."

"Every Home has had a cutting edge," muttered the sheriff. "I'm worried . . . is what I am. I'm worried mighty bad. I don't like the way that he looks. I don't even like the way that he smiles."

"Oh, that's all right," said Tom London. "He's feeling a little strange, just now. Everybody feels strange and upset when they come out of jail. That's only natural."

"Here we are having a drink to him. That's kind of funny," said the sheriff. "I dunno that I oughta drink to him, though."

"Do what the rest do," said Tom London. "That's the easy way out of everything."

He smiled as he said it, but the sheriff sighed. Sheriff Wayland was the most honest man in the world, and one of the bravest, but he was not exceedingly clever, and now, as he had admitted, he was very worried, indeed.

They filed into the barroom with the others. The bar was thickly lined.

Then, Dave Loomis said: "Fill 'em up, boys. There's the glasses, and there's the whiskey bottles. Help yourselves and fill 'em high. Speakin' personal, it's a good day for me, when Barry Home comes back. His father and his grandfather before him, I knew 'em both, and they knew me. Barry's had his bad luck. We all know about that, and there ain't any doubt that the best thing is to forget about it, and take Barry for what he was before ever anybody doubted him. Barry, I'm lookin' at you."

"Wait a minute," said Barry Home. He held up his hand. Every glass was frozen in place, most of them halfway to the lips, as

Barry spoke: "I want to say this, fellows. Dave Loomis is a kind man, and always was a kind man. I'm glad to drink his liquor and to drink to him. But I've got to say that I suspect a good many of the people in the room are not exactly friendly to me. That's all right. I don't expect them to be. But I'd simply like to know where I stand. If there's a single fellow here who doesn't feel that he's my friend or that I can be his friend, I wish that he wouldn't take this' drink."

He looked carefully about the room and a battery of eyes was turned upon the faces of Rance Tucker and Tom London.

Rance Tucker seemed to be in a quandary. He raised the glass, and he lowered it. He stared straight ahead of him, then flicked his glance to either side, like a speaker stuck for want of the right word.

In the meantime, however, Tom London said cheerfully: "It's all right, Barry. I suppose that you have some bad thoughts about me, but I have none about you. Here's to you! Here's in your eye, Barry Home!"

With a fine, flourishing gesture, he downed the glass of drink. Rance Tucker, with a sigh of relief, followed his example.

# Chapter Six
## "Frank Talk"

The delight of Dave Loomis overflowed. He beamed upon the entire company, his face reddening as he looked about him. While he cheered on the festivities, other men ordered drinks, the constraint disappeared from the faces of nearly all, and even the sheriff seemed to be relaxing.

As for Tom London, he walked up to Barry Home, and the latter met him in a corner of the room, smiling. Tom held out his hand. Barry took it instantly.

"I'm glad that you've done that, Barry," said the man of mystery. "After what your ideas were at the trial, I thought that there might be some black blood in your heart."

"Because you shifted the blame for the robbery on my shoulders?" said Home calmly.

"Come, come, Barry," said the other. "You don't stick to that point of view, do you?"

"Come, come, Tom," said Barry. "Where's your sense of humor? When you say that, can't you smile a little?"

They spoke quietly. People three yards away could not make out what was being said. The more vital the words, the lower the pitch in which they were spoken.

"You never explained your theory to me," said Tom London, his eyes frank and curious. "What is it?"

"Are you still riding the same horse?" asked Home. "The big dappled chestnut, I mean."

"The very same," said Tom London.

"The same one whose trail led from the place of the robbery of the Crystal Creek coach?"

"You mean," said London, smiling tolerantly, "that the horse's trail was like the chestnut's? There was the same barred shoe on

36

the near front hoof. The chestnut had a touch of frog, you know. Never bothers him now, but I keep the barred shoe on him, just in case."

"My theory is this," said the young man. "You and Tucker probably had your horses shod in the same shop here. Why not? Tucker's gray mustang with the barred shoe on the near front hoof and yours. That was odd enough to cause the two of you to comment on it. Now, then, when you heard that they were on the trail of your horse, after the robbery, you remembered the gray mustang that also had the barred front hoof. Isn't that simple?"

"So far it sounds simple enough, if it were true," said Tom London. "Go on, old son, I like to see the way your brain works."

"All right," said Barry Home. "I don't mind showing you just how my head works, Tom. My idea is this . . . as soon as you heard they were on your trail, you got hold of Tucker and made a proposition to him. If he would run the blame for the robbery onto somebody else, then you would give him a good split of the profits of the robbery. Maybe ten or fifteen thousand."

"Ah? Go on, Barry. You work it out so smoothly that I almost begin to believe that I must have done something like that," said Tom London.

"Of course, you did," said the ex-convict. "And then you easily worked out the details of the rest of the story with him. Nothing hard about that, I should say. In the first place, he got up in the middle of the night or early in the morning, to fit in better. He happened to hear a horse snort, and he looked out the window and saw the gray mustang being ridden into the corral. The corral gate squeaked. He waited there at the window and saw the rider clearly. It was Barry Home, the same Barry Home whom Rance Tucker had begun to hate because he lost so much money to me at seven-up, whenever he had a game in the evening. That's the story, Tom, and after the story was cooked up, you got Rance Tucker to stick to it."

"It's a good enough story," said Tom London. "I remember that your lawyer tried to work up your case along those lines, though, so I'm not surprised to hear it now."

"No, you're not very surprised," he answered. "I simply wanted you to know that I stand on the same ground, but more strongly."

"What's given more strength to your case?" asked Tom London.

37

"Why," said Barry Home, "haven't you looked into the eyes of poor Rance Tucker tonight?"

"What about 'em?" said London.

"They're as blank as the eyes of an owl at midday, but there's a little red glitter rising up in 'em from time to time."

"What does that tell you, Barry?"

"Why, that he's half crazy. That's what it tells me, Tom. What does it tell you?"

"Simply that he knows that Barry Home is a dangerous man to have for an enemy, and that he's going to watch you, to keep from being hurt. But you don't mean to say that you really still stick to the theory of the frame between me and Rance Tucker, do you?"

"Yes, I still stick to that."

"By thunder," muttered Tom London suddenly.

"Well?"

"I wonder if I have it?"

"Have what?"

"Why, the right theory, and I think I have, Barry. It's humped right into the middle of my brain, and I'll swear that it's right."

"Fire away."

"I'd better wait and try to work this up."

"Just as you please."

"Well, I might as well tell you what I'm guessing," said Tom London. "It's this . . . that Rance Tucker himself may have drifted over and stuck up that stage."

"Ah?" said the young fellow.

"That's what I mean. Think it over. It fits together well enough. Rance Tucker may have wanted a bit of extra hard cash. I never knew a rancher in my life who didn't need hard cash."

"He had some payments coming due about that time, but they were only for four or five thousand dollars," said the young fellow.

"That's all right. He couldn't have known that particular stage was so loaded down with gold, could he?"

"Go on," said Barry Home.

"Why, that's all there is to it. He's in a little pinch. He decides that he'll work himself out of it with a gun, instead of with mortgages and banks. So he takes the gray and rides over and turns the trick."

"I could understand that," agreed Barry Home, nodding his head.

"Of course, you could understand it. And Rance Tucker was a rough devil when he was a youngster. There are plenty of stories floating around about his work in the old days. Oh, in a pinch he can be a fighting man."

Barry Home nodded, but with a frown that carried no conviction whatsoever.

"Then," argued Tom London, "listen to the rest."

"I'm listening, all right."

"Why, the day after the robbery, he hears that they're on the trail of his horse with the barred shoe and that drives him crazy with fear. He decides that he'll hang the blame on you, because he doesn't like you. That's all there is to it."

Barry Home looked into a shadowy corner of the ceiling, like a man conceiving a distant and difficult thought. Then he shook his head again.

"Rance Tucker," he said, "is more the type of fellow who fights when his back is against the wall, or when he's half crazy . . . when he's drunk, say, or when he's pinched in a tight corner and can't get out. Then he could be a devil, I suppose. I saw him cornered by his big red bull in a field one day, and he laid the bull out by pulling up a loose fence post and slamming the bull over the head with it. He could fight, but he wouldn't go out to do a trick like the stage robbery."

"He was in a corner," said London. "He needed the money. That's enough of a corner to make him rob a stage, I guess."

"Maybe, maybe," murmured Barry Home. "I'm glad that you suggested it, at any rate, because I want to go over everything fairly."

Tom London suddenly narrowed his eyes. "You've got something on your mind, Barry, of course," he said.

"Yes, I've got something to do," said the other.

"Well, good luck to you."

"I'm going to tell you what it is, too," said Barry Home. "You've talked frankly to me, and I'm going to talk frankly to you."

"That's the straight thing to do," said Tom London. "Particularly if you've got something against me."

"Why, it's this way," said Barry Home. "I spent three years in the pen."

"Of course. I know that."

"And I went up for a job that I didn't do."

Tom London nodded. His interest was intense, so that his jaw set hard and his nostrils flared a little.

"Three years is a long time," went on the boy. "It's such a long time that I decided, while I was in prison, that I'd get the man or the men who had railroaded me."

"That's natural," commented the other. "I suppose every fellow in the same situation feels the same."

"And swore by everything holy that I'd never give up the trail."

"That's swearing by a lot."

"It is. And it means a lot," he replied. "And that's why I'm telling you, London. In spite of what you've said, I still think you may have had a hand in the job. When I find out the truth, if you're in it, I'm going to do my best to send you west."

"That's frank," nodded London.

"It is," agreed the young man. "It makes a square deal and a fair fight between us. If you can cover up your trail, good. That is, if your trail needs covering. Otherwise, I'll run down the devil who railroaded me, and I'll kill him. What happens to me after that, I don't care."

Tom closed his eyes as he nodded. "You mean business," he said soberly. "And I don't blame you. I'm thanking you for telling me that I'm still on the suspected list."

He held out his hand, and for the second time that evening Barry Home gripped it firmly.

# Chapter Seven
## "A Gesture"

London drifted to another part of the barroom. And Barry Home now had the attention of Dave Loomis himself. A big man was Dave and fairly well blocked the eyes of Barry from the rest of the room, yet, with side glances, he managed to keep track of the movements of the others in the place. Prison experience helped him here, the sort of experience that enables a criminal, at one of the long dining tables, to catch the attention of another criminal with a single glance, and then to carry on a complicated conversation by means of signals made with the head, gesture of the hand, and a few significant words tapped out in a code with a spoon against a plate or a cup, all done in the most haphazard way imaginable. With the farthest corners of the senses, as it were, Barry Home had learned to note matters in detail, though with the most inconsiderable glance of the eyes.

It seemed to Dave Loomis that Home was giving him his full attention, but, as a matter of fact, he was studying all the crowd, either from side to side, or with glimpses over the shoulder of Loomis into the long mirror that extended down the bar. It was in that reflection that he saw Tom London pass Rance Tucker, far down the room, and let his arm graze against the side of the rancher.

Rance Tucker paid no heed apparently. But surface indications are another thing that convicts learn to disregard. When, a moment later, Tucker finished his drink and left the room, Barry did not hesitate.

He walked out into the lobby in time to see the broad back of Rance Tucker disappearing through a door that led onto the side verandah. He could not directly follow without calling too much attention to himself, because every man in the room was sure to be aware of the bad blood that existed between himself and Tucker. But why had Tucker gone out there into the whirling snow of the storm?

The cold was growing momently more bitter. The draft that flowed under the doors and across the floor was like a stream of ice water. People were continually shifting their position and shrugging the shoulders of their coats into different wrinkles. Why should Rance Tucker step out of the hotel to the southern verandah?

Well, there would be shelter, here, from the full blast of the wind, for one thing, more than on any other side of the house. In addition to that, it was the side nearest to the stable. If a man were suddenly to decide to go out and hitch up his horses, he might go either through the back hall and around the corner, or straight over the southern verandah.

Barry passed through the hall that led in such a narrow compass past the dining room. He would have avoided the pantry, but, as he was stepping by it, the door flew open and the girl, with a loaded tray, stepped out before him.

When she saw him, she came to a halt, with her head held stiff and high and her eyes darkening soberly at him.

"Barry," she said, "are you getting ready to raise the devil around here?"

"I'll never raise the devil again," he said. "I'll never be breaking the law, Patty."

He would have taken the weight of the tray from her. She shook her head and frowned to warn him to get back.

"I don't trust you, Barry," she said. "You've started on poor Lew Tucker, already."

"Why," he asked, "you know how that happened, don't you?"

"Yes, I know," she answered gloomily. "He tripped and fell down on his chin. Wasn't that just it?"

"You could believe it, if you wanted to," he responded.

"Show me the backs of your hands," she commanded.

He held them out obediently.

"How did you get that welt across your fingers, just in front of the knuckles, Barry?" she asked.

"As I was walking down the road," he said promptly, "I was swinging my hands to make the walking easier and keep up my circulation. You know, the wind was cold."

"I know the wind was cold," said she, eyeing him carefully.

"As I was swinging my hands, this one whacked across a stripped branch that was sticking out of some shrubbery."

"Where did it happen?"

"Down at the beginning of the trees."

"The shrubbery's on the left down there, coming this way," said the girl.

"Perhaps it happened farther up toward the hotel," he suggested.

"Perhaps," she answered. Then she added: "Look here, Barry, whatever else it was, it wasn't good sense to tackle Lew Tucker. It let everybody know that you're on the warpath. If anything happens, you're going to be jailed for it. Anything!"

"I know that, and that's why nothing is going to happen."

"Oh, Barry," murmured the girl, "you're going to smash things up, I know. You're going to ruin your own life, for one thing."

He slid a hand under the tray and took the weight of it. "I'm not going to break the law," he insisted.

"But what are we going to do?"

"Make an easy living."

"Easy livings are not honest. That's the fact of the matter."

"Look at the way your Uncle Dave lives here," he said. "That's both easy and honest, I'd say."

She shook her head at him, frowning with pain. "You don't mean that sort of living. I know that you don't."

"I've made up my mind," he answered. "You see how it turns out."

"I feel pretty sick about you, Barry," she replied.

At this, the faint smile disappeared utterly from his face.

"Pat," he said, "do you give a rap?"

"I give several raps," she said and nodded.

"Really?"

"Yes."

"You mean that you . . . that you . . . well, that you really care about me, Pat?"

"Why should I say so?"

"You shouldn't. I know that you shouldn't." Then he added: "I told you that there was a time when your letters were the only thing that kept me from going crazy. I meant that. I mean it, now, when I say that, if I could put the world in a balance, with you on the other side, you'd outweigh the rest of the world for me, Pat."

"You were always a good, friendly sort of a liar, Barry," she answered.

"Don't you think that I mean it?"

"Not a whack."

"I tell you, it's true."

"Prove it," she said.

"There's a tray between us," he said. "Otherwise . . ."

"I don't mean foolishness. I mean, you really step out and prove it, Barry . . . will you?"

"What sort of a reward is there at the end of the trail?" he asked her.

"There's that better half of the world that you were talking about a while ago."

He straightened to his full height, his shoulders hunched a little forward in the attitude of one prepared to receive the shock of a very heavy blow.

"You're talking about yourself, Pat?"

"I'm doing that. Are you interested?"

"Give me a chance to prove it, Pat. That's all I ask. Except that I'm a dog, if I let you care about me now."

"I wrote to you for three years because I thought you were getting a bad deal," she told him. "I thought you were the underdog and that your life was ruined. Then you came back here tonight, and I could tell from one look that your life wasn't ruined. No, no, you are a lot more apt to dig in and do some ruining on your own account.

"I liked you before, and now the trouble that I feel on account of you, Barry, is aching away inside me every moment. If you honestly wanted me, you could have me in a minute, Barry. I'd go around the world blacking your boots. I'm not proud. But if you want me, you've simply got to go straight."

"What do you mean by going straight?" he asked her.

"Being an honest man in the eyes of God and yourself. What do you mean by going straight?"

"Never bringing myself to the attention of the law. That's what going straight means to the rest of the world."

She shook her head. "I knew that it was something like that. You've been hurt, and now you're going to pass the kick along. Give me the tray at once, Barry."

"Are you going to walk out on me like this?" he asked her.

"I'm not walking out on you. It's only that I saw the poison in you, that's all. If you're not honest, Barry, I wouldn't follow you around the world. I wouldn't follow you one step. Not if you were the king of England!"

"Sunday school stuff rubs out and wears thin, before the finish," he said.

"This idea of mine won't rub out and wear thin," she assured him. "It's as close to my heart as my blood is."

"You're thinking of children and all that, eh?" he asked her.

"That's what I'm mostly thinking about," said the girl. "Let me go by, Barry."

"Wait one minute longer," he pleaded.

"Well?"

"I'm going to think over what you've said," he declared.

"You say that you'll think it over. But you don't mean it. You've made up your mind already. Somebody's going to die for the years you spent in jail. Rance Tucker or Tom London, perhaps. I know what you have in your mind. Everybody knows, for that matter."

He sighed, and stepped back. "You think you're walking out of my life, Pat," he said. "But you can't. If you care a whit about this jailbird, he's going to keep you caring."

She uttered a short exclamation and hurried past him down the hall.

# *Chapter Eight*
## *"In the Barn"*

There was in Barry Home a cold devil that had been born three years before and nourished by the brutal cruelty and injustice he had received during the intervening time. It was generally the topmost spirit in his breast, but now, for an instant, it shrank down and died within him, and all that was kind and warm-hearted in him sprang alive.

He had almost cried out to her. If he had done so and she had turned to show him the suffering in her face, he would have been changed forever. But he did not cry out. He saw her push open the swinging door of the dining room, and again he strove to speak, but again the devil in him throttled the words, and they were unspoken. As the door swung shut behind her, making a faint moaning sound upon the rusting hinges, he sighed. With that sigh the kindlier impulses died out of his heart, and left it cold and calm again.

She was gone from his sight. Yet, for a moment, he laid his hand against the side of the wall and considered. It seemed to him that he could see her more clearly than ever, not only face and body as they were, but as if through a veil of glowing flesh and blood, the whole spirit and all that he saw of her was gentle and true, brave and womanly. Yet, the impulse that already had been mastered in him once would not master him again so quickly. He turned down the hall once more.

His business was not with women, no matter how fine they might be. His business was what he had promised himself that it would be, one day in the frightful darkness of the solitary cell, when he was eating out his heart. No—the truth is no heart was left in him on that day when the dark, cold panic of the grave had overcome him in a rush, and he had wished to fling himself at the door, screaming for mercy, for help, and for freedom, one glimpse of the fine, pure light of the day!

Then, when he had mastered that desire to surrender, as he grimly took hold of himself with the last iron atom of will power that was left to him, he had gone down on his knees and promised that he would do certain things when his term expired, if that time ever came.

During the remainder of his imprisonment, every trouble was easier to bear, even when he looked forward to a prolonged term, for he felt that he had been to the bottom of the pit, and that, thereafter, nothing could wring the sinews of his soul as they had been wrung before. To him, the promise of what he would accomplish when freedom came was like the hope of spring in the dim, cold heart of winter.

So that unforgotten moment came back over him again and, turning down the hall, he went swiftly to the back of the hotel and out through an entrance not far from the kitchen door. As he stepped into the open, the wind cut at him with a saber stroke, its cold edge penetrating to the nerve and the bone.

But what of it? Very little, indeed, to a man who had been manacled in a blizzard with a twelve-pound sledge hammer to swing to keep himself warm and with a rock pile to use his energy upon. He merely shrugged his shoulders, rested his head for an instant against the wall, already snow-encrusted, and looked out toward the barn. There was one dim light glowing in it, showing through the cracks around one of the windows. If he followed that light, perhaps he would find Rance Tucker. And might not Tom London be with the rancher?

He went at a run, sprinting lightly along. And so he came to the corner of the barn and paused, with the wind beating about him. There was not much snow falling, and that was so very dry that it shook off from his clothes at a shrug of his shoulders, but it added to the biting cold of the first winter blizzard. There was a sliding door at either end of the barn, as he knew. But he could not risk pushing open the one nearest him. Little by little, he worked it back, but only a fraction of an inch. Then, staring through, he made out suddenly the face of Rance Tucker, not a yard away.

He almost cried out in his astonishment and bewilderment at this sudden apparition. Looking again, he saw that Rance was alone, sitting upon the grain bin, whittling long, thin slivers from a stick of wood and scowling thoughtfully at his work. Beyond him extended the long line of horses in their stalls, a dozen of them, at least. What was the meaning of this lonely vigil of Rance Tucker?

Barry could not enter the barn on this side to find out, and, if he remained there in the open to spy on the man, he would soon be frozen. He ran to the other side of the barn, pushed open the other sliding door a little, and looked into the thick, solid velvet of utter darkness. That was what he wanted, and, slipping inside, he pushed the door shut behind him. Then, closing his eyes, he tried to remember exactly what this side of the barn had been like in the old days. It might have changed in the interim, but, as it was before, there had been horse stalls part of the way and other stalls at the farther end where cows were kept in the bitterest of the winter cold. At each end, crosspieces nailed to big uprights that fenced in the mow led upward to the top of the mow. Yes, he could remember all of that very clearly.

Ahead of him, he heard horses stamping and snorting as they worked their muzzles deeper into the feed of the mangers—wet horses, for he could detect the unmistakable odor. Feeling down the wall to his left, he reached the side of the mow and presently located the ladder that led upward. Up that he climbed, with the hay bulging out and scratching him as he worked on. But now there was vacancy before him. He reached out, probed empty space, and found that he had come to the top of the hay.

He stepped from the ladder, and sank to his knees in the soft fluff. It was sweet to his nostrils, and the place was gratefully warm, as though some of the heat of the long summer had been harvested and kept there with the hay to prepare for the savage length of approaching winter. He was not conscious of a light at first, but, standing quite still for a moment, he finally was able to make out a dim glow from the farther side of the mow. That would be the lantern that was burning there, giving Rance Tucker enough light for his whittling that was now being so very thoughtfully conducted.

He began to cross the top of the mow, but presently collided with something that barked his shins. He fell forward, and hard, cold iron slithered up the side of his neck. Lying still, feeling about him, he discovered that he had tripped over a big pitchfork, left lying on its back with spear-pointed, tiger-toothed prongs sticking up two feet and a half. One of them might have passed well enough through his throat; one of them might have glided easily through his heart, and that would have been the end of his endeavors in this world.

He sat up, after a little time, and smiled faintly in that darkness. It was a very odd world, to be sure. The dangers that are plotted with human cunning may be far smaller, indeed, than the dangers that are cast in one's path by chance. At last, he stood up and went forward again. His feet accustomed themselves, as of old, to the art of walking in deep hay, which consists of taking short steps, as when walking through soft sand and waiting for the resilient rebound of the compressed hay to lift and help one forward. He smiled again, remembering how he had worked, on a time, stowing away hay in that very barn.

Patty Loomis had been a mere youngster of eleven at that time, and hardly worth the notice of a fully matured man sixteen years old. He had been very proud to work with experienced laborers making hay. He had been praised, most of all, for his willingness to work on top of the stack inside the barn and stow it away under the roof, with no breath of air stirring and the dreadful heat of the sun pouring through the shingles of the roofing above him. He had been praised for that. He smiled as he remembered the big Irishman who, leaning on his hay fork, had called to the others.

"Look at Barry, now, will you? He's a whale, when he gets on the end of the pitchfork, is what he is. For the size of him, I never seen such a lifter!"

Oh, they had worked him hard enough, in those days of his youth. Yet it had been a pleasant time for Barry Home. How he had gloried in the excess of his strength as he never would glory again until that happy day when his hands were on the throat of the man who had engineered his trip to the prison—Rance Tucker or Tom London, one of that pair, or both! He hardly cared which.

Then, stepping on, he came close to the edge of the mow. It was difficult to come to the very side of it, for the hay on top of the mow, being the loosest, was very apt to slide beneath a weight, and might throw him down into the mangers below, a most excellent way of breaking bones. So he lay down flat and, inching forward, at last was able to part a projecting tuft of the hay and stare down at the scene beneath him.

Rance Tucker had not moved apparently. The heads of the horses were almost entirely lost in the shadows made by the stall partitions. One of the mustangs, perhaps outworn by a long day's work or else a very fast eater, was lying down already. Then the sliding door of the barn opened, and Tom London stepped inside.

# Chapter Nine
## "Thieves' Conference"

"Thought you'd changed your mind about coming out," said Rance Tucker. "Wasn't it here that you said meet you, in case there was a need of us talking?"

"I said the woodshed," said Tom London, "but, when I didn't find you there, I came on out here."

"Well?" said Tucker.

"Nobody else around here?"

"Nobody," said Tucker.

Tom London lifted his head and looked straight at the spot where Home was lying at the edge of the mow above him.

"A barn is a damned silly place to talk in," he said. "A thousand men could be hidden away within earshot of us."

"Yeah, and who would be hidden away on a night like this with the Loomis stoves going so fine and the Loomis whiskey so good?" asked Rance Tucker.

"One man would," answered Tom London.

"You mean the kid?"

"He's not a kid any longer," said London.

"Aw, damn him!" said Tucker. He shut his knife with a click. "I'm tired of thinkin' about him," he concluded.

"So am I," said London.

"Well?" asked Tucker.

The out-thrust jaw made his head tilt back a little, so that Barry could examine his face more clearly. It was not an ugly face, really, but a face that showed hard endeavor and a strong will, yet unbroken by life. He seemed to await suggestions.

"You saw me talking to him?" asked London.

"Yeah, I seen you, and you seemed to be having a good time out

50

of it. I wonder what he did to Lew? How'd he manage to handle Lew, I wonder."

"He's strong," said London. "I tell you, he was a soft kid when he went to prison, but he's had three years of hell. You can see the whole of the three years in his eyes, if you look."

"I looked into 'em, right enough," declared Tucker. "There wasn't no other place that a man could look. It was like facin' a double-barreled shotgun, I tell you."

"Worse," said London. "A lot worse. And he'd kill quicker and more surely than a double-barreled shotgun, too!"

"I'll put my faith in a shotgun even ag'in' Barry Home," said Tucker. "I wonder what he could've done to Lew?"

"Why, hit him out of time, that's all. Lew didn't stop to argue. He just left."

"He'll be back. He's got pride, that Lew of mine has," declared the father gloomily. "And he'll be back, mind you, London. You can bet on that."

"I'm glad that he's coming back," said London. "But he's young, Rance."

"He's young, but he's a man."

"Nobody's a man till he's thirty," said London, with conviction, "or until he's had a few years in prison, some place."

"You got both of them advantages, maybe?" asked Tucker, with a twisted grin.

London looked down at the other without answering, and, although his face was utterly in shadow, Barry could guess that he was smiling.

"This is pretty far West to be asking so many questions," said London.

"Maybe that's true," said the rancher. He added: "What was you talkin' to Barry Home so hard and fast about?"

"I was trying to change his mind for him."

"Change his mind about what? About you being the robber?"

Tucker actually laughed, and, as he listened, the mirth ran like a freezing poison through the body of the listener.

"That wasn't his idea," said London.

"No?"

"No, it wasn't."

"Couldn't the young fool see that?" asked Tucker.

51

"He couldn't. He's had three years to think everything over, and that's too long for a brain of his sort, I suppose."

"He's got a good enough brain to handle Lew," scowled Tucker, unable to forget his son's unhappy experience. "What's his idea?"

"That you turned the trick by yourself."

"Is that what he thinks?"

"Yes, that's what he thinks."

Barry Home listened with interest to the lie. He could see the point of it clearly. A queer sense of omniscience came over him, and he began to guess that his theory about the robbery had been entirely accurate.

Rance Tucker slid from the top of the feed box and stood shaking his fist at the air—also, in the direction of the man he was cursing.

"Damn that fool," he said. "Why would he think that I'd do a thing like that, and me a respectable rancher and everything?"

"He was working for you, then."

"A lazy, worthless hound he was, too," commented Tucker.

Again the listener smiled. Nothing is right about an enemy, he had learned long ago, and with pleasant contempt he looked down on the face of the big man.

"He knew you needed money, that you had debts."

"I had some debts. I had land and cattle for 'em, too!"

"Stolen money would pay 'em off as well as the land and the cows, and you'd miss that kind of money less. That's what you used, after all."

"Not then. I wasn't such a fool. I sold cows. But the next season, I bought back twice as many." Tucker laughed gleefully. "I covered my steps all the way. That's what I did."

"This is the idea of Barry Home," said London. "He thinks that you needed the coin, and that you planned the robbery, and put it through. Then you framed him, when you heard that the search was for the trail of a horse with a barred shoe on the left forefoot. That would bring the hunt pretty close to you, perhaps. You took no chances. You sprang the story to the sheriff. You talked about looking out the window and seeing him ride in. Then you planted the loot in his room."

"Well," said Tucker, "he was bright enough to guess part of it, anyway."

"Yes, he was bright enough. He's no fool. That's one of the things I wanted to tell you."

"Well, when was any Home ever a fool, when it came to making trouble for their betters?" said Tucker, with a snarl. "Is that all he said?"

"No. The most important part is coming."

"What is it?"

"He told me that he wanted to give everybody a fair warning. He warned me, because he said that he once suspected me. He'll warn you before the evening's over."

"Of what?"

"That this is a death trail. He's going to kill the man who sent him to the pen. He's sworn to do it. He told me that of his own free will."

"He wouldn't tell you that . . . he wouldn't put a rope around his neck, in case he . . . he managed something," muttered Tucker.

"You never spent three years in prison. It makes a little difference in the way a man does his thinking and his acting. If he can kill you, Tucker, he'll die happy."

"And let you out, eh?" said the rancher.

"Never fear. I'm standing by you, man," said London.

"I think you are," said Tucker gloomily. "You're standing by me. What's my interest is yours, in this play of the cards."

"But you were paid for your work," said London. "You held me up for half of the whole loot."

"Held you up? Wasn't I taking half the risk, then, by covering you up?"

His voice rose high in the argument. "You took your half of the risk after the stage was robbed," assented Tom London. "But that's over and done with. I don't talk about spilled milk."

"Anyway," said Tucker, "I never cashed in on my whole half."

"Why not?"

"There was the diamond stickpin and the woman's necklace, the pearl one with the diamond clasp. I didn't know how to sell 'em. If I went to a pawnbroker, he'd cheat me. Besides the things were pretty well advertised through the papers, d'ye see? If I tried to get rid of 'em, I might be spotted. And then the goose would be cooked."

"So you still have 'em?"

"Yeah. I still have 'em. Five thousand dollars' worth of stuff, and more, according to what the papers printed about the missin' articles."

"Where do you keep them, Rance? In the bank?"

"You'd like to know, eh?" asked Tucker, sneering. "But I don't keep 'em in the bank. Never mind where I do keep 'em. No man would find where I've put 'em, and yet . . . ." He broke off with a laugh of triumph. "And yet," he said, "it's an easy thing to find 'em, too, for a man that knows." He laughed again.

"All right," said London. "I'm not planning to rob you, Rance. I don't go after small things like that. It's not my game."

"Five thousand bucks is small to you, eh?"

"Yes. And now, about young Home."

"That's what I wanta talk about. If he's on a blood trail . . . and I would've guessed it before . . . are we to let him run with his nose to the ground till he finds something out?"

"No," said London. "We're not! We stop him."

"When?"

"Tonight."

"With what?" said Tucker.

"With a bullet through the brain," said Tom London.

# *Chapter Ten*
## *"The Moving Hay"*

Tucker showed not the least emotion, when he heard this announcement. He merely began to nod and to frown. At last he said: "In the hotel, eh?"

"Why not?"

"That's as good a place as any," said Tucker. "But it's kind of clumsy. I mean, there's so many chances of other folks hearing and seeing."

"The hotel is the best place in the world for me," said the robber. "I've worked it before, Rance, as you ought to guess. I know every corner and nook of it, and I have a few passkeys that will open every door in the place, and not a sound heard." He made a gesture of confidence, as though the matter were already accomplished. "Nothing could be better for me," continued Tom London. "No matter where he may sleep in the hotel tonight, I can open the door for you, Rance."

"Open the door for me? Open the door for yourself!" exclaimed Tucker. "Why should I do the job?"

"Because he's after you."

"Bah," snorted Tucker. "He'll be after you, too, before he's done. It's your job as much as mine. It's more your job, in fact."

"Why?"

"Robbing and killing is your business," said the rancher.

"It's yours when you need it . . . you can rob and kill in a pinch as well as anybody, Rance," said Tom London angrily.

"Can I?"

"Look, man, look," protested London. "I know all about you. I know everything that you've done. I had to find out everything. And I have found you out. I had to have a hold on you, in case of a pinch. Well, Rance, you know what you've done in the past."

"What have I done?" asked Rance Tucker, half sullenly, half defiantly.

"D'you want me to go all through the yarn of what happened to young Barnefeld?" asked London.

The rancher was silent, staring, and again his jaw thrust out, but he did not speak.

"It's all right," said London. "How you got your start in life doesn't make any difference to me. Not a bit! It might interest other folks, but not me, so long as you play fair and square with me, Rance, and never are tempted to turn state's evidence, say, or some little trick like that."

"I'm not that kind of a sneakin' hound," declared Rance.

"Of course, you're not," replied London, "but I don't want you to change. And I suppose this is the reason why I'm no fitter than you are to do the job on that young fellow tonight."

"Listen. I'd like to know how you found out about Barnefeld," muttered Tucker. "And that's not admitting that I had any hand in it."

"Nobody would have thought of looking up that old story," said London. "Nobody except those that already knew you had stepped a little on the shady side of the law. I knew that already, so I looked back and found out fast enough that, just after Barnefeld was robbed and murdered, Mister Rance Tucker began to look about for a small piece of land to buy. Then I got on the trail and went to the shack that's still standing at the corner of the Berryville Trail and Chester Road, and down in the cellar I found. . . ."

"Wait a minute," said Rance Tucker huskily.

"All right," said London. "I don't want to talk about it, either. Looking at that by match light, in the middle of a howling night as bad as this, made my blood curdle, all right. I don't want to talk about what you've done in the past. But I want to point out that you qualify for this job tonight as well as I do."

Tucker answered: "You've kept your hand in, London. You're surer than me with a gun and, from your own account, him that tackles Barry Home, he'd better be damn' sure with his weapons."

"True," said London. "The best answer is, we open that door and go inside together. I'm going to take my revolvers, Rance. I'll carry the lantern in one hand, and you can get the riot gun out of the store. No, I'll steal that for you as a starter, to show that my heart's in the right place."

"How'll we cover the thing up?" asked Tucker. "We're sure to be suspected. Everybody knows that he hates us, and, therefore, that we're sorry that he came back from jail. Everybody will have a look at us as soon as the body's found."

"Rance," said Tom London, "suppose that there's a mountain lion running at your heels and a wolf pack away off in the distance. Do you hesitate about killing the mountain lion because you don't know how you'll handle the wolves afterward?"

Tucker shrugged his shoulders.

"Besides," said Tom London, "I have ideas of how we'll be able to dodge, when people come hunting for us. It's the little matter of establishing an alibi, and I'm an expert in that line, Rance." He laughed, exulting. "No matter what the other evidence might be," said London, pursuing what was apparently a favorite subject, "no matter if the prints of the murderer's feet go in blood from the dead man to your own parlor rug, and your thumb prints are on the throat of the corpse, and your knife is found in the side of the man who's dead . . . no matter if all of those things are standing out against you, it makes no difference if you have old man alibi standing beside you, when the sheriff with his posse knocks at the front door." He broke off and laughed again. "I've alibied myself out of a dozen hangings and twenty lifetimes in jail," he concluded, "and I know how I can alibi myself out of this trouble, too."

"And me?"

"Yes, you, too. Look here, Tucker, you don't think that I'm the sort who lets down a partner, do you?"

At this, the vicious element in Tucker became only too evident. "I'll tell you what I'd expect out of you," said the rancher, "and that is everything that saves your neck and lines your pocket. That's all I expect, and it's each man for himself, as soon as this damned Barry Home is dead. Trust myself in your hands and to your alibis? I'm not such a fool!"

"Good," Tom London answered calmly.

And in the quiet nodding of his head it seemed to Barry Home that he was seeing the most dangerous quality that a criminal can possess—imperturbable coolness under every circumstance. Long was the road that London could travel in this world. That conclusion had barely come to Home, when it seemed to him that he was seeing the two men below more easily than before. In fact, his face was now in plain view of them, if they should look up. Then he was aware that he had been sliding forward and was still moving little by little, gradually, steadily. He was not slipping over the surface of the hay, but the hay itself was in motion, a considerable width of this top layer having been unsettled by his weight.

Softly, rapidly, he began to turn his body to the side, but at the first motion the forward impetus of the hay redoubled. It began to shoot away under him, threatening to cast him straight down into the mangers beneath. In the hundredth part of a second that remained to him, he chose between two things. One was to make a vast effort to reach the wooden upright that was nearest to him; the other was to try to swing about so that he could at least drop feet downward. If he fell, there was no doubt as to what London and Rance Tucker would do, no doubt in the world. They would simply thank the fortune that delivered him into their hands, and that would be the end of Barry Home. So he flung himself sidewise toward the upright. The hay shot out from underneath him and went down in a great cloud.

The frightened horses pulled back from their mangers, snorting and squealing as though the sky were falling on their heads, and the voice of London shouted: "There! Look! It's Home!"

The left hand of Barry Home had missed the upright entirely. The right had caught hold, however, and, as a gun spoke beneath him and a bullet tore through the hay at his side, he jerked himself back to the safety and darkness at the top of the mow. Instantly the lantern was extinguished below him. He heard a muttering of voices, the grinding of the wheels of the sliding door on the runway, the whistling of the icy storm through the aperture, and then the heavy slamming of the door.

He was alone in the barn except for the animals. All the information that he had gained was now more than counterbalanced, since his enemies had learned of the fullness of his knowledge. There had been a vast advantage for him, that was now totally relinquished, for they would understand that he had overheard their mutual admissions, their plans for his murder. They would be on guard. If they were dangerous before, they would be doubly dangerous now that they knew that he was forewarned and fully aware of their admitted guilt.

So, lying prone in the hay, Barry Home gritted his teeth together.

He had a wild impulse to descend at once, rush to the hotel, borrow or steal a gun, and turn it loose upon the precious pair. But what was gained if he killed them and, in turn, was hanged for that crime? For a moment, his brain whirled. Something had to be done quickly, but the very need of haste paralyzed his wits, and he could accomplish nothing.

At last, he fumbled his way down the edge of the hay mow, found the ladder of crosspieces nailed to one of the great uprights, and descended. He would have to find his plans as he walked blindly back toward the hotel.

# Chapter Eleven
## "Into the Storm"

When he reached the back of the hotel, he went into the kitchen a moment and found Mrs. Loomis standing at the inner door, ringing a great, brazen-lipped bell with all her might. She had a happy expression on her face. Why should the woman be ringing this bell in the middle of the night, unless she were utterly mad? Then he remembered—no matter how much had passed since the coming of twilight and that moment when he first saw Loomis in the distance—the actual time that had passed had been very short, and the meal, which was in course of preparation on his arrival, was merely ready for the table. It was the supper bell which Mrs. Loomis was sounding.

Patty came swiftly to him and touched his hand.

"What's the matter, Barry?" she asked him. "And what have you done?"

He looked down at himself. He had not been too abstracted on the way from the barn to neglect the obvious precaution of brushing off the hay that stuck to him. There was no sign of it on his clothes. Whatever she saw was in his face, and certainly in his heart there was murder to match whatever she could guess.

"You have a horse, Patty, haven't you?"

"I have one," she said.

He looked down and saw that her eyes were troubled as she searched his face again.

"I want to borrow it," he said. "Which is it?"

"The blue roan gelding on the near side of the barn," said Patty Loomis. "What . . . ?" She did not complete her question.

"It's all right, Patty." He nodded to reassure her and saw that far more than a mere gesture was needed to make her happy about him. A lump rippled up in her throat and fell again.

"I suppose it's all right," she said. "But you're going to stop and take some supper before you leave?"

"No supper. I have to ride three pretty brisk miles, and ride 'em now."

"You'll be back before long?"

"I'll be back before very long. Good bye, Patty." He glanced uneasily around the kitchen as he spoke.

"You want something else?" she asked.

"Yes, but . . . ."

"You want a gun?" said the girl.

He flushed, and then set his teeth.

"I want a gun," he murmured.

She was off in a flash, gesturing toward the side door. There in the hall he waited, and she came to him with her hand beneath her apron, and, when she took it out, she was carrying a long, heavy-barreled, single-action Colt.

"The kind you like," she said.

He handled it fondly. At the touch of his fingers on the roughened grip, confidence ran warmly through his body, and that unforgotten delight of battle wiped out all fear of consequences. No man in the world could be trusted, perhaps, but this was a friend that would not fail him. Then he saw the girl, so pale with fear that her eyes seemed darker, and he wondered at her.

"It's in good shape," said Barry Home. "I see it's loaded and clean and well oiled."

"Yes, it is," she answered, the haunted look never leaving her.

"By thunder," said Barry Home suddenly, "if it weren't for the solemn oath I've made, I wouldn't leave you now, Pat. I'd stay here with you, and never raise my hand in my whole life except to make you happy."

A pitiful smile plucked at her lips and was gone again. She nodded. "Yes, Barry," she said.

"It's your father's gun?"

"Yes," she whispered, overcome with emotion against which she kept on fighting.

He closed his eyes and saw again, for a moment, the picture of Hal Loomis, the brother of Dave, but very different from the hotel keeper was that big, burly, adventurous man who had trekked from the deserts of South Africa to the snows of Alaska, hunting for gold, laboring with the strength of a giant to find treasure for his family, and never succeeding, but getting, instead, a long series of hard knocks. Fate had never daunted him with her hard strokes, however, and to the end he had fought hard and cleanly.

It was the gun of Hal Loomis, now, that he gripped in his right hand. And it seemed to Barry Home that the ghost of the dead man stood with a troubled face behind his daughter and looked sadly, reproachfully, at him above her head.

Home thrust the gun inside his coat. "It's going to come out right," he declared.

"Yes," she murmured, and again she nodded, and again the wave of apprehension widened and darkened her eyes.

He put a hand on either side of her face and stood close while an agony of tenderness wrenched at his heart. "You wait, Pat," he said. "The time's coming when I'll be able to show what you mean to me. You've given me a horse and a gun tonight, and I'll promise you this, I'll use 'em for no wrong thing. I'll never shoot till it's my life or another man's."

"Good old Barry," she said, and smiled again at him in a way that made the tears rush into his eyes.

He had to hurry out from the house, breathing deep and hard to restore his self-confidence and remove the aching pity from his heart.

Then he was in the barn again, lighting the lantern that swung a little back and forth on its wooden peg near the door. Of course, it was the pressure of a draft that moved it, but it was to Barry Home exactly as though the hand of Tom London had that very instant hung it in place.

By the lantern light, he looked up grimly toward the place where he had lain stretched out on the top of the mow. Looking down, it had seemed to him that he had been at a very secure distance. A neck-breaking distance, almost certainly. Looking up, however, it seemed that Tom London could not possibly have missed his shot. There was the beam he had reached, and by which he had managed to snatch himself back to safety and darkness. Down on top of the manger he saw lying the spilled mass of the fallen hay, with two horses working happily away on it.

The blue roan was one of them, a mustang built long and low, with plenty of driving power in his quarters and a fine, muscular slope to his shoulders. He was not a pretty horse, but one that looked serviceable, such a horse as one could expect the daughter of big Hal Loomis to select for herself.

He got the saddle off the peg on the wall, and the blue roan tried to kick it out of his hands. That did not either alarm or annoy him, but brought a grin to his lips. He could almost have told the horse by the manner of the beast. She was always selecting the worst-mannered horse in a whole herd, then gradually reforming it until it became as wise and gentle as a household pet. She had been doing it with one horse after another from the days of her childhood, and here was another instance.

As he finally got the saddle in place and wedged the bit at last between the angry teeth of the gelding, he told himself that nowhere in the world could another girl be found like Patty Loomis, a perfect mate for him. There was nothing under heaven that he would not do for her—nothing except to give up the vow that he had made long ago in the solitude of his cell.

That was what he told himself fiercely, and softly moved his lips. All the while it was as though she were standing at his shoulder, silently, as she had stood before him in the hall, grieving with all her heart at whatever terrible danger he was intending to face, but loyally helping him to the extent of her ability. Aye, there was a woman for him or for any man.

He gave the cinches another tug, put out the lantern, and led the mustang to the barn door. The gleam of that lantern might well have been seen at the hotel and, if Tom London or the rancher, Tucker, noticed the light, either one of them or both might be waiting now outside the barn. He hesitated, thinking of this, before he pulled back the sliding door.

When he thought of all that lay before him in the bitter cold of this night and its darkness, he realized that, if he kept pausing for every possible thought of danger, he would never get through to the morning, he would never be able to execute any of his plans. So he thrust the door boldly open. The blue roan grunted and pulled back, as the wind knifed into it. A tarpaulin, hanging near the door, flapped loudly in the rush of the air.

The sliding fingers of the cold pried under the ribs of Barry Home and got at the pit of his stomach. Brave man or coward, no one could face such whip-driven cold as this without something more than the apparel he was wearing. The snow was coming faster, riding the wind with a scream, and cutting the skin of his face as it struck him. It was such a night as to make one wonder what, other than raving idiocy, would make any man leave shelter for the open. But Barry Home did not hesitate. Only, first, he took the tarpaulin hanging beside the door and tied it around his shoulders. Then he led the mustang out, closed the door, mounted, and left the corral for the open road.

The wind, in the meantime, gathered force and leaped on him with a yell, when he had gone through the corral gate. Through the tarpaulin and through his own wretchedly insufficient clothes, the chill of the storm soaked like water through paper. He gave himself some comfort by remembering what he had read of the gigantic Patagonians, those filthy savages who endure a weather that is continual storm and ice in nakedness, with only one bit of leather, like a shield, strapped to their bodies, and turned toward the prevailing wind. He was better than that, at least, in his equipment, as he started riding through the blizzard for the house of Rance Tucker.

# Chapter Twelve
## "At the Window"

The wind had shifted so that it beat straight in his face all the way to the Tucker house. It was increasing in force until, in the throat of the pass, it came at him with such violence it threatened to lift him out of the saddle. It seemed wonderful to him that anything so cold could have such buoyancy.

How the mustang managed to keep going was a mystery to the rider. He flattened himself along the neck of the strong-hearted gelding and kicked it in the ribs now and then, by way of encouragement, and at every kick the horse shook his head and freshened his trot. A trot was all that could be managed with safety, now that the road was wet and frozen underfoot and doubly treacherous where the snow had drifted across it in the hollows. Sometimes, as they went on, the wind scooped up a cloud of the fallen snow and sent it with hurricane swiftness like a great, flying, ghostly mist into the face of Barry.

Had it not been for the tarpaulin that covered his shoulders and the upper part of his body, he knew that he would have had to give up the journey before he had covered the first half mile. Even as it was, when the first mile had ended, he was certain that he would be a dead man before he went over the next two. But he could remember other miseries of cold almost as great. Every winter there were sure to be a few occasions when a rider would be forced to venture his very life for the sake of the cattle on the range. So he was well inured to this exposure; moreover, experience hardens the mind.

The second mile brought him into the pass itself, where his courage failed him for a moment. Perhaps he would have turned back, after all, except that the blue roan, shaking its ugly head, bored resolutely on into the teeth of the storm. That roused his heart with admiration for the poor beast that could have no understanding of the purpose for which this adventure was undertaken, which was supported and urged along merely by the will of the rider and perhaps by a somewhat perverse determination to conquer every obstacle that could be presented.

Out of the pass, the country widened into rolling hills, and the wind, no longer compressed in a funnel, raged less furiously. He was able to sit up straight on the horse, and he began to swing his arms to quicken the circulation as he came to the house of Rance Tucker, lying long and low, a big, black hulk. All was familiar ground to him here. He had worked long enough for the thrifty rancher to have a map of the layout printed in his mind. It would be useful to him now.

In the first place, he had to cache his horse. He went behind the woodshed where it abutted on the smokehouse, where the hundreds of hams and sides of bacon were cured every year by Rance Tucker, who raised his own pigs to feed his own crew and had something left over to sell cheaply to the Loomis store. The junction of the two sheds formed a perfect windbreak, and, when the rider threw the reins, the blue roan cuddled up contentedly into the angle thus formed, as though this were exactly the sort of stabling it was used to. That was sufficient shelter, at least, to keep the tough brute from any danger of freezing.

Barry Home remained there beside the horse for a moment, jumping up and down and thrashing his arms about against his body until he was in a glow. He waited with his eyes closed, also, until the wind strain was gone out of them. He practiced passing the revolver out of his coat and back inside it a score of times, to make sure that he was familiar with the lie of the weapon. When he was ready, he wiped his eyes, settled his hat firmly on his head, and then turned the corner of the smokehouse into the screech of the gale again.

A moment later he was beside the leeward wall of the house, with only the howling of the wind overhead, as it shot across the roof of the house and sped away, sloping rapidly down to the ground again. Here, there was no snow upon the ground, and he could give thanks for that, because it would be easy for his feet to grow numb while he waited out here, slowly exploring.

He tried the light in the kitchen first. Rubbing away a frost of cold mist in a lower corner of a pane, he looked through the spy hole and saw the whole room easily, while the white frosting secured him from discovery. Mrs. Tucker was there at the sink, a tall and bony woman with what seemed a curving rod down her back but what was in reality her spinal column, sticking out from the starving flesh. It was said that Mrs. Tucker was not in the habit of cooking for herself when her men folk were out of the house. She fed them well enough when they were present but, for her own part, a glass of milk and a few crackers were enough to suit her, or the trimmings of meat left on a leg of mutton after most of the carving had been completed. On bits and scraps she was pleased to maintain herself when she was alone, and well could Barry Home remember the starved and forbidding eyes with which she followed the trencher work of the men at her table while she sat erect at one end with her mouth pinched into a straight line and the devil in her glances.

She was not, in fact, washing up dishes after her supper. She was busily scrubbing at the sink, but through the window he could see that she was using the empty evening to rub up all of the kitchen pots and pans. With her sleeves rolled up to the elbows, she attacked the pots with a huge rattling, scrubbing at them with a brush and sand first, and then polishing them off to shining dryness.

Well, there were certain virtues in such a woman, Barry Home supposed. But he did not wish to find them again in any woman he married, any mother of sons of his. It seemed to him that the evil that had spread abroad through that house had almost entirely sprung out of her. Evil she was, and to evil she gave birth.

As he watched, the door was flung open, and young Tucker came striding into the kitchen. Not a sound did his footfall make on the floor, so loud was the shouting of the storm outside in the ears of the watcher, and he heard not a whisper of the loud cry of Mrs. Tucker, although he could see the opening of her mouth and the straining of her lips as she ran toward her son. Black was the face of Lew Tucker and solemn his look. What would he tell his mother?

Barry shrugged his shoulders and shook his head. Whatever else might happen that night, it was plain that Lew Tucker had received a frightful blow to his pride; otherwise, he would not have shrunk from his father in time of need. Why had he lingered on the way?

What had he been doing? Well, perhaps he had been sitting in the darkness of the barn, after unsaddling his horse, holding his head between his hands, in thought, pondering his downfall and his shame.

There was some pity in the heart of Barry Home as he turned from the kitchen window and walked along the side of the house to the next lighted window, that opened out from the living room. Somewhere in that house were the articles of the loot that the rancher had named to his partner, Tom London. If he could find them, Barry Home could reverse the judgment against himself, and thus punishment would fall where it had been so long and richly merited.

Where was he to search? He had gathered from the story of the rancher that the stuff was hidden, at least in part, in some open and obvious place, where the eye was not likely to recognize it. Otherwise, Rance Tucker would not have laughed with such exultation. Furthermore, his assurance must have been absolute, or he would never have confided so much to Tom London. But still there was hope in young Barry Home that he might be able to penetrate to the heart of the mystery.

He looked through the living room window as he had looked through the kitchen window and saw it not too brightly illuminated by the lamp with the circular burner that was suspended above the little round center table, the light made more brilliant by strands of clouded glass beads that hung from a circular frame all around the lamp. Beneath that glow he saw the books and could name them— the velvet-covered, brass-studded album of family portraits, PIL-GRIM'S PROGRESS, the book of the flowers of the wayside and the field, and the battered, ancient dictionary that, so far as he could remember, had never been opened except to look up populations that had been outgrown twenty years before. He grinned sourly as he surveyed the rest of the room, the empty fireplace—in spite of this weather—and the stiff-backed chairs with moth-eaten plush covering the seats.

There had been no happiness during the months he had worked for the Tuckers, only the satisfaction of holding down a place where few cowpunchers would stay more than a few weeks at a time, underfed and underpaid.

He tried the window with his hand. It seemed fast, at first, but then it shuddered and finally rose a little. It must not be allowed to make a sound that would be audible at the farther end of the house. He was about to push it up a sufficient distance to enable him to climb inside, when something made him turn his head, and now he saw three riders coming rapidly down the road from the pass.

He must not be seen against the lighted square of the window, so he crouched down close to the ground, and saw the riders swing in through the gate to the Tucker house. One of them was surely Rance Tucker. The heart of the young fellow quickened. If ever a man sensed the near approach of fate, it was Barry, as he saw the three shadows proceed to the barn, dismount, and pass into the darkness of that building.

# Chapter Thirteen
## "The Glass Fringe"

He was in a quandary once the three had disappeared and a light gleamed inside the barn from a lantern. He might slip out to the barn and try to overhear what was passing there, as he had spied on London and Tucker. But probably they were coming straight back to the house. And he might do something with them now. If he recognized them in time, he could shout a challenge and open fire—on London and Tucker, yes, and perhaps he could kill them both, but the third man? That complicated everything.

Besides, even if the third man had not been there, it was no good, this shooting business. If anything happened to London and Tucker, the blame would be attributed to him as directly as though a thousand pairs of eyes had seen him do the shooting. What was his triumph of revenge, then, if he passed from freedom back to prison, and from prison to the hangman's rope?

Savagely he brooded as he crouched in the cold and saw the door of the barn open again. Out came the trio. The barn was dark again behind them. There came a pause in the storm's uproar, and he heard distinctly the rumbling of the wheels of the sliding door on the runway.

As the three came closer, he recognized two of them. The larger man was Rance Tucker, he was certain, and even more unmistakable was Tom London from a certain grace of carriage that he retained even when leaning against the wind. Slowly they came on, slowing almost to a halt from time to time, as the force of the storm staggered them. They came very close and, staring hard, straining his eyes, the young fellow made sure of the third man. It was the sheriff!

Barry set his teeth, for the thing became clear. Tucker and London, when they knew that they were overheard, had made up their minds that they were in immediate danger of their lives. They had cooked up some sort of a story to interest the sheriff, and now they were gathered together to watch out this night in safety, this night, at least, under the broad shield of the law. All Barry's difficulties from that moment were doubled and redoubled.

They entered the house. Presently they came into the living room. In the entrance hall, they had taken off their coats. But their faces were blue and red with cold, and they began to stamp and strike their bodies with their hands. Tucker made angry gestures toward the empty hearth. His son came in. Everyone was speaking. Mrs. Tucker appeared, her ugly face illumined as she embraced her husband on his safe return. Then the party trooped through the farther door, evidently going in to take advantage of the warmth that the kitchen stove would offer to them.

Rance remained a pace behind the others. As they disappeared through the doorway, the watcher at the frosted window saw through his peephole how the rancher paused, swept his big hand through the strands of the glass beads around the hanging lamp, then, with a sly smile of content, followed the others.

The watcher shook his head. He had a vast sense of defeat. With four men inside that house, all armed, all undoubtedly on the lookout to ward off danger directly threatening them from him, there seemed nothing left but to get his horse and return to Loomis, with the single advantage that the storm would then be blowing at his back.

And then he knew that he could not return. He could not leave these detested enemies any more than a starving wolf can leave the trail of a bull moose, though it knows that it is far too weak to pull down the prize when it has been brought to bay. So he lingered there, shuddering with the cold, trying to think. He could form no plan. But somewhere in the house there was the proof that would shift blame from his shoulders to those of Rance Tucker. He must find it. He could not trace it, if he remained there in the outer night. No, he must enter.

After he was inside, inspiration might come to him, he felt, so he rounded to the front of the house, tried the door, found it unlatched, and entered quickly, sliding through a narrow aperture and shutting the door behind him again. Even so, he heard the whoop of the wind go with a hollow and a whistling sound through the house. Would that alarm the inmates of the place?

A noise of voices arose suddenly from the back of the house. He recognized the heavy tones of Lew Tucker, saying: "The front door was opened, then. I know the way the wind come in." The door to the kitchen was ajar. Lew Tucker stood in the gap of it, frowning, and looking across the living room toward the darkness of the hallway.

"Don't be a fool, Lew," said the voice of Rance Tucker. "That was the howl of the wind comin' down the chimney. I seen the smoke and ashes puff out of the stove."

"Somebody opened the front door!" insisted Lew.

"Well, go and see, then," urged his father carelessly. "You ain't gonna take my word for it, so you go and make up your mind for yourself, will you?"

"Yes, I will," growled Lew.

He drew out a big Colt to assist him in the search. Barry Home shrank back against the wall, rolling his eyes wildly from side to side. There was no other door opening into the hallway, he knew, except that of the living room. Where could he hide himself, then? There were only the long, dripping overcoats and slickers that hung against the wall, but for a good reason he would not use that refuge.

Lew Tucker, in the meantime, was striding straight on.

Barry Home groaned, his throat swelling and aching with the suppression of the sound. It was not young Lew Tucker that he wanted. It was the father of that young fellow. But there was Lew coming, armed, and with a resolved face.

Home slid back into the darkest corner, and there he squatted on his heels against the wall. Chance would have to help him now. As for his own revolver, he drew it with a numb, cold hand, and held its muzzle down, beside his knee.

Then Tucker stood in the door and moved his head, staring about him, gun held at the raised ready position for firing. Plainly he meant business of the most serious kind. He stepped forward. Exactly as Barry Home had expected, he brushed aside the wet overcoats, found nothing, and finally with a shake of the head turned away. He reached the doorway, jerked his head sidewise, and looked straight at the spot where Home was crouched.

A thousandth part of a second was Lew Tucker from death at that instant. Then he went on slowly, and Barry Home was blinded by a rush of blood to the head, and staggered by the pounding of the pulse in his temple. He stood up, trembling and breathing deeply. He heard the kitchen door opening again and the sound of voices rolling out toward him.

"Well, Lew?" asked Rance.

"I guess I was wrong. If that door was opened, it was closed without anybody coming inside."

"You look in the hall?"

"Yes."

"Nothin' anywhere?"

"No, not a soul," said Lew Tucker, and closed the door on his own last words.

Barry Home smiled as he listened, and then glided into the living room. He glanced at the empty hearth, not that he expected to see the warmth of a fire flickering there, but because everyone else had looked in that direction on entering the room. He had no instant to waste on odd details by glancing here and there, but he made sure of the emptiness of the hearth first of all, gritting his teeth at his own folly at the same moment.

Then he stood under the flare of the lamp. How perfect a target he was for anyone who opened the door of the kitchen at that moment. Then he did as he had seen Rance Tucker do. He drew out the bead fringe that dangled around the lamp. What was the meaning of that caressing gesture on the part of the rancher? What was the meaning of the sly and exulting smile of the man?

He could find no reason for that either and, leaving the string of glass beads to clash softly together as he stepped back, he removed himself a pace and looked uncertainly toward the door of the kitchen. Out of the other room came the steady rumble of men's voices, with the shrill overtone of Mrs. Tucker cutting through with an opinion, now and again.

There was reason for him to tremble. Though he did not actually shake, every nerve in his body was painfully on the alert, reaching out, probing on all sides toward possible danger. That right hand of his, now recovering from the cold, tingling and throbbing with heat, was eager to snatch out his revolver. One gun against four, that was not an easy game, even for Barry Home fighting for his life.

He could see, now, that when he examined the beaded fringe

under the lamp, he was not in exactly the same spot where Rance Tucker had stood. He moved to the same place, thrust out his hand, and placed it under the dangling strings of glass beads. Even then he would not have found a difference, if his eyes had not been sharpened by keen necessity. As it was, however, he could see that whereas the other strings turned dark and cold in the shadow of his hand, one of them appeared faintly luminous and of a softer, creamier texture of light. They were not glass at all. They were pearls!

# Chapter Fourteen
## "Sparks"

He glanced up from them, suddenly, to the larger bit of cut glass from which the particular string of beads dangled and saw that it was a good bit smaller than the other pieces of glass around the lamp, the headpieces from which the strings dangled. It was cut in many more facets, and it cast out a spark of fire, instead of the duller flash of the other bits. It was not glass any more than the string of beads beneath it. It was the valuable stickpin diamond!

No wonder that Rance Tucker had said that he had hidden the little treasures where no man could find them, though they were easy enough to locate, when one only knew the key. He himself might have searched through the house forever, and vainly, except that he had chanced to be on hand to see the gesture of Tucker. But now he knew, and he reached up his hand to strip away the prize.

He checked himself. It was not the possession of that thing that he really wanted. A few thousand dollars mattered nothing, as a matter of fact. What was important was that, while this string dangled here, it was proclaiming with every flash, with every gleam of jeweled light, that Rance Tucker had a share, at least, in the robbery of the stagecoach to Crystal Creek.

No, the value of the evidence lay simply in the place where it hung in view, if he could bring the eyes of authority to glance at it. It meant, in a single flash, the removal from his own shoulders of all implication in the crime for which he had suffered for three years. It meant his reëstablishment as a respectable citizen. Respectable citizen? His upper lip twitched with disdainful scorn as he thought of the phrase. He knew, he thought, what respectability amounted to now. As he had told the girl, it was merely the ability to hide the evidences of crime. So London and Tucker had done. For three years they had continued being respectable, while he, poor fool, suffered every pang short of damnation.

Breathing deep, he stared at the little string of pearls and the diamond above them. How simple it was. How clever. He almost stopped hating Rance Tucker, in his admiration for this stroke of cleverness.

A shot that shattered a pane of glass in the window through which he himself had looked, not long before, cut short these speculations. He felt the whir of the bullet past his face, and then turned and dove for cover.

Not toward the hall door, for that was too far away, but just to the left of the living room fireplace there was another doorway that opened on the stairs that led to the second story. At that door he aimed himself, like a projectile, running low, his shoulder bunched and the muscles hardened. He struck the door. It crashed before him as the second and third bullets plunged into the woodwork that framed him. And forward he pitched onto the broad lower steps of the stairway. In his ears was the yelling voice of Rance Tucker from outside the house: "I got him! I nailed him! I nailed him! Run him down, damn him! I got Barry Home!"

People were coming with a rush from the kitchen, as Home, more than half stunned, picked himself up and staggered up the stairs. He got to the first landing, where the steps turned and wound upward at a new angle, before the people from the kitchen rushed in and reached the broken door that he had battered down.

He turned and fired, not at them, but above their heads, and heard the shriek of Mrs. Tucker. He was still bewildered by the shock he had received, so that, as he ran on up the steps to the hall above, he could only vaguely hear the clamor of the voices and wonder if the bullet by any chance had actually struck poor Mrs. Tucker. Then he was in the hall above. They were not following. He stood still, in the cold, clammy darkness, and listened to their voices.

Rance Tucker was already in the room, shouting in triumph. "The third shot, I nailed him. I split his back open for him. He's a dead rat. I nailed him fair between the shoulders!"

There was so much confidence in his voice that Barry Home actually slid his left hand up behind his back toward the shoulder blades, and he started as his finger touched moisture. No, of course, that was simply melted snow. And Rance Tucker was enjoying the same illusion that hunters have when they swear they have seen half a dozen bullets strike the bear, and yet the bruin is scampering rapidly away through the brush, unscathed.

"I don't see any blood," said the voice of the sheriff.

"There mightn't be any blood on the floor, but there's blood oozing down his clothes and his body. There's blood being pumped right out from his heart this minute, red blood, lifeblood!" shouted Rance Tucker. "Tom, he ain't gonna bother us no more!"

"I hope you're right," said London.

"Right? You hope I'm right? I know I'm right. I don't seem such a fool now, do I, comin' out from the kitchen into the cold again? No, I got an instinct. I can tell when things are goin' wrong!"

"He'll get out of the house and away," said the sheriff.

"He'll die before he gets fifty steps," said Rance Tucker, filled with confidence.

"We've gotta keep watch. There's a moon blowed up over the mountains now, and it gives plenty of light," said Lew Tucker. "We gotta go and lie out and wait, some of us."

"You'll be freezing yourselves to death, you crazy things," said Mrs. Tucker.

"Lew is right," broke in the sheriff. "We can't take any chances. If it's Barry Home, and, if he's in this house, he means to fight his way out, unless your bullet got him, poor young fool."

"Poor young murderer, you mean!" said Mrs. Tucker. "The blood-thirsty young scoundrel. I hope. . . ."

What she hoped remained unknown. For now the sheriff broke in with a crisp, clear voice: "Rance, you and Lew and Tom London get outside and watch the house. Stay there for an hour. You'll have moonlight to do it. Use shotguns. Shoot at any shadow that tries to get free from the place. Understand?"

"I understand," said Rance Tucker. "But you won't need to wait for a whole hour. He's running blood, I tell you. His blood is soaking through the flooring, some place in the house. I split his wishbone, boys. I was kind of unsteady, seeing him first, but the third shot, I nailed him. I seen him go crash, when he hit the door." He laughed in his exultation.

The voice of the sheriff cut in again: "Get out there on the double. Barry Home is a tough man. It's hard to kill Barry Home with one bullet. Get out there, now, and look things over. Be sharp, too. He's gonna slide through your fingers, if you don't look out. If it's only to drag himself away and die in some hole or corner where he'll never be found. If you wanta find your dead man, get outside. I'll hold things down in here. Before you're froze to death, one of you come back in. Rance, you're the oldest. You come back inside after an hour, and I'll go out and take your place. We're gonna have to keep a watch on the outside of the house all night. When the morning comes, we'll start in searchin' for the body."

"It's a waste of time," said Rance Tucker. "I split his wishbone for him, I tell you."

"Go and do what you're told to do by somebody that knows," said Mrs. Tucker. "Don't go and dispute with the sheriff, Rance!"

"Come on, Pa," urged the son.

"Oh, I'll go," said Rance Tucker. "Only, it's a big night for me. A big night when I've bagged Barry Home, and don't you forget it!"

"All right, Rance," said Tom London, who spoke very little at this moment. "The main thing is for us to keep from freezing while we're out there in the open. We'll need all the coats and slickers that you have in the house."

"They're in the hall, stacks of 'em," said Mrs. Tucker. "And I'll fire up the kitchen stove and get some coffee to boiling for you boys. I'll fetch it out to you. There ain't no more comfort than hot coffee in the cold."

"Make it good and strong, Ma," said Lew Tucker. "Not that dishwater that you're likely to serve up."

"Only," said Mrs. Tucker, "are you sure that murderer ain't gonna come down from upstairs and break in on us? Are you sure that you hurt him bad enough to take the fight out of him?"

"Him?" said Rance Tucker. "You take my word for it. He's lying on his face dead, somewhere up in the hall. That's all. He's dead, right now. But I guess we'd better play safe, like the sheriff says. That's the best way, to play safe when you're up against Barry Home!" He laughed again at the end of this speech, as though he had said something very witty.

It was mere excess of joy and animal spirits that brought the merriment forth.

Then, standing frozen to his place in the upper hall, Barry Home heard their muffled voices as they got into coats and slickers, then heard them stamping through the door. He did not attempt to get through a second story window to the ground. That would be difficult and dangerous business, while the outer walls of the house were iced over with sleet. For his own part, he had formed another, and what seemed to him a much better, plan.

Mrs. Tucker was already in the kitchen, to judge by the rattling of iron. That seemed to indicate that she had opened up the stove and was loading it with wood again. She would soon have the coffee pot on, steaming and boiling. In the meantime, the front door slammed heavily, the weight of the wind hurling it shut with a crash, while the breath of the storm whistled and screamed through the house.

Barry Home took advantage of that uproar to make, rapidly, the first three steps of the descent down the stairs.

# Chapter Fifteen
## "A Slow Descent"

The living room was, undoubtedly, the crucial place to hold from a tactical point of view, if one wished to make sure of what happened in the house, and the sheriff was very right in remaining there. Barry Home was glad for almost the same reason for, according to his present plan, it was the sheriff that he wanted to get at.

But he made his descent cautiously. From the living room there came no sound whatever for a time, and, meanwhile, he was coming down the stairs, but in such a way that his procedure would have appeared extremely erratic to anyone not initiated. For he never moved until the wind caught hold of the house and shook it from head to heel with a furious blast. Then he ventured softly down, two or three steps at a time. After this he would pause, motionless, two or three minutes, until another blast of the hurricane descended on the place.

After twenty minutes of these precautions, he got finally to the bottom of the stairs. And now he stood beside the broken door. Inside that bright frame was the room with Sheriff Bert Wayland waiting, gun ready, eyes keen as a hawk's. A formidable man was Bert Wayland, not one to talk a great deal, but he could shoot straight and fast. His record was long. There were many deaths to decorate the length of it.

That was the reason why the young man hesitated long moments until the door of the kitchen opened, and the voice of Mrs. Tucker, husky with excitement, said: "Well, Mister Wayland, is everything all right?"

"Everything will be all right, so far as the house goes," said the sheriff, "till you hear a gunshot, and I drop dead. I'm watchin' that doorway, yonder. I'm watchin' it as though the devil might stick his head around the corner of it almost any minute."

"Good for you," said Mrs. Tucker heartily, "because a devil is what he is. I can't understand why the prison should go and turn loose a killer like him. Prisons is the place for 'em, and no place else!"

"Maybe," said the sheriff.

"I'll be fetching you in a cup of coffee, Sheriff Wayland, in a coupla shakes," said Mrs. Tucker cordially, and slammed the kitchen door.

That instant, surely, the eyes of the sheriff would wander toward the place where his hostess had disappeared. That instant Barry Home glided into the frame of the broken door and leveled his gun, hip-high, and saw the glance of Wayland, as he had expected, swinging back from the kitchen door.

The sheriff was seated in a straight chair, well to the side of the center table, so that the glare from the lamp, shining down, would not trouble his eyes in taking aim. His gun rested on his knees. But he made no effort to raise it when he saw that he was covered, and by whom.

Many things had been said of Barry Home, first, second, and third, but never had any man suggested that one of the three was that he failed to shoot straight. The sheriff, at least, cherished no such delusion.

Without moving his gun hand, Wayland's head rose as he stiffened a little in the chair, and his nostrils flared. He had the attitude of a man steeling himself to receive a frightful shock of a bullet that would strike over his heart and tear its way through his life.

"Lean over and put that gun on the floor," said Barry Home.

The sheriff obeyed.

"Now stand up, turn your back to me, and hoist your hands."

Again the sheriff obeyed.

Barry Home went to him and laid the muzzle of his revolver in the small of the sheriff's back. He nudged it hard against the spine of the helpless man.

"You see where you stand," said Home.

"I've been beat before," said the sheriff. "Only tonight I was a fool to trust Rance Tucker. He split your wishbone, did he?" He groaned as he spoke.

The left hand of Home went deftly over him. There was not a bulge to indicate another weapon.

"That's all right," said Barry Home. "Now come over here."

He steered the sheriff with a hand on his shoulder until he came to a certain point, facing the hanging lamp. Then, stepping forward, he laid the muzzle of his gun against the sheriff's breast.

"You don't need this much light to murder me by, Barry, do you?" asked the sheriff calmly.

And Barry Home wondered. He had seen men die, young as he was, and in the prison he had heard many tales of death. Yet there was something both terrible and fine in the calm of the sheriff, who was taking his turn under the muzzle of a gun. How would he, Barry Home, react in a similar situation? With his left hand, he reached out and fumbled behind the glass strings of beads.

"Look at this, not at my gun," he advised. "There's your answer!"

"I don't see nothin', Barry," said the sheriff, as calmly as ever.

"Look again, at the string that hangs from the cut-glass bit that's smaller than the others. See anything now?"

"Yeah. It's smaller. The beads are bigger, though."

"Reach out and break that off from the frame," ordered Barry Home.

"It's pretty nigh funny enough to make me laugh," said the sheriff, "though I know that I'm gonna catch thunder and lightning in a minute."

"You're wrong," said Barry Home. "You'll see how wrong you are in another minute. But do as I say."

The sheriff obeyed once more and stood gravely, holding the dangling string of beads with the diamond at the top of them in his hand.

"Don't look at me," said Barry Home. "Look at the stuff in your hand."

"I see it," said Wayland.

"Look again. Is that stuff glass?"

The sheriff stared, and then started. "By thunderation," he muttered under his breath.

"That stuff," said Barry Home, "was all described by the papers at the time the Crystal Creek stage was robbed. A pearl necklace, and a diamond stickpin. Worth a couple of thousand dollars apiece."

"By thunderation," repeated the amazed sheriff.

"Pull yourself together," said Barry Home. "Tom London and Rance Tucker should have served that prison sentence, not I. You remember that I always swore I had nothing to do with it? London robbed the stage. You remember the horse trail business? London and Tucker framed it together to put the blame on me. Tonight, in the Loomis barn, I heard them talk the whole thing out. The diamond and the pearls . . . Tucker was afraid to sell for fear he'd be traced through 'em. He had this idea for concealing his stuff, and it was a good idea, I'd say."

"Good idea? It's a great idea!" said the sheriff. "It . . . it's a good enough idea for a book. But hold on, Barry. You mean to say that the state was wrong, and you were innocent all the while?"

"That's what I mean." He quietly put up his gun as he spoke. "Take your Colt again, Wayland. Call in Rance Tucker. Show him that stuff and ask him where he got it. And watch his face."

The sheriff drew in a great breath as he scooped up his gun. For a moment it seemed, from his savage face, as though he intended to turn his bullets upon the young fellow, but what he said was: "The hounds, the dirty hounds! And a poor kid went to prison and hell for 'em, eh? Oh, Barry, I'm a sad man, when I think what a fool I've been. A sad man."

He went to the front door, opened it, and, as the wind whistled into the house, his voice was heard calling, faint and far away: "Rance! Oh, Rance Tucker, come in!"

Almost at once Rance Tucker was entering the house, and the whistling of the wind was shut out as the front door closed.

"Wayland, have you got him?" exclaimed Tucker.

Barry had slipped back through the broken door and waited, peering out through the safe mask of shadow. He saw the two come into the room, the face of Tucker eagerly expectant.

Suddenly the sheriff held the string of beads before him. "Where'd you get this, Tucker?" asked Wayland sharply.

The jaw of Rance Tucker dropped. "Damn you!" he whispered, and caught at his gun.

He was far too slow in his movements to match the skill and training of the sheriff. Now he stood at bay, his hand on the butt of the gun, his jaw set, his eyes wild, covered by Wayland's gun, as Barry Home stepped through the doorway.

"It's a plant . . . it's a plot," muttered Rance Tucker, as he saw the face of Barry Home. "Home, he came here and put the stuff up there with the glass beads."

"You know too well where it came from," said the sheriff. "Cover this fellow a minute, Barry, while I go and call the others."

He stepped to the front door, and once more his voice rang into the night, more loudly than ever.

"Tom London! Oh, Tom! Come in! I've got him! Lew Tucker! Come in, Lew!"

Someone came running.

"Be careful, and mind what you do," the voice of the sheriff said in caution. "Give me that gun, Lew. Now go ahead in and see the man we want. Why doesn't Tom come, too?"

The door of the kitchen flew open at the same moment that Lew Tucker stepped in from the hall, and there they saw Rance Tucker standing, covered by the supposed thief, and the sheriff assisting at this outrage. But the very fact of that assistance struck the pair cold.

"There's the thief," said the sheriff melodramatically, but most unnecessarily, as it seemed.

Mrs. Tucker had been drying her hands on her apron. She began to moan, saying: "Oh, Rance, I always knowed that God wouldn't let it be with such an honest young feller as Barry Home. You should've picked on that worthless Slim Ferrar."

"I'm gonna say one thing," said Tucker at last. "You've got me, but get the man that done the real job. Get Tom London. He robbed the coach!"

# Chapter Sixteen
## "The Pursuit"

But no matter how loudly the voice of the sheriff had run through the night, Tom London had not appeared.

"He's gone!" Barry Home said suddenly, and pointed toward the window.

What meant something to him, and very little to the others, was the small round eye of darkness, through which the bullets of Rance Tucker had sped not so long before. A man could have seen a very informing tableau by looking through that peephole, at any time in the last minute or so, and what would keep Tom London from taking such a glance as he came running to answer the call of the sheriff?

"He's gone," repeated Barry Home. "But he can't go as fast as I'll follow. Wayland, swear me in, make me deputy for this one night. Swear me, and I'll chase him to the rim of hell!"

Never was an oath administered more swiftly than at that particular moment.

And with the response trailing in the air behind him, Barry Home bolted from the house. As he ran from the door into that terrible blast of the wind, he saw what he expected—the silhouette of a horseman, galloping up the road toward Loomis with the gale helping him on. And the horse that he rode was a Thoroughbred.

Groaning, staggering, with a blindness of rage and of helplessness, Barry Home rushed to where the long, low-built blue roan had been left. Soon he was out on the road, and there was the shadowy form of the fugitive not so far ahead, strangely close, as though he had halted to make some adjustment of his saddle and then had gone on. But the blue roan was flying at full speed.

The wind had shifted a few points; the sky was scoured clean of clouds; and the moon poured a steady flood of silver into the pass as Barry Home rushed his horse up the trail. Well shod was the roan and sure-footed as a mustang has to be in the West, and he strode mightily on, the wind giving him wings.

Now Home could tell why, to his unutterable amazement, he gained ground. As he drew closer, he could see the long-legged Thoroughbred slipping and sliding in the treacherous going. The surface of the road had been whipped clean of all snow by the force of the wind, but the earliest fall, that had melted, had turned to ice, and it was over a surface of ice that the cleated shoes of the gelding were beating, biting in to get a good grip and sending him swiftly and safely along.

Ah, trust Patty Loomis to have a horse that was a horse! And a rage of self-confidence swelled up in Barry and mastered him. He rode well forward, jockeying the good mustang, holding it with an iron hand, one hand, and that the left, because the right hand had to be nourished in the warmth of his body against the moment when it would be needed to grasp the handle of the Colt.

He could see before him how Tom London was riding his horse all out, now glancing back over his shoulder, now flogging the poor, skidding Thoroughbred to more frantic efforts. Given one good mile of clear going, and there would be no doubt of how that exquisite mechanism of flesh and blood would speed away from the blue roan, but now the Thoroughbred was caught at exactly the wrong moment and the low-running mustang made every stride a winning one. Tom London knew it, finally. He pulled up his horse at the side of the road, swung down to the ground, and drew his revolver.

It was still a good distance, fifty or sixty yards. There were two ways to manage the thing, to pull up the mustang in turn and shoot it out at long range, or else to charge straight in, trusting that the motion of his gelding would upset the aim of London as much as it unsteadied his own hand. The second course was the only one for Barry Home. And as he snatched out his revolver, it seemed to him that he was merely an instrument in the hands of a greater fate that would control this battle.

There was no doubt in him. Calmly and coldly, but with the whole long agony of three discredited years weighing down upon him, he watched the gun of Tom London, as the robber fired. And he saw the moon flash dimly on the buttons of the man's heavy overcoat. Then he fired in turn. There seemed to be no effect. It was merely that Tom London had lowered his own weapon and seemed to be looking curiously at the charge of his enemy. Then his knees sagged, and he leaned over very slowly, put out a hand toward the road, and collapsed.

He was dead. The certainty of it was in Barry Home before he could rein up the gelding, and then turn back to the place. Tom London was dead, and his horse was backing away from the horrible smell of blood.

They had sat long over the table at the Loomis hotel, because there was much to discuss out of that day's happenings, and the sudden disappearance of London, Rance Tucker, and Barry Home, to say nothing of the sheriff, was enough to cause every man to hazard some conjecture. There was the pale, drawn face of Patty Loomis, too, to cause the whispers to be lowered still further, as she circulated about the long dinner table, laden with plates or platters. There was, too, the somber look of Dave Loomis, sitting miserably at the head of the table robbed of his customary cheerfulness.

But three miles, even through bad weather, does not take a galloping horse much time. And they were still sitting about the table at the Loomis hotel when the door opened, and the sheriff looked in.

"I want to swear in a coupla deputies," he said briefly.

Patty Loomis, with a moan, put her hand against the wall to steady herself.

The sheriff said to her briskly: "It's not to get Barry Home, Patty. Barry Home needs no getting. There never was a time when he ought to've been got. Tom London robbed the Crystal Creek stage, and Barry's killed him for it . . . killed him resisting arrest, as an officer of the law. Rance Tucker went halves with London for putting the blame on poor Barry Home. And it's Rance that I want watched tonight. Any volunteers? Patty, I think Barry went around the back of the hotel."

She found him in the kitchen, sitting with his head resting in his hands. After she had looked at him a moment, smiling sadly and happily as well, she went to him and laid a hand on his shoulders.

"I know, Patty," he said. "I'll be all right in a minute. But I'm still a little sick. I've thought all the time that it was my business

87

only. Now I see that fate or something had a hand in it all the while. Patty, I've killed a man."

She was perfectly silent. Her face was grave. And she looked above and beyond him, as one who knows that happiness is near, but that it must be fought for to be kept.

# *Slow Bill*

"Slow Bill" first appeared in Street & Smith's *Western Story Magazine* (10/13/23) under the Faust pen-name, John Frederick. In it, Faust has his protagonist, young Jim Legrange, so in awe of his successful millionaire father and so fearful that he cannot ever fill his shoes, that he travels to Truro, the now nearly abandoned town where his father got his start and about which he has heard many stories. Unexpected discoveries are made when he meets up with Jack Rooney, one of the few remaining inhabitants of Truro.

# Chapter One
## *"Legrange Comes to Truro"*

Legrange, as he went up the cañon, was a very picture of one of those adventurers of the earlier days who had moved in the gold rushes from the California to the Montana fields and back again. Sometimes those men had gone alone, sometimes in small groups, sometimes in a caravan of a hundred, pressing eagerly ahead, fevered for the sight of "color," so that those who fell by the way remained where they had fallen and nothing said. He wore a loose felt hat, whose brim slopped down around his face, a flannel shirt, whose sleeves had shrunk until they were far too short, and which he, therefore, wore turned up to the elbows, exposing brawny fore-arms on which the first sunburn was already deepening to strong bronze, blue overalls, rubbed almost white across the knees, and stout, shapeless boots. In his hand was the hammer for chipping rocks, and, as he went, he now and again knocked a corner from a boulder and looked with understanding on the fresh surface that was revealed to him.

To be sure, there were no pounds of powder in the pack upon his burro, no boxes of caps, and no spoon to dig up the débris from a drill hole. Nevertheless, the round pack was in just such a shape as the gold hunters might have made when they were new to the trails and the ways of the mountains. It was lumpy and deformed and sat clumsily upon the back of the little animal.

And, just as the contents of that pack differed from the contents of the packs of the gold hunters, so the contents of the mind of young Jim Legrange differed from the minds of the adventurers. He was not hunting for a fortune. His father had made one large enough and too large, that he would inherit. But his college train-ing as a geologist enabled him to read a story in every stone, a

91

story with sentences and chapters, a million years in the writing, perhaps.

Yet it was not as a mere geologist that he was making this lonely expedition. When the dusk came on, he looked up to the lofty slopes and to their dark covering of pines with the fired eye of an enthusiast and dreamer, and he paused now and again to listen to the chanting of the stream that wound down the gorge, leaping into a waterfall here and there, then rousing deep echoes that called back from the sheer face of a cliff.

To Legrange they told an old story that had been related to him by his father many and many a time in the long evenings at the ranch house. Those tales had told how, in the earlier days, the older Jim Legrange had left his home in the East and gone out with the gold hunters, sighting his course between the mountains and viewing the world between the ears of a burro. Out of those adventures Legrange had gained the money that started him as a rancher. The ranch had grown like a weed. The cattle had multiplied again and again. There were tens of thousands of acres in the domain, and the millions of the elder Jim Legrange were rolling up year by year.

He had gained the nest egg in the hunt for gold which he had found. But, more than that, he had gained a stock of wisdom concerning the ways of the world and had sharpened his eyes to look into the hearts of men. That wisdom was the truer basis upon which his fortune was erected. And the stern school through which he had passed had tempered and formed his character. To young Jim his father was a demigod. The youth half loved and half worshipped him. No other men like him were living now.

When the rancher talked of the earlier times, it seemed that a race of giants had roamed the mountains, committing strange and mighty crimes, performing equally gigantic feats of heroism and self-devotion, failing a hundred times, succeeding once, and making the one success far outbalance the failures in the eyes of the days to come. What faces and hands those men had had who sat around the campfires where his father had heard them talk and where he had talked, himself.

Eventually, he had determined to use a summer exploring deep into the mountains, through all of whose recesses his father had wandered. He was hunting something more precious than gold. He was recreating some part of the atmosphere of the life of that father whom he adored. He was coming to know him more and more intimately. Each bold gorge, each rough-faced mountain told him how the nature of that father had been built up strong and rugged and stern, but beautiful in its harmony and beautiful also in its achievements. For how big was the soul required to take a small fortune among the mountains, winning it like a gambler who plans one dollar to win a thousand and then step down into the sober and exacting life of a ranchman and roll the beginning into a great stable estate, capable now of supporting a university, say, and doing untold good for the world at large. His father had begun as an adventurer, but now he had become a law-abiding, quiet homemaker. He was an example of citizenship to every youth on the range, and by the force of his personal influence he was like a king.

Like a king, indeed, he seemed to young Jim Legrange, and sometimes the younger man trembled at the thought that he must one day, as the sole heir, try to sit upon the throne. What a difference men would discern in them then. How greatly would he suffer by the comparisons that they were bound to make. And now and again there came to him a great and desperate temptation to resign the whole of that wealth and give the world the work of his father before he, a weaker-brained and weaker-handed man, should mar or diminish it. A dozen times he had chosen the site of the college that he would found. A dozen times, half sick at heart, he had willed the ranch and all of its beautiful highlands, its little streams, its long lake, its huge and solid mansion, into the hands of strangers. For he himself must go forth to make his own way, step by step, even as his father had done before him.

Yet it is hard to resign a throne, and hardest of all to make a man know that his son will not carry on his work. When, for the first and last time, he opened his design to his father, the older man had not spoken in reply, but had sat silent, stricken, as though the words were cutting him to the heart. And he had gone about thereafter for days with a stamp of suffering upon his face.

Indeed, it made the heart of young Jim bleed merely to think of that occasion. And it was because of it that he was making this immediate journey into the mountains. He wanted to place himself in his father's boots, if he could; he wanted to knock out the walls of his mind, so to speak, to expand his spirit. So, with the young ghost of the man his father used to be beside him, he strode up the valley, eyeing the falling of the evening, the red passing of the sunset, and then the slow settling of the darkness.

But he could not pick out a spot to camp. There was always a bend of the valley wall just ahead of him, where the calling of a waterfall or the rushing voice of a rapids spurred him on to make just a few steps more. And then he was lured yet a bit higher up the valley. The poor burro would have paused long before, but the club of Jim—he had hours before discovered that a mere whip meant nothing in that burro's life—whacked the little fellow along. And so they came around a sharp elbow turn and stumbled almost into the very midst of the old town of Truro.

A homesick Cornish miner had given that name to the place. It spilled out on either side of the stream, a long, narrow mass of shacks, where twenty thousand people might once have lived. Time had quite crushed it. All the outskirts of the place had fallen into the saddest disrepair. There were fallen roofs and knock-kneed walls and drunken chimneys. It seemed as if one strong breath of wind would knock all flat like a house of cards. But in the center of this large and dreary ruin there was still a little fire of life. Smoke rose bravely from three or four chimneys, and toward that sign the young traveler made on.

As he went, a song was ringing in his brain, an old tune that his father used to hum to himself as he rode the range, a little jigging tune, and, set to that tune, the stories which his father had told him of Truro thundered across his mind. Under yonder mountain's head he had seen the Indian and the Negro fight until both lost footing and rolled to the bottom of the gorge, leaving a red-splotched trail behind them. There was the big blasted pine, from whose withered limbs they had hung the three Mark brothers, whose gang had pillaged and murdered near the mining camp for weeks. And now in the town itself the passage of thirty fierce mountain winters since his father had lived there could not hide from the discernment of Jim Legrange the sites of his father's stories. He could pick them out one by one. And when he passed the long front of an immense shed, in front of which a single line of aspens waved, his heart leaped into his throat, choking him. It was the place of Captain Loftus, the gambler—"the square gambler," they had always called him, until that famous affair of the roulette wheel.

He went on again. A drop of rain stung his face. He looked up and saw that the evening was turning black. Yes, just as his father had many times described it, the head of Mount Samson was lost in a rushing mass of clouds that in an instant blocked the horizon from side to side. Then, with one peal of distant thunder, like a signal gun, the musketry of the shower started. It fell in volleys. It crashed among the trees, and it dropped with a heavy and mournful roll, like the roll of death drums upon the roofs of the deserted houses. It brought up a faint, musty odor, thick in the nostrils of Jim Legrange. He knew it was only the odor of decaying wood, and yet it seemed to him that it symbolized the transitoriness of all life.

The rain was nothing. If it wetted him through and through, he merely shrugged his shoulders at it and went on, for he had other things to think of; and, if his body was cold, his brain was on fire. So he came to the center of the town. It was exactly as his father had a hundred times described it. The two streets came together in a crooked, oblong plaza, and around this plaza the chief life of the village had centered. There had been twenty thousand people here, and each of the twenty thousand had been spending quantities of money everyday. This plaza had been a center of swirling life, and in a week men lived more here in Truro than in seven years, perhaps, in other lands. From diamonds to whiskey there was little which a spender wished that could not be bought here, all at quadrupled prices, to be sure. But what do prices matter, when gold is being dug out of the ground? Prices are names. They have no weight.

In the very middle of that open place Jim paused and stared about him. He knew every corner, it seemed to him. Alas, the whole roof of the old Centralia Place, where his father had often slept, had fallen in. And yonder was the blacksmith shop in front of which Denver Jack and Rawlins had fought with knives and guns, a terrible duel to a double death.

Jim Legrange went on again. He was not as happy as he had expected to be when he first started for the mountains. Instead, there was a mixture of sadness and of a fierce revolt. For supposing that times had been changed, might not he, as well as his father, have risen to show his strength and fight his way with the best of them and the worst?

He stepped into the general merchandise store. Ah, how changed it was. Its widespread roof still stood, but the long, sweeping aisles were vacant now, and the goods, that had once been piled in all directions and risen to the roof, were shrunk to a little stock in a corner near the stove. There was a little food—bacon, flour, and such necessities. There were some cloth, medicine, harnesses, picks, and drills, but the whole stock was hardly more than a handful.

Beside the stove sat two old men, white-headed, white-bearded, round-shouldered with age, with long, bony hands, from which the flesh had dropped away, and great, bony wrists. The boots on their feet seemed old enough to have a character of their own, and they were big enough to be stepped into and out of by the owners.

This was McCreary's Store! This was that famous site of so many fights and of so many frolics. On the edge of that very table yonder, perhaps, his father had slapped down the money when he had made that famous bet with Jack Sterner. This was the place where the men had swarmed and crowded in to tell tales, or to hear them. This had been the very center of the life of the town of Truro. And this was all that was left of the famous store that huge Bill McCreary had founded.

"Howdy," said a cracked voice to Jim. "Were you wanting something or other at the store?"

"Yes," said Jim Legrange sadly. "I do want something."

"What is it?" asked one of the ancients.

"Only old Bill McCreary himself could tell me," said the gloomy youth.

"Well, sir," said one of the poor wrecks of humanity before him, "I'm McCreary. What is it?"

# Chapter Two
## "Like a Little Kingdom"

The hair prickled upon the scalp of Jim Legrange. It was not a mere disappointment to him—it was a horror. For, having buried that famous Bill McCreary in his thoughts long before, he could not readjust himself to the knowledge that McCreary was not dead, but living, though living as a pitiful caricature of the self that had once been so mighty of hand and of will that all the rough spirits of Truro were pacified before him.

"You?" said Jim Legrange. "Are *you* McCreary?"

The old man shrugged his shoulders with impatience.

"And why not, son?" he asked grimly. "Why not? Ain't I got his face and his voice? Have I stole 'em from somebody else? If I did, I bought something that ain't worth much." Then he laughed so heartily in so cracked and quavering a voice that he had to press his hand against his side and finally drop feebly into his chair. His ancient companion had been moved to equal mirth by this clever remark, and in their uproar neither had been capable of remarking the scorn and the sorrow with which Jim Legrange was eyeing them.

"What might you be wanting with McCreary?" asked the storekeeper.

Legrange tore his thoughts away from the distant past.

"I'll tell you another time," he said hastily. "Just now what I most require is a bed for myself and a shelter for my poor burro . . . together with supper for us both."

At this McCreary scratched his chin a little wistfully. "They ain't a man living," he said, "that can say that I turned him away hungry from my door. Not a man living. But when it comes to supper *and* a bed, I'm afraid that it lets me out. Eh, Pete?"

Pete nodded a lugubrious head. "Old Jack is the man for him," he said.

97

"Old Jack," echoed McCreary, "is the man for him."

"Is Old Jack's a hotel?" asked Legrange.

The two old fellows looked at one another and then shook their heads.

"In a way of speaking," said McCreary, "it *ain't* a hotel."

"But," said Legrange, "if it's a hotel and not a hotel that he keeps, will you tell what he *does* keep?"

"A house," said McCreary.

Legrange flushed with anger, yet he could guess that the old fellows were not baiting him, but their age-enfeebled minds were wandering away from the subject to which he tried to hold them.

"How is it a hotel?" he asked.

"Because he takes in folks that need a bed."

"And how is his place not like a hotel?"

"He don't take no pay."

"A kind and respectable fellow," said Legrange. "God bless all such, say I! Where is he to be found?"

"Right up Landers Cañon. You take the first turn."

"I know the way. I could find it in the blackest night."

He smiled upon their wonder. Indeed, from the stories of his father the whole map of Truro, with its environs, was printed in his mind. How he could astonish these men, if he were to tell some of the tales that he knew about them. For if the one was McCreary, the other could be no other than that inseparable crony of his from the old days—Pete Martin, the stage driver, tamer of horses and men. But it was necessary to learn something more about his host-to-be.

"Hold on," called McCreary. "If you go up the cañon, you're taking a chance that he may not be able to put you up."

"How's that?"

"He may have his man by this time of the night. They's a good many of them vacationists that wanders along when it comes about this time of the year, and, when they hear about Jack Rooney, they mostly pops in on him."

"His *man?*" queried Legrange.

"He don't take no more'n one man every night."

"Small house, eh?"

"Nope, he's got a good-sized cabin, fine and snug as ever you seen."

"But only a bunk for one more?"

"Plenty of bunks, if he wanted to use 'em . . . but it's just the way of Rooney, that's all. You can't start in by changing the ways of old men, you know."

"Old?" cried Pete indignantly. "Why, Rooney ain't no more'n a boy, and that you know as well as I know it, McCreary. How you take on with your talk."

"Not old compared with you and me, Pete," said McCreary gently, "but to the eyes of a youngster like our friend, here, I'd say that he was fair to middling old, right enough."

"Well," said Legrange. "I suppose I must start on. Jack Rooney is his name?"

"That's his name."

"And he puts up one man every night?"

"Every night that one comes his way. He'll put 'em up, with no questions and no money asked. And, after they've stayed the night with him once, they ain't welcome never to come back no more afterward. That's the way with Jack Rooney. He don't like to put up a man twice."

Legrange turned fairly upon them at the door. The more he heard of this Jack Rooney the stranger the story grew.

"Look here," he said, "the man must be a freak. You mean that he takes in everyone without question?"

"I mean just that," said McCreary.

"But suppose that a robber came down the road."

"Oh, Jack would take him just the same."

"Has he been cleaned out of money a dozen times?"

"Him? Jack Rooney cleaned out? Son, it's plain that you're a stranger in these here parts. Nope, Jack Rooney ain't been cleaned out yet."

And with this he turned a knowing smile upon Pete, and Pete smiled knowingly in return. It presented yet another side of Jack Rooney to Legrange.

"What's the business of this man?" he asked curiously.

"He ain't got no business to speak of."

"I mean, what does he live on?"

"Well, he raises some chickens, and he's got a couple of cows for milk, and he keeps a few hosses running in his pastures. He sure lives snug, does Jack Rooney."

"He sells eggs, I suppose."

99

"Sells eggs? Who'd he be sellin' 'em to in these parts, except half a dozen here and there? Nope, he raises 'em for his own use and the use of them that he puts up by nights. He raises his own vegetables, too, and his own berries. He's got a right smart bit of work to do around his place to keep things up, I'd say."

"A right smart," agreed Pete Martin in a groaning voice at the mere thought of physical exertion.

"His family helps him, I suppose."

"Family? Good land, man, he ain't got no family . . . not old Jack Rooney!"

The picture grew stranger and stranger.

"But," said Legrange, "he has an income that supports him, I judge?"

"I dunno," said the storekeeper solemnly. "There's some that says one thing, and some that says others about how that he comes to get his money. But all I got a right to know is that, when he comes down here to buy, he pays with cash and pays on the spot. Always gold. Nothing less."

Legrange started. Here, indeed, was a breath of mystery that belonged to the time of which his father had spoken so often. And how delightful it would be to return to his father's ranch bearing with him a story of Truro as strange and as exciting as any which the elder Legrange had ever recited.

"He always pays with gold! Perhaps he has a little treasure of his own laid up?"

"That's what other folks has said, and that's what other folks has thought," said the storekeeper. "And some of 'em has gone up there in the cañon to pry around and find out what they could find out. But none of 'em had no luck . . . none of 'em had no luck!"

And, with his companion, he burst into an ironic laughter so violent and so prolonged that the tears came into his eyes.

Legrange left him and went back into the night to find the burro. That wise little beast had tucked himself under a wide projecting roof, and, with one ear rocked forward and another hanging back, and with his feet braced, was sleeping where he stood. Legrange scratched the wet ears, with a touch of compassion and affection for the queer little brute that had been his companion for two weeks. Then he prodded the burro up the street.

As they went on, he turned in his mind the information that he had received. He was to request lodging, so it seemed, of a queer fellow who lived in utter solitude, supporting himself with what he could raise with his own hand and out of a store of gold which he had laid by, or which—as the grim hint of the storekeeper might have seemed to imply—he secured by unknown and mysterious ways which might not be strictly according to the law. This was strange enough, but added to this was the habit of receiving any stranger who passed, so long as there was only one, and of never taking in the same man twice; the picture grew both queer and complicated.

So he went on up the cañon. Here at least there had been nothing to rot, and he found his way easily. For it was all mapped clearly in his mind. He knew the first bend and the second. It was above the second bend, a full three miles from the town, that he came upon the house of Jack Rooney.

How he first saw it he could never afterward forget. The rain had ceased, and wind from a new quarter of the heavens had scattered the clouds here and there and let the moon look through—not her clear face, but rather a ghostly and uncertain light that showed the scurrying of the clouds and made the dark earth less thick with shadows. By this light he saw the house of Jack Rooney. One light burned from one window, and a paler light came from an open door behind the main body of the house.

He saw a long, low roof line, so long, indeed, that he rubbed his eyes and looked again, and with the second look he discovered that it was not the roof of the house alone, but the roof of the whole group of houses and several sheds combined. He turned the burro in at the entrance path. On the one hand, berry vines were lifted in high twining masses upon frames, and the new-fallen rain had struck out the sweet odor of the fruit and rolled it heavily through the damp air. On the other hand, there was the sharp scent of cabbage and of other vegetables on a broad patch upon his right. Beyond this vegetable patch, the forms of cattle were slowly venturing out from sheds, under which they had taken shelter, and were beginning to munch the grass again.

He came still closer up the path. There were evergreens clustered here and there about the house. And farther away he saw the regular rows and the pruned heads of the trees of a small orchard. A sudden peace rolled over the mind of Legrange. In the nearer distance he could hear a faint bleating of sheep. A dog growled softly in the yard, as he passed. It was like a little kingdom sufficient unto itself. Here was the simple life made both delightful and independent. And Legrange found himself smiling through the dark, in spite of his weariness.

Through the open doorway, in which the light was shining, he saw the form of Jack Rooney himself, and Legrange paused at once for closer observation.

# Chapter Three
## "The Picture"

It was the door of the creamery, and, by the light of a lantern hanging from the roof of the building, he saw a man well past the middle fifties—perhaps he was even more than sixty years of age. His hair was white and might have indicated an even greater age, but his carriage was so alert, and there was such life and youth in his manner, that it took many years from his apparent time of life.

He was skimming pans of milk, scooping off the cream with a curved tin skinner and dropping the yellow clots of cream in a great brown earthenware jar that stood beside him. Presently he was finished. The cream was in the jar, and the mouth of the jar was tied across with a wet cloth, and the skimmed milk had been poured into a large pail. It was at this very point that something from the outside—though Legrange could have sworn that he had not made a sound—seemed to catch the attention of Jack Rooney.

For he whirled softly and quickly to the door, and Legrange saw a type of the bulldog in faces—low and wide of brow, wide of jaw and small of nose, and with high cheekbones and labor-thinned cheeks. And, as he listened, Jack Rooney stared downward to the ground.

There was something so animal-like in that attitude of wary attention that Legrange felt a chill creep through his blood. But almost at once the other came through the door and called out, throwing up a hand by way of greeting.

"Hello, stranger!"

"Here!" answered Legrange.

Jack Rooney hurried inside the creamery and came out at once again, carrying the lantern. The screen door banged behind him. He strode down the wooden walk, with the shadows of his legs walking gigantically beside him. Now he passed the swinging gate and was clasping the hand of Legrange.

103

"Out in a rain like this one!" he cried. "Well, well, son, I'm mighty glad that you've landed here. We'll have you dried out and feedin' in a jiffy. You come right along with me. Got a hoss?"

"Here," said Legrange, "is my burro."

"Ah," said Jack Rooney with an odd accent, "that's something that ain't so often seen now in Truro . . . a burro all packed up."

He led the way back to a barn, where he opened a door and showed them into a stall for the burro. There he held the lantern, while Legrange unstrapped the pack. And there he pitched into the manger more food than three burros could have munched. After this he jumped down and refused to let Legrange carry the pack to the house. It was no light weight, and worse than its weight was its widespread clumsiness. But Jack Rooney, though he was far from a big man, managed in some deft way to bring the pack upon his left shoulder and arm, and then he walked along, carrying the lantern in his right hand and chatting as easily and with as good a breath as though he were quite unburdened.

And this is a man whose hair was white! It made Legrange blush for shame. They went into the house through the kitchen door. Legrange stepped upon a floor composed of great stone flags, so industriously scrubbed that the rock had been whitened. He saw a stove newly blacked and polished with an absurd care, so it seemed to the young visitor; and he saw along the wall well-ordered lines of pots and pans, each burnished and each looking in some strange way at home and in place. In that passage through the kitchen he noted, too, the clean sink and the spotless drainboard. And at the window, a delightfully surprising touch, were flowers growing in a window box. The lantern light touched dimly and pleasantly upon pink blossoms.

They entered the dining room, with half a dozen stiff-backed chairs pushed against the wall and the round table placed under a hanging lamp. They went on again and came into a living room, where Legrange saw a laid fire, and through this to a bedroom, where the host deposited the pack upon the floor.

"Here you are," he said, without so much as a shrug of the shoulder to show that he was glad to be relieved of the load. "Look around here and get yourself fixed . . . try to make yourself feel fair to middling at home, son. I'm going to get you a snack of something to eat. Have you got any dry clothes in that pack?"

Legrange assured him that he had, and, when his host stepped from the room, he looked around him to examine the surroundings with a greater care. It was not a large room, but it seemed to have been planned rather with an effort toward homely comfort than toward spaciousness. The one narrow window was screened across with the network of a climbing vine, and the rafters along the bare ceiling sagged perceptibly downward. The very door was lower than the average, so that a man stooped, as it were, into a place of snug comfort. And it was all the more a charming surprise because out of such masculine roughness of background there had been developed such a touch of feminine delicacy. There was a little fireplace. There was a large chair, handmade, but so cushioned and formed that it was, nonetheless, comfortable. And over the fireplace there was even a little shelf of books.

Presently he was changing his clothes, and then he stepped out into the hall and was greeted with the most surpassing fragrance to the nostrils of a hungry man—the odor of frying bacon. He could hear it hissing in the pan, and in his mind he could almost hear the bubbling of the eggs that must be frying at the same time. An instant later a breeze brought to him the scent of coffee that was just coming to the boil. Indeed, it was close to a miracle that the cooking of a meal could have been brought to a climax so soon, and it came into the mind of Legrange that old Jack Rooney must keep his suppers ready in the pan, prepared each day for the chance guest of the evening.

And half smiling, half mystified by the thought, with all it implied of eager geniality and good nature, he stepped out to the living room and began to examine it more closely. But he took not one step past the door. For, looking him full in the face and clear as a ghost of the reality, a picture of his father stared across the room.

Legrange dropped into a chair and stared again. But, after all, it was not so amazing. Perhaps his father had been very well known in Truro in the old days, though he had always insisted that the rôles he played were nameless and unnoticed. That might spring out of his modesty. Nay, it must spring from some such thing, for here was a man of the old times who chose to keep a picture of Jim Legrange, Senior, hanging over the fireplace in his best room. And the heart of the son began to thrill and to swell. Before that evening was ended, who could tell what strange and magnificent stories of the courage and the prowess of his father he might hear? He drew a great breath at the thought.

As for the picture itself, it was a facsimile of one that belonged to Jim's mother. It showed the elder Legrange as he had been a full thirty years before, erect, wide-shouldered, keen-eyed, with long and curving mustaches, sweeping like miniature sabers upon either side of his mouth. There was a military erectness, a military pride in his demeanor. But the picture that the younger Legrange knew was only an ordinary photograph; this was a huge, life-size enlargement. It had even been tinted. Indeed, in that dim light, it seemed that his father was standing in the flesh before him. That had been the first startling reaction.

Here he whirled suddenly upon his heel, for he had felt the weight of eyes watching him from the rear. It was old Jack Rooney who stood in the doorway, smiling and nodding. Yet, it seemed to Legrange that the smiling had only very suddenly begun, with his own turn to the rear, and that the eyes of Rooney were still grave and attentive.

"You like that picture, I guess?" he asked.

What made him secretive just then was not hard to decipher, for, though the first impulse of Jim was to cry out that it was the picture of his own father that hung upon the wall, he decided that he must keep that relationship secret for two reasons. The first of these was that, if he confessed that he was the son of him upon the wall, old Rooney might be tempted to tell less or more than the truth of what he knew about Legrange. The second was that, after drawing out all that Rooney knew, he could surprise the veteran by simply giving his name.

"Why," said Legrange, "that's a sort of wild-looking fellow. He must have been able to lift his share."

The glance of Rooney lingered upon him, just a fraction of a second, as the lash of the whip seems to linger along the flank of the lagging horse.

"He could lift his weight," he said with a significant lack of emphasis. "He was a man!"

"What was his name?"

"You'll know his name when you hear it . . . that is, if you was raised west of the Mississippi."

"That so? Then let's have it." And he waited, setting his teeth to keep back his smile.

"That," said the old man, "is a living picture of Slow Bill."

# Chapter Four
## "A Man Comes to Town"

With that he turned upon his heel and walked out of the room, saying: "Come along! There ain't no use keeping a gent standing around when his stomach is empty. Come along, stranger. What was it you said your name was?"

"Legrange," murmured Jim. "James Legrange is my name."

And he followed in a haze, scarcely conscious of what he did. For a new apprehension had come to him, and it staggered him even to conceive it. It occurred to him that there might be a new reason for the silence of his father concerning his own share in those events among the mountains and the mines. Perhaps in those early days there had been deeds done which would not bear the retelling after so long a time and among men of peace. Perhaps in his youth the sedate rancher had sometimes allowed the wild temper, that often showed in his glittering eyes and in his set jaw, to go loose. The very possibility made young Jim turn pale. The more he thought of it the more probable it was. For Jack Rooney had mentioned Slow Bill in the manner of one who announces a national celebrity.

They were in the dining room now. He cast an eye over a table steaming with hot food. He smiled mechanically. Mechanically he expressed his gratitude to his host and his amazement that such a meal could have been prepared so quickly.

"It's having things ready and doing things simple," explained Jack Rooney, not without pride. "I aim to have good chuck around these diggings, and I aim to get it onto the fire and off the fire onto the table pretty quick. Why not? The way that women folks got of killing time and pestering around a kitchen, thinking about what they got to do next, sure never looked like sense to me. I never seen no sense to it, and I thought that I'd see if it couldn't be done more

108

simple. Well, sir, I worked it out so that it *is* more simple. I do up my house every day. Do as much work as a woman does. Bake my own bread . . . try some of that there, Mister Legrange. Ain't it light, and ain't it white? . . . and I do the washing, scrub the floors every Saturday afternoon, and sweep 'em every other day of the blessed year . . . milk the cows, make the butter, raise the chickens . . . all of them things that women folks make such a pile of fuss over.

"I'll tell you, son, that a woman sure knows how to make propaganda. She can talk about herself and what she does all day and every day till you'd think that men would begin to wake up and to see that it ain't all true. But men are just nacherally born fools when women come around. Women talk about men's work being only from sun to sun, but women's work being never done. Say, Mister Legrange, it sure does rile me to think of folks swallering that sort of guff! I do a woman's work on this here place, and then I do a man's work, too. And if anybody was to ask me whether I'd rather wash a set of dishes, or else to handle a two-hoss plow that was dancing and jigging along through hard dirt and trying to yank your arms out at the shoulders, or whether I'd rather do a little washing than to mow ten tons of hay into a hot barn, with weeds down my back and dust up my nose . . . well, man, I'd tell 'em that when I want to *rest* I come in to do the housework!"

In this vein Jack Rooney talked, at the same time passing to his guest the platter that contained more bacon and eggs than even his stalwart appetite could consume, or pressing upon him a deep-dish apple pie, or persuading him to a great plate of hot rolls, flanked with a dish of golden honey.

And Jim Legrange ate hugely, listened, nodded, and heard not a word. His brain was too busy striving to untangle the mystery and the dread that had come upon him—the mortal fear for the repute and the fair name of his father. Not that he could conceive the elder Legrange doing a mean or a low thing, but that he feared what the consequences of that wild temper in the wild head of a younger man might be backed with a power of hand which was still proverbial along the cattle ranges.

He said at the first pause in the easy, drifting talk of his host: "But Slow Bill . . . I hope to hear about him."

"You'll hear about him," chuckled Jack Rooney. "You'll hear

about him, and I'll be a pile surprised if you're the first one that gets away from this here house without knowing an earful about Slow Bill. But there's a proper time for listening to a proper yarn, and that's not while a gent is putting chuck into his stomach. Slow Bill was worth watching and listening to when he was living, and he's worth hearing about and smoking a pipe over, now he's gone."

"He's dead?" asked Legrange, the younger, signifying with a gesture that he could eat no more.

"Aye," said Jack Rooney meditatively. "I reckon he's dead by now. But come into the other room, and we'll have a fire and more about Slow Bill. Ah, there's the rain again. How Bill loved to lie awake in the shack and listen to the rain. 'It makes a background for a man's thoughts,' he used to say. He had queer ideas, had Bill!"

Rooney rose from the table at that instant to lead the way, or else he could not have failed to notice the violent start of his guest. How many times had Jim Legrange heard his father speak those very words?

In the living room the fire was roaring in a trice, and, when the first rush of flames through the kindling wood had subsided, and when the logs were beginning to burn with a faint whispering hiss of oozing sap, Rooney packed his pipe, lighted it, and started his narrative.

"He come in with the stage," said Rooney. "There wasn't no road to speak of, but the Cartright brothers had found road enough for *their* wheels to run on, and so they'd started a line to the bottom of the cañon, where the rocks begun to grow big. A coach would last out about two trips before it had to be junked, but the prices that they charged made it good business, even when they were chewing up running gear at that rate. Well, the stage come in, and the boys was there to see it. Off gets the rest of the passengers, and the last one down was a tall gent, with shoulders as wide as that door yonder, and eyes as quiet as a steer's in a spring pasture. He gets down slow and careful and stands up and brushes the dust off'n him, and he sure was dressed neat . . . almost neat enough to be a gambler.

" 'Well,' says the driver, 'I'll take the rest of that pay right now, partner. You can get that lock worked off'n your bag right now. I ain't got no time to spare.'

"And he points to a big carpetbag with a lock onto it that the stranger had hefted down.

" 'Is there a locksmith here?' he says.

"The crowd puts up a laugh at that.

" 'You ain't in New York now, Bill,' says someone.

" 'I imagine not,' he says. 'Besides,' he says, 'now that I come to think of it, my money isn't in that carpetbag.'

" 'Where in thunder is it?' yells the driver, Sam Kewan, and a hard man he was!

" 'I've forgotten,' says the stranger.

"There was another laugh, but Kewan was getting peeved.

" 'I'll have that coin,' he says, 'and I'll have it quick.'

" 'I'm sorry,' says the stranger. 'I'll pay you when you come back on your next trip.'

" 'Why, curse your eyes,' says Sam, 'd'you mean to say that you've beat your way up on me? Then I'll have that bag for security.'

" 'You're welcome,' says the stranger.

"Sam jumps down from his seat and kicks the lock plumb open . . . and inside there wasn't nothing but rocks wrapped up in paper. Sam picks out one and heaves it right at the head of the big young gent.

" 'Look out, Bill!' yells somebody, and Bill jumps just in time.

" 'My friend,' he says, 'it seems to me that you're a trifle hasty with your rocks and your guns!'

"Because now Sam had his gat out and was cussing enough to make a muleskinner plumb ashamed of his vocabulary.

" 'I can use ten dollars' worth of your dancing,' he says. 'Start prancing, you hound, or I'll shoot the feet off'n you!'

"And he sends a chunk of lead into the pebbles at the feet of Bill.

"We all backs up. And we seen Bill push the hat back on his head and look at Sam sort of thoughtful, like he didn't know what to make out of such acting up and carrying on.

" 'I'm a slow man,' he says, 'to be angered. I hope that was a joke, Kewan.'

" 'Joke . . . nothing!' says Kewan. 'Dance, you big tenderfoot!'

"And he shoots again and trims a corner off the toe of Bill's foot. Bill puts his foot up on its heel and looks down at the hole that's just been blowed in his leather, and all is dead easy and quiet as you or me sitting here right this minute. Then he looks back to Kewan.

" 'It seems to me,' he says, 'that you'd better put up your gun, or you'll be doing harm.'

"It got another laugh from the boys, and Sam goes plumb crazy, he's so mad.

" 'Wait a minute,' says somebody, 'maybe Bill ain't got a gun.'

" 'I don't need one, I'm sure,' says Bill, quick as a flash. 'It has just occurred to me that there is something to be done here.'

"And with that he walks right in on big Sam Kewan, takes the gun by the muzzle, and jerks it out of Kewan's hand. He tosses it twenty feet away. Kewan just stares at him. And the rest of us was dumbfounded, too. Looked like Bill was walking right· into a chunk of lead when he done that.

" 'Remember,' says Bill, 'I'll pay you on your next trip up.'

"And he turns on his heel and saunters off.

"You'd have thought that Kewan would have run after him and started a fight, because there was nothing but temper and fight in Sam. He didn't need no guard with a sawed-off shotgun when he was driving the stage. But he didn't make no move to start any trouble. He just walks over slow and easy and picks up his gun and shoves it back into the holster. His face was red and white in patches, he was so mad. But all the time it was easy to see that he was thinking about something.

"He goes back and climbs up onto the box of the stage ag'in.

" 'Boys,' he says, 'Bill . . . he's kind of slow, but it looks to me like a man has come to town. Giddap, Beck!'

"And he scoots that team right out of town.

"But that was how Slow Bill got his name. He wasn't knowed as anything else, after that. He took to it, himself, and always introduced himself as Bill. But, when the stage come up the next time, there was Slow Bill, waiting for it. He'd worked them tender hands of his raw, but he'd earned his fare in gold dust, and he paid it right into the hand of Sam Kewan. Sam gives him a grin.

" 'Bill,' he says, 'seems like I owe you a pair of boots.'

"Slow Bill looks down to that hole in the toe of his boot.

" 'Why,' he says, 'I guess I can afford to throw in a pair of boots for interest.'

"And, after that, we knowed that we had a man with us, and that he was a square shooter, too!"

# Chapter Five
## *"While the World Moved"*

Here the narrator paused to tamp down the tobacco in his pipe and shake his head, smiling over the recollections which were beginning to swarm in his mind; and young Legrange felt as if he must burst with the happiness of hearing such words spoken of his father. It was what he had always guessed must be true. The very moment such a man as his father appeared, no matter in how rough company, his strength of character must assert itself and his utter fearlessness.

But here the story commenced again, and it rolled on for hours, with endless anecdotes of the deeds of Slow Bill—how he had performed in the dance hall, the gaming house, the gold field; how he took his losses manfully; how he made his winnings gracefully; and how the respect and the love of the entire community were centering around him.

"But what became of Slow Bill?" asked Jim Legrange at last.

"Well," said Jack Rooney, "that's what I been wishing to learn all these years. That's why I got that picture hanging over the fireplace in that room. If Bill is living, I say to myself, some day he'll come back here and look up the places where he used to cut such a figure. Or if Bill don't come back, then maybe somebody that's seen him will come through and recognize him by that picture."

"Why," said the guest, "it seems to me that you would have made it your business to find out about Slow Bill after he left the camp."

"These thirty years I've made it my business," admitted Jack Rooney.

The heart of the younger man jumped. Here was faith and fidelity and affection greater than any he had ever heard of.

"Did you never leave Truro to get trace of him?"

113

"For a year I didn't do nothing but ride on his trail and camp on his trail. But there wasn't nothing come out of it. Sometimes I seen somebody that had had a glimpse of Slow Bill. But I run all the clues down, and they didn't lead to nothing. The thing of it was that I never knowed the right name of Slow Bill, though him and me were pretty thick. I never knowed his name, and so I didn't have no luck when I tried to find him. You see?"

"And you've been here ever since?"

"I lost interest in things when Slow Bill dropped out of sight."

"Didn't he tell you where he was going, or when?"

"That wasn't his way. He'd sit and think things out slow and easy, but, when he made up his mind to start, he didn't ring no bells to let folks know."

"And so he simply faded out of your sight one day?"

"Yup. Him and me had been partners."

"Really?"

"Yup, we sure had. But one day I seen him, and the next day I didn't. That was Bill's way."

"And you've never heard a word from him since?"

"Nope. I been here sitting and waiting, but nothing in the line of news of Bill has ever showed up. I didn't have no interest in going other places. I made my little stake right here in Truro. I seen the rush start and seen it finish. I got sort of fond of the cañon. So I set up shop right here and been here ever since. But Bill ain't showed up, nor no news of him."

"Maybe he's dead long ago."

The old man shook his head.

"Nope," he said, "he ain't dead."

"What makes you so sure?" asked Legrange, thrilling strangely in the face of such conviction.

"Because, son, there wouldn't be no justice in the world if I was to be left sitting here for thirty years and all for nothing!"

Legrange could endure it no longer. He reached suddenly from his chair and laid his hand on the arm of Jack Rooney.

"My dear friend," he said, "you're right. Slow Bill is alive!"

Jack Rooney clasped the arm of his chair and blinked at his companion. He had lost color, and the pipe shook between his fingers.

"Oh, Lord," he whispered, and again, "oh, Lord! You know him?"

"Know him? I'm his son, Jack Rooney!"

He had expected an outburst of exclamations. How poorly he read how great emotion will affect a man. For old Jack Rooney sank his chin upon his fist and began to nod to the fire with unseeing, staring eyes.

"You're the son of Slow Bill?" he murmured to himself. "Well, well, well, well! Here's part of Slow Bill come back to Truro!"

He stood up, wandered to the mantelpiece, found a match, relighted his pipe, and then stared at Legrange through a mist of smoke. A sudden thought struck him.

"Bill wasn't married when he was up here."

"No, he married my mother after he came down from the mountains."

"How old are you?"

"Twenty-five. They'd been married for three years when I was born."

"My guns," said the old miner, "while Bill was seeing you born and raised and growing up to a man . . . while he was doing that, I been just sitting and waiting up here." He stopped short. "Why," he said suddenly, "I've got to be an old man . . . an old man!"

And Legrange suddenly knew that the hermit had never before realized it, so swiftly had the years marched past him.

"Not old," said Legrange kindly. "You have more strength and more energy than half of the young men I have known!"

"Then Slow Bill's name was really Legrange?"

"Jim Legrange."

And still young Jim waited for the outburst of joy, but it did not come.

"Well, well, well," sighed the miner. "It don't seem real somehow. What become of Slow Bill?"

"He brought down the stake he'd made in the mines and put it into cattle."

"Got to be a rancher, eh?"

"Yes."

"Things prosper with him?"

"He's become very rich."

"You don't say!"

"Everything that he put his hand to turned into money."

"Hmm! Well, that's mighty fine for Bill!"

115

"When you see his ranch, you'll be astonished to see what he has done from such a small beginning."

"Didn't he have a pretty good-sized stake when he come down from the mines?"

"Not more than ten thousand dollars."

"Ten thousand! Why, son, ain't ten thousand dollars a lot of money?"

"I'll tell you," said Jim Legrange, hunting for some way of expressing to the other the size of his father's fortune at the present moment. "I'll tell you. Last year Dad built a barn that cost thirty thousand and spent fifty thousand leveling and checking some land for irrigation."

Again he failed to hear gasps of surprise and exultation.

"It's queer . . . it's mighty queer," was all that Jack Rooney muttered.

"Why?" said Legrange.

"Your dad must be a millionaire!"

"Several times over."

"And all made out of that first stake he brought down from the mines?"

"He didn't have a cent to start with except that ten thousand. Everyone knows that. He made all the rest out of his wits."

"And luck?"

"No luck about it. He took his hard times with the rest of them. But when the dry spells came, it was always found that Dad had saved up a lot of water in his tanks, and, when bad years came, he had stacked up feed and hay . . . in spite of all that, he nearly went under twice in two great dry spells. He came through with his cattle as thin as famine. But, after all, the bad times were a blessing to him in each case. He had been almost drained of resources, but his neighbors had gone down in whole ranks. Not that Dad had not done his best to help them. But since he survived, he was able to buy in land as cheap as dirt on all sides, and half-starved cattle by the thousands, too weak to have lived if he had not taken them. So that the two greatest strides he made were during times that ruined hundreds of other people."

"And, I suppose," said Jack Rooney, "that some folks hold that against him? Some folks may grudge what he got during them bad times?"

"They can't grudge my father. I imagine that you could ride for two hundred miles around his ranch without hearing a bad word spoken of him."

Jack Rooney nodded slowly. "Rich and happy and settled down with a family of children growed up."

"No, I'm the only one."

Jack Rooney looked slowly at him, surveying him from head to foot.

"Well, lad," he said gently, "you're enough."

And Jim Legrange thought that it was at once the greatest and the most subtle compliment that he had ever received—to be so recognized by one of those great men who had known his father.

"And with a happy wife?"

"Aye, she and father are the happiest pair in the world, I imagine. Here's a picture of them on their wedding day."

He took a locket from his neck. He snapped it open and showed the pair of pictures that it contained. Jack Rooney took it in such a trembling hand that Legrange looked sharply up at him. But the head of the old miner was bowed over the faces. "It ain't possible," he was muttering. "He couldn't have done it."

"Done what?" asked Legrange.

"He couldn't have been so lucky," sighed Rooney. "Why . . . why . . . it seems like I been standing still and waiting and letting the world turn around, while everything moved on it except me. But he sure got a mighty pretty girl, eh, Legrange?"

Young Jim took back the locket, and he thought sadly to himself that this was the sharpest of commentaries upon human weakness of mind. After waiting thirty years to see his old partner and companion, Jack Rooney could not keep the poison point of jealousy from touching his heart at the very first thrust.

Jack Rooney had gone back to his chair, and for a long interval, a whole minute, perhaps, he said not a single word, but cast up around him a dense screen of smoke. Young Legrange, hurt, astonished, rose and bade him good night.

"Go along," said the miner, "go along and sleep and leave me be. I got more things to think about than you'd ever guess. Having dreamed about a thing for thirty years makes it tolerable hard to see a dream come true, old son."

Jim Legrange smiled, patted him affectionately on the shoulder, and went to bed obediently, where, in spite of his happy heart, he was instantly asleep and did not waken again until the sun was high among the mountain tops. He leaped out of bed with the guilty feeling that he had far overslept his time. When he had dressed and come out into the house, he found that his breakfast stood near the stove, ready for cooking, but that old Jack Rooney was not in sight.

He cooked his own meal, therefore, and went out afterward to find his truant host. It was the cracking of a revolver that guided him. He came over a ridge and saw in the hollow old Jack Rooney blazing away with a heavy Colt. His target was a black stone thirty steps away, but even at that considerable distance the marksman was blowing off the projecting corners with an uncanny accuracy.

# Chapter Six
## *"Legrange Takes the Road"*

The 'puncher who rode down for the mail spurred all the way back to the ranch house as soon as he had it in his hand. For among the letters he had seen one addressed to Legrange in his son's hand-writing, and he knew that letter would be eagerly opened. He arrived on a lathered horse, therefore, and two minutes later Legrange had the letter in his hand.

He went at once into the library, where he might read it undis-turbed, and, as he went, he pinched its fat sides again and again. Certainly there was nothing that stirred him more than a letter from his boy, and such a thick letter as this had come to him hardly ever before.

"Blood will tell. Blood will tell," muttered Legrange, as he cut the envelope carefully open. "He's full of love for those moun-tains! Full of it!"

And, indeed, across his eyes were already rolling pictures of the black forest washing around the edges of the upper mountains, leaving the sides bare at timberline, a mark as level as the mark of the sea along the winding shore. And in his nostrils there was the delightful freshness of the evergreens which he had not breathed for a full thirty years—like thirty centuries it seemed to the elder Jim Legrange.

He had the letter open at last, and he read:

**I was hardly into the shadow of the mountains, when I decided to cut away from the route which you and I had planned for the trip.**

"Good," murmured the rancher. "I've always despised men who stayed to beaten paths in the mountains."

**Instead,** continued the letter, **I turned straight to the left under Mount Cousin and went bang into the Truro Cañon.**

Here the hand of the rancher containing the letter dropped suddenly to his side, so that the pages brushed against the floor. And for a long moment he stared out the window, as though he saw ghosts passing across it.

"Mount Cousin . . . the Truro Cañon," he whispered to himself.

Then, as though forcing himself against his will, he raised the letter and continued his reading.

**I went straight up the Truro Cañon until I struck the town. And there I found . . . but I can't hesitate and stop over the details. I have to get into the main drift of important things. Within half an hour after I reached Truro I was on the way to see the best of your old friends in the mountains . . . I was on the way to see Jack Rooney himself, and to hear wonderful stories about Slow Bill!**

Here the hand of the rancher fell again. The fingers relaxed, and the pages scattered carelessly across the floor. He remained in that manner for some time. Then he dropped to his knees, as though blinded, and fumbled around the floor until he had gathered all the sheets again. After that, he read feverishly on and on, hunting for things which apparently the missive did not contain, though every word and almost every look of old Jack Rooney had been set down by his son. How the glories of Slow Bill were dwelt upon and underlined, and with what a passion of admiration for a man who could not only do what his father had done, but who could keep from telling the stories of his deeds to his own son.

But all of this the rancher read through with a whitening cheek until he came to the tale of how the locket with the two pictures had been shown, and the strange effect that it had had upon Jack Rooney. At this the elder Legrange groaned, crushed the letter to a crumpled mass, and threw it into the fireplace. But, before the flames could catch on the paper, he snatched it out again and read and reread the narrative.

A step came to the door of the room. He turned and saw Mrs. Legrange, very girlishly slender and with still a shadow of the beauty of her youth. Time could not dim it; neither could it corrupt the love of Legrange for her. Though sometimes he told himself that the reason he loved her so ardently, so freshly, was because he had always known that he could not win her whole heart. For the greater half of that was lost before she ever saw him.

"They tell me you've heard from our boy, Jim," she told him.

"From Jim?" he said huskily. "A letter from Jim? Not at all . . . not at all! Not a word from the rascal. He's too busy with the burro's pack, I suppose, to waste any time writing letters."

"You really haven't heard a word?" she murmured, and he saw a shade of trouble in her eyes. "You . . . you don't mean that you're keeping bad tidings from me, Jim?"

"No, Nell, no. On my honor!"

She hesitated an instant longer, and then with a wan smile of reassurance she went on down the hall. She was no sooner gone than Legrange struck his hand across his forehead.

*The first lie*, he thought to himself. *How many others will follow? But at any rate she must never know.*

He crossed the room, closed the door softly, then hurried back to the fire and burned the letter in it, burned it with such care that, when the paper had turned to a coal, he was not contented until he had scattered the flimsy texture of the ash to dust.

After that, he began pacing the room back and forth, making up his mind, and, as his mind became more and more fixed, he took longer steps and lighter ones. He stood straighter. Years seemed to fall away from him until at last he was as formidable a figure as that Slow Bill who had first appeared in Truro, seeming taller because he was less heavy of flesh, and with a grimmer face, now that the mustaches were gone and the straight line of his mouth was fully visible.

He went to his room, and there he stepped first to his gun rack. Time had been when every weapon in that rack had been as familiar to his hand as the grip of a friend. But that time was long since passed, and he shook his head and gritted his teeth when he thought of it. For though to his son that scene of Jack Rooney with the Colt revolver had meant nothing, to Legrange, the elder, it meant more than all else.

But now there was nothing else for it. He must meet Rooney, and he must meet him before Rooney had told the whole tale to his son.

After that, he selected from the rack the very oldest gun of all, antique in fashion, but still the most familiar of all to his touch. For that was the very weapon that he had worn in Truro in the old days. And he felt that, if luck were to befriend him in the crisis, it would stand by him when he wielded that weapon.

He made his pack small and compact, then he went downstairs and found his wife.

"Jim!" cried his wife, the instant she saw him with the gun belted at his hip. "There *has* been bad news!"

"Not really bad," he told her, "but surprising."

"Of our boy?"

"No, it has to do with me only. I'm riding out for a few days."

He bade her farewell hastily and was gone. In the corral he caught up his best horse, less fiery than the steeds he had ridden in the old days, but with a softness of gait and a sureness of foot which he had come to appreciate more in the passing of the years. Then he started. He did not head straight for the mountains, however. He went first through the town to his lawyer.

"I want my will drawn up," he said. "Frame it to please yourself, except that half goes to my wife and half to Jim. Here's my signature at the foot of the sheet. I'm in a hurry."

"Bad news, Legrange?"

"Not bad, I suppose, but I'm taking a journey, and at my time of life a man never knows when the end will come, old friend. Isn't that true?"

So that was ended, and he mounted again and rode down the street of the town. And every ten steps he was forced to wave a greeting to a friend, and to call out a cheery word. They came out of their houses, out of their shops, to see him pass. Women smiled to him from open doors. Children shouted to one another to come to see him pass. And yet he thought mournfully to himself that, if the truth were known, these smiles would turn to sneers of contempt and hatred. He would be loathed as much as he had been praised.

All the work of the thirty years, he could see now, had been built upon a foundation of sand, and now the shock was at hand that would shake them all to the ground unless he could conquer Jack Rooney, as he had conquered other men in days gone by.

He passed out from the town. Yonder the blue head of Mount Cousin pressed against the sky, seeming near enough, and yet there was a weary way before he would begin to climb its bulging, rounded sides. He touched his horse with the spur and went at a rapid canter. And, as he rode, he weighed his life, as men will do, two or three times during their existence. He could find no real evil in it, except for the two great sins. But did not two such sins outweigh a whole multitude of good deeds? For what that was really good could be built upon crime as a foundation?

By the evening he was high up on Mount Cousin. There he halted and made his camp, for even a horse as staunch as the one he rode could not keep on both day and night. His supper was crackers and cold water. And before the sun was up, he was on his way again in the chill of the morning, with the horse, unused to such continued labors, grunting protests at the steep grade.

All that day he went on. In mid-afternoon he frightened a rabbit from a thicket; catching at his revolver, he tried a snap shot. The rabbit bounded into the air and fell. Slow Bill rode on. He had no need of that meat, but he had seen that some of the old cunning was still with him, and his hand had not lost all of its former agility. That was why a faint, stern smile began to play at the corners of his lips. And he was still faintly smiling when he came up Truro Cañon in the dusk of the day and saw the expiring town stretched before him.

# *Chapter Seven*
## *"Just Words!"*

There was no rain falling this night, but the wind was carrying a piercing mist in its arms, and out of that mist Jim Legrange entered the general merchandise store, where he found the same stage and the same actors upon it that his son had seen. They did not recognize him, and he was glad of it. Like his son he inquired for a hotel, and, as they had done before, they mentioned that the only place in the valley where he could get a bunk was in the house of Jack Rooney.

"But there ain't no room for you there tonight," they told him. "Old Jack has up and busted his rule all to bits. He used to take in a gent for only one night. But he's kept a young feller up there for three days now. Maybe Jack'll bust his other rule, too, and take in two instead of just one."

So they pointed out the way to him, and he went up the cañon until he came to the fragrance of the berry patch and passed between it and the vegetable garden to the door of the house. There he rapped, and there he heard the latch lifted. But the door was not opened by Jack Rooney. It was Jim Legrange, Jr., who stood before him. He uttered a cry of surprise and of happiness and seized his father by both shoulders.

"Dad, when Jack Rooney sees you, he'll be the happiest man in the world. He doesn't even know that I've written to you!"

So he led his father in and then stood back to see the old companions confront one another. However, there was nothing but disappointment for him. He had expected such a reunion as would have done his heart good to witness, but, instead of exhibiting the

124

slightest emotion, the man who had waited thirty years to see Jim Legrange merely rolled out of his chair and shook hands with a sort of limp indifference.

"Well, Bill," he said, "here you are ag'in, and, allowing for them mustaches chopped off, looking plumb nacheral, I'd say!"

"Heard you were up here, Jack, amusing the kid with your yarns," answered his father in the same manner, "and so I thought I'd drop in and say hello again."

He took a chair removed from the immediate neighborhood of the fire.

"Draw up close, Bill," said the host. "I guess you got sort of damp coming up the cañon."

"Just a mite," said the rancher. "But I got a thick skin, as you might remember out of the old days."

"Well, well," said Jack Rooney, and he also pushed his chair back into the shadows.

After that, to the amazement of young Legrange, the two sat without uttering a syllable for a full five minutes, and he began to grow more and more restless. And yet, when he reflected upon it, this was exactly how such old companions might act. They were smoking busily, and beyond doubt their thoughts were equally busy reaching into the past and wandering by the side of one another through unforgettable adventures. Suddenly he felt that his own presence was a clumsy intrusion upon their privacy. Perhaps the two veterans would remain half the night in silence, if he were to remain, but, if he left, they might speak a word from time to time.

Cautiously he rose, bade them good night in a voice that received no answer from either of them, and went back to the doorway. There he turned for a final look at them. The room was very dim now, for the fire had not been replenished with wood for a long time, and the illumination was only a steady and dull light around the hearth, or an occasional leap when a small draft struck the flames up toward the chimney. And the forms of the two miners were lost in the haze, but their big hands and their faces were blocked out in red light and red shadow, very roughly, with blurred lines, as though made with soft chalk in a hasty sketch.

125

He looked on them for a long instant, and then he went back to his room, feeling that he had trod upon holy ground—feeling, indeed, that he would ever remain a better man for having witnessed this solemn occasion.

In fact he had been gone from the room for a full ten minutes before either of them spoke. It was then Slow Bill who stirred in his chair to knock the ashes out of his pipe.

"Well, Jack?" he asked.

There was no answer. Five minutes more dragged out an endless length before there was a second sound, and again it was Slow Bill.

"Jack," he said, "we might as well get at it and get it over with."

"What?" said Jack Rooney.

"You know."

"I tell you, I don't."

"That's cutting corners on me. Of course, I know why you've been sitting here for thirty years, Jack."

"Tell me why, then?"

"You've been waiting for me."

"That's it. And here you are!"

"And what you want, now that I'm here, is murder."

"Are you sure of that?"

"Of course, I'm sure. You want to pay me back, and death is what you want to repay me . . . naturally enough."

"Lemme tell you," said Jack Rooney. "During the first five years what nourished me and kept me living was the hope that I could catch you sometime and kill you slow and careful, squeezing out your life little by little . . . seeing you die bit by bit. I would have relished that the first five years. I used to dream about hearing you confess and yell and beg me to kill you quick."

Here he made a pause and slowly refilled his pipe. But for all of the slowness, and for all of the steadiness with which both of the men stared at the fire and never at one another, it was plain that there was a new spirit in the room, and that the two were watching one another with a hair-trigger intentness.

"The next five years," said Jack Rooney, "I spent considering how any way of killing you could give you as much pain as I had gone through. And I seen that it couldn't." He sighed and shook his head. "Since then I've lived on here twenty years, Bill. Twenty years is a considerable long time, but during them twenty years I been spending all my spare time thinking of that problem and working it back and forth. I was beginning to think that there wasn't no justice in the world, and that I'd *never* meet you ag'in. But, if I did meet you, I wasn't no ways sure what I'd do. Just lately the idea come to me."

He stopped again. Each one of these pauses seemed an interminable space to Jim Legrange. And in each interval he stirred in his chair and seemed a dozen times on the verge of speaking, but never saying a word.

"Well," he said at last, "what is the great idea, Jack?"

The other answered obliquely. "I hear you've growed to be quite a man in your part of the world?"

"What do you mean by that, Jack?"

"I mean that you've piled up a lot of land and money."

"I've had my share of luck, if that's what you mean."

"Not luck! Not luck! I hear it's been all good hard work. You've played square with other folks, and you've made your coin by hard digging."

"I hope that's true." He was more uneasy than ever.

"And I hear that you got the respect of everybody around you. I hear that nothing much can be done in them parts, if you ain't asked in to give advice."

"I can't say as much as that."

"You're mighty modest, Bill. But then, come to think of it, you always *was* modest."

"Thanks!"

"I hear that you're the biggest man on the range."

"Ah," said the rancher suddenly, "I begin to see what way you're drifting."

"You do?" remarked the other curiously. "You was always a deep one, Bill. You was always able to see right plumb through me. Go on and tell me what I got in my head right now."

"Why, Jack, you know that I got my start out of money of which half should have gone to you. You've been spending thirty years of torture up here in the cañon. Isn't that right?"

"Thirty years . . . it's a long time, now you come to think about it."

"Of course, it is! You've been waiting for me here, and I've been down on the range making money. Can you guess how much money I've made?"

"A million, Bill?"

"A million? How much was taken out of the old Willoughby diggings, first and last?"

"Everybody knows that. Close to four millions."

"Well, Jack, I could turn my property into four million dollars' worth of gold, and still I'd have a bit left over to live on pretty comfortably. About enough to make another million, Jack."

"Five million dollars!" breathed Jack Rooney.

"And that's not half of the facts. I have credit for just that much more. If I had a deal I wanted to swing through, I have enough credit in the banks and with the rich men on the range to make about anything that I want."

There was a groan of admiration from Jack Rooney. "That's mighty fine," he commented.

"But it's as good for you as it is for me."

"How d'you make that out?"

"Jack, the claim you have against me is something that mere money can't altogether pay. But I want you to think this over. I'll give you, in any way you want it, a half interest in that ranch and in everything that I have. I'll give you better than half. I'll give you three of the five millions. If you want it in cash, I'll sell out and turn over the three millions in gold to you."

Jack Rooney was silent.

"You understand what it means, Jack? You can put it out at six percent very easily. All in first mortgages! And that six percent will bring you in a hundred and eighty thousand dollars every year. Think of it, Jack! It's a pretty fair salary for the amount of time you've been waiting. The very first year you'll make enough on the interest to have paid you six thousand dollars a year for every one of the thirty years. For every month you've been sitting here and waiting, you get more than five hundred dollars. That's what the very first year of the income means to you. And after that there are other years. Let those figures soak in on your brain, Jack."

He spoke this earnestly, hastily, beating the facts with his right fist into the palm of his other hand. And he leaned forward to decipher the expression upon the face of Rooney, as he completed his statement. But the face of Rooney was securely veiled at this moment in shadow and smoke from his pipe.

"Suppose I have three millions," said Rooney, "what would I do with it?"

"What would you do with it? Good God, man, what do other people do with it?"

"How many folks do you know," asked the old miner, "who have tied up their lives to a few cows and chickens and an old shack and a hoss or two for thirty years and waited? And, having waited here so long, I dunno but what I've got sort of used to this place. I used to hate it, Bill. I used to think of other folks in the towns having their good times. I used to see everybody leaving Truro and going down to the valleys . . . and getting married . . . and raising their families . , . and forgetting the mines except to spin yarns about 'em in the evenings, so's their kids could take it all in. I used to think about them things till it seemed to me that this wasn't no better than a prison.

"I come a hundred times close to leaving during the first five years, but I stayed on, and finally I stopped regretting. I been thinking all these years that I been putting up with this here place just because it was a trap that I'd make you walk into one of these days. But, dog-gone me, if it don't seem as if I'd come to like it for its own sake. That's the truth of it, old son. I'd sure hate to part with it. Because there's part of me that's rooted in the ground here, it seems, just like the trees are rooted. And I done the planting. If I had three millions, I'd have to leave here. I'd have to start down to a city. I'd have to go some place to spend that there money. I'd be a plumb fool just to stay here. And what would I spend it on? I ain't got sense enough to spend fifteen thousand dollars a month. And I'd be leading a poor life watching the smart gents get my coin away from me, smooth and easy. I'll tell you the straight facts, Bill. Three million dollars to me is just words. It don't mean nothing to me. The whole lot of it wouldn't buy my old team of hosses, Jim and Dandy, from me, that I do my plowing with. No, sir, it wouldn't buy them hosses. Three million dollars wouldn't buy my berry patch. Bill, in the old days money meant something. Now it ain't nothing but a pile of metal that's too soft to even make a shovel out of. No, Bill, I ain't selling out. You ain't got enough money to buy one room in my house . . . let alone me!"

# Chapter Eight
## "In His Own Coin"

He finished that strange speech in a sort of ecstasy, with his head raised and his eyes shining. And in that moment Slow Bill, leaning low in his chair, clutched at the handles of his old Colt. But something held him back; his hand was like lead.

Perhaps it was awe of this man to whom an immense fortune was nothing. And there was a frozen amazement in his eye. He had felt that, having grown great himself during these thirty years, he was coming back to a pygmy. But it seemed to Slow Bill that the partner, who had been clay in his hand in the old days, was now equipped with an equal, or even with a superior, strength. He had always half despised Jack Rooney as a gullible and easy-going dolt. Jack Rooney had worshipped him as a man of power and a distinguished figure in the camp. Jack Rooney had loved to see the eyes directed toward his companion when they walked down the street together. And Slow Bill had regarded him with that sort of half-pitying affection with which an older man regards a younger and weaker one. But now he felt that his own stature had diminished, and that Jack Rooney had grown mightily.

Rooney was speaking again. "Besides," he said, "I ain't working at no easy job during these thirty years. I been living on poison, Bill. With all your coin, could you bribe a man to take poison, Bill?"

And Legrange sighed and stared down to the floor.

"Bid higher," said Jack Rooney. "Maybe I got a price . . . I dunno. But three millions ain't even a beginning bid. I got to be paid . . . in cash . . . for the friends that I gave up . . . for the fun that I missed . . . for the children that ain't around me. I got to be paid . . . for a wife, Bill!"

At this Slow Bill leaned back in his chair, with a breath so

131

deeply taken that it was like a groan. "I knew that was coming," he said, "but will you hear me say something about it, Jack?"

"Talk, talk, talk," said Jack Rooney. "I been wondering all this time how you'd excuse yourself. I knew that you'd have some way of working out . . . or of trying to. Let me hear you talk, Bill. It gives me a chance to see what sort of stuff you're made of."

"You've turned pretty hard," said the other slowly. "That's not surprising. To begin with, of course, I know that I've done the worst and the lowest thing that one man can ever do to another.

"It started with that picture you had of Miriam. I suppose you've forgotten about it. You used to pull out that picture of the girl you'd left behind you and tell me how wonderful she was. Do you remember that?"

"You can hurry past that," said Jack Rooney huskily. "You can trust that I remember it all well enough."

"I can't hurry past it. You see, Jack, you never could understand how I could look at a picture as lovely as that one and remain indifferent. But I put on a face of stone simply to keep you from seeing how I'd been waked up by the first glance at her face."

"Was that it?"

"Yes."

"I used to be bothered," said Jack Rooney calmly enough, "at the way you'd look at that picture and then shrug your shoulders and say that she was pretty enough. It used to make me mad . . . but I used to wonder what sort of woman you *would* like. I used to more'n half believe you when you said that you'd never marry."

"Do you remember," said Slow Bill, "that I began to urge you to go home and get married?"

"I remember," said Jack Rooney soberly. "And I've thought of it a thousand times in the past couple of days . . . since I learned that you were the man who married her in the end. Why did you keep after me to go home and be married?"

"Because I was hounded day and night with the fear that someday I'd slip out of camp without a word to anyone and rush for your home town and make a dead set to win Miriam, while you were away. I kept urging you on. Oh, what a torture it was! I kept telling you that money was nothing. You said that you had to have enough to establish a home before you could go back to her. I used to declare that poverty was the way to begin a life with a woman. Sometimes I'd have you on the verge of packing and starting."

"But the next morning there'd be the hope of striking it rich that very day," said Rooney.

"As a matter of fact, when you found the gold, it was because you had started up the cañon to go on the home trail."

"I'd half forgotten that!"

"You stumbled onto color on the banks of the creek. You tore back to town to get me."

"In those days I thought you had to share everything with me. In those days we was really partners, Bill."

"Jack, it cuts me pretty deep to hear you say that. Anyway, the devil was in the luck. You twisted your ankle, like a wet rag, just as we were starting."

"That's right. It hurt, too."

"So I left you to take care of yourself, because you were begging me to hurry on and clean up that gold before someone else might find the place."

"That's true, Bill."

"I went double-quick up the cañon. I found the place. And it was exactly what you thought it might be . . . a little pocket of gold in the sands. It took me a day and a half to clean it out. Never washed such stuff in my life. It was like lifting money out of a purse rather than actual work. But there were forty pounds of good gold in that lot."

"Forty pounds, Bill!"

"And while I took it out, it made me drunk with thinking of the possibilities. You know the stuff will do that, Jack?"

"I know . . . worse than red-eye ever was."

"A lot worse! Before I was through, I was a crazy man. I had money for the first time since my father went bankrupt in Boston. I had money, and I was on the way up the cañon and pointing toward your home, a thousand miles away." He drew a great breath. "Jack," he said at last, "there was a crazy idea in my mind. You had started for home. You had been stopped by gold. You had come back for me. I said to myself that it was fate that had stopped you, and that I was the man who was being called . . . that this was my opportunity, which could never come back to me again . . . that a man had to take his chances when they came. And when I told myself that I was worse than a dog to do what I had in mind to do, still I could not help saying to myself that all was fair in war . . . or in love!"

"In war or in love," admitted Jack Rooney. "But between partners, Bill?"

Slow Bill was struck back in his chair. There was another interval of pause—a deadly silence.

"Will you tell me one thing?" asked Jack Rooney, and his face was twisted with agony, as he spoke.

"I'll tell you what I can."

"True?"

"I've done you too much harm to lie to you about things now."

"When you went to her . . . ?"

"Don't start with her. You'll drive yourself frantic."

"I got to know. When you went to her, did you tell her that I was dead?"

"No!"

"You swear that?"

"I do."

"Nor that I was married to another woman, nor in love with one?"

"Jack, on my honor, I didn't mention your name. I didn't even tell her that I was the Slow Bill you'd written about to her. I told her only my real name. To this day she thinks that I only knew you as a man about the camp."

"You got her . . . just by talk, Bill."

"Just by talk," admitted Slow Bill.

"Well," said the smaller man at last, "it's just by talk that I got to strike back at you."

"Talk?"

"By going to your wife and telling her the truth, and by letting the folks in your own country hear the straight facts about what you done to me, Slow Bill!"

# Chapter Nine
## " 'The Turning of the Screw' "

One could see that announcement take effect upon Slow Bill. It made him stiffen and straighten. It made him reach toward his gun and then let his hand swing loosely away from it.

"No one would believe you, Jack."

"They would, though. I'd hound you till I got you in the middle of a crowd, and then I'd make you face me while I told the yarn. And they'd see the truth of it written plain in your face!"

The rancher shrugged his shoulders.

"You don't know me, Jack," he said. "I can hold my expression."

"You can't see yourself now, Bill," said the miner. "It ain't any use. When you see me, you'll go to pieces."

The rancher shrugged his shoulders again.

"Call in your boy, then, and let him hear me talk, and see what that does to you and your fine airs, Bill."

At this Legrange started violently. "You mean you'd start by telling about this to my Jim?"

"Say, Bill, where else would I begin?"

The horror faded slowly out of the eyes of Legrange. "Do it," he said. "My boy believes in me as he believes in the Bible."

"I can't shake him?"

"Never!" Legrange sat down very calmly and lighted his pipe afresh. "I grant you one thing," he said. "If my boy will believe you, every human being in the world will believe you. If you can convince him, you can convince anyone."

"There's the old Bill talking out in you," said Jack Rooney without passion. "In them old days you used always to think that you couldn't fail . . . that nobody could beat you. I used to believe you always, too. And I was a fool for doing it. So was the rest of 'em in

Truro. There was a plenty of 'em that could have handled you, Slow Bill, but they didn't never have the nerve to step out and try it."

Slow Bill sneered. "That was it," he said. "They didn't none of 'em have the nerve to step out and try it. I looked a bit too big to them."

But he smiled after a lordly fashion, as though there were other and greater reasons also why the men of Truro in the old days had not dared to confront him. Jack Rooney watched him with a mild eye of mere observation, but his mouth was setting more stiffly every instant. He moved suddenly toward the door.

"Wait!" called Legrange.

Rooney turned to him.

"Where are you going?" demanded Slow Bill.

"To call your son."

"Very well, Rooney. Suppose we make a wager on this?"

"About what?"

"That Jim will or will not believe you."

"I'll bet on that, Bill."

"If you can persuade him, you can go on talking as much as you wish. It will make little difference to me after that. But if you fail, you're to swear never to speak of what you know."

Rooney hesitated, but he hesitated only an instant. "I'll take that bet," he said, and straightway opened the door and called: "Legrange! Oh, Legrange!"

Almost instantly there was an answer, and then a sound of a door opening and closing. The heavy footfall of the young man was heard in the hall, and then he appeared before them, alert, smiling, plainly delighted to have been called back to such a meeting. His smile, however, wavered and grew dim when he marked their faces.

"Sit down, Jim," said his father, "unless you're too sleepy to talk. I want Rooney to know you as well as he knew me in the old days. I've been trying to persuade him to come to the ranch to pay us a visit. I want you to help me talk to him. The old chap has grown so firmly rooted here that he can't see his way to coming away with us."

And with this he turned upon Jack Rooney a smile of the most genial warmth. Rooney in turn blinked at him, like an owl confronted with a shaft of light. He had not been prepared for dissimulation so smoothly acted out.

As for young Jim Legrange, he was as pleased as though two kings had asked him to join in their debate. And eagerly he pressed Jack Rooney to come down to the ranch, because, having been companions in their youth, his father and Rooney should have the privilege of growing old together, of hunting together, of talking together, of discussing their old history and making their new. If Rooney did not care to give up his independent existence, he could build a cabin in any one of a score of outlying valleys among the hills, and there he could live in the most utter freedom, as wildly as in Truro Cañon, but with friends and civilization just around the corner when he chose to return to them.

Jack Rooney, listening to this appeal, could not budge his gaze from the face of Slow Bill. At last, he lifted one hand to hush the younger Legrange.

"Son," he said, "you don't know what you're saying. You been called in here to be a judge, and what you're going to judge is between me and him . . . between me and your father, yonder."

Young Legrange glanced from one to the other. In the face of his father he saw worry and bewilderment.

"What the devil are you talking about, Jack?" asked the elder Legrange. "Is this a new sort of a joke that you've invented?"

Jack Rooney shrugged his shoulders. "You start pretty well, Bill," he admitted. "But you ain't going to be so spry when I get through with you." He turned squarely upon young Legrange.

"Son," he said, "you been looking over my place for a couple of days. What does it look like to you?"

Young Jim turned from the smile on his father's face and regarded Jack Rooney gravely. There was much behind this. The whimsical look of his father seemed to mean one thing; the deadly gravity of Jack Rooney meant quite another.

"It looks to me like a very comfortable little home, Mister Rooney," he said, "but not a whit better than half a dozen places that we could fix for you at our place."

Jack Rooney raised his hand hastily again. Indeed, it was plain even to young Legrange that there was a more subtle and more dangerous matter to be judged than merely the removal of Rooney to another dwelling.

"That's what it looks like to you . . . a home?"

"And a very comfortable one, Mister Rooney."

"All right, son. That's what I wanted it to look like . . . just like a home. But d'you think that was what it really was?"

"Why not?" asked young Jim.

He turned a baffled glance upon his father; and the latter, shaking his head and smiling leniently, pointed significantly to his head, as though to suggest that poor Jack Rooney's brains were a little addled. Perhaps that was what had happened in the long and lonely years that he had spent by himself in Truro Cañon. And, perhaps, the very shock of the coming of his old friend, Slow Bill, had been the thing that had finally unseated the reason of Jack. At least, it was an anxious mind and one filled with pity that young Jim turned to his host again.

"If not a home, then what is it?" he asked again.

"A trap!" said the miner.

"A trap? But for what?"

"For Slow Bill."

"What!"

"A trap for Slow Bill!" cried Rooney, shaking his fist furiously above his head. "For thirty years I waited for him to walk into it, and finally he come."

"My head is whirling," stated young Jim. "What do you mean?"

"Just what I'm telling you. That I made this place, and that I sat down in it, thinking that someday someone would come through that knowed something about Slow Bill. I got that picture of Bill, and I hung it over the fireplace in this living room. I put it up there so big and bold that everybody had to see it, and, if anyone should come along that knowed Slow Bill in the old days, they'd be sure to recognize him, and, if anybody knowed where Slow Bill was living lately, they might recognize him and let me know where to find him."

"A trap?" murmured young Jim. "Why, Mister Rooney, you might call it a trap. But, of course, you didn't intend Dad any harm?"

Jack Rooney smiled in such a way that Jim could never forget it.

"Not more'n death," he said. "Not more'n death, young man. All I set that trap for was to get him where I could kill him slow and kill him sure."

"Kill him!" cried Jim Legrange.

"That's the right word. But, finally, I seen that killing wasn't the best thing. It come over me just the other day that the right thing to do was to tell the world the sort of a gent that he was. And that's why you're here . . . to listen to my yarn. If you believe me, I go down and tell other people the truth about Slow Bill and the particular kind of skunk that he is. If you don't believe me, I shut up and stay put right where I am."

"Ah," sighed the boy, "is that it?"

And he cast an understanding glance toward his father. The latter smiled in return and made a brief gesture, as though to indicate that he desired his son to humor the old veteran in every way possible without actually yielding to his wishes.

# Chapter Ten
## "Ghosts Out of the Past"

"You got to go back to one day when I was starting up the cañon for home . . . thirty years back," said Jack Rooney. "The reason that I was quitting camp was because I was plumb in love with a girl back in my home town. And every time I pulled out her picture and showed it to my partner . . . that was Slow Bill . . . he used to tell me that I was a fool to let a girl with such a pretty face go around loose without a wedding ring on her finger to show other gents that there was a claim staked out. And Slow Bill, he kept after me so long that pretty soon I couldn't stand it any longer. I had to bust out and light away on the long trail, traveling light and streaking all the way.

"But when I got halfway up the valley, I kneeled down by the side of a boulder along the creek, and I took a drink, and, when I was leaning over the water there, drinking, I seen a little bright sparkling of gold, and I scooped in with my hand and pulled up a handful of sand, and in that sand there was raw gold. I reached down ag'in and swashed my hands around. Dog-gone me, if that there place wasn't burning up with gold!"

The miner paused and drew on his pipe a couple of times, just to see if the tobacco in the bowl were not long since burned out.

"The fever hit me," he continued. "There I was without nothing to pan that stuff. And if I left it to get the tools, anybody might come along and see what I'd seen. I sat there for an hour, going through agony. Then I made up my mind that I had to take the chance. I streaked it back for the camp. I found my partner, Slow Bill. I told him what I'd found, and him and me started up the cañon ag'in, to get that gold out, and we had our pan and the other fixings with us. But, just as we got started, if I didn't do a fool trick and turn my ankle plumb over. I couldn't walk.

140

"Slow Bill carried me back into the shack and would have stayed to fix me up, but I cussed him and made him go along up the cañon to get that there gold, and Slow Bill sure humped it away and out of sight.

"I lay there gnashing my teeth at my luck to be away when I was making the biggest strike of my life . . . maybe making myself famous by opening out a wonderful big new field, where other gents besides Slow Bill and me would get rich. But, while I was lying there and wondering about things one way and another, seeming never to get well, news come to me . . . that was three days later . . . that Slow Bill had been doing a little job panning stuff on the banks in the creek and had finished his job and had gone on *up* the river. About a hundred gents made a rush to see what he'd found. Them that come first to where he had done his digging found out that there was just a trace of color here and there, but there wasn't enough gold left to make a wedding ring out of. Slow Bill had cleaned it out, and all it had amounted to was just a little pocket of gold, richer'n sin while it lasted, but mighty quick to finish up.

"Well, says I to myself, old Slow Bill ain't nobody's fool. He's just turned loose and drifted up that there creek to see if he couldn't locate the mother lode that them gold sands was washed down from.

"I turned that idea over in my head. Maybe old Bill would find it, and then him and me would be rich and famous ever after. And dog-gone me, if it sure didn't warm my heart. A week went by. I was getting around easy, just walking with a mite of a limp. But still there wasn't no sign of Bill coming back. And I says to myself that maybe something has happened to Slow Bill. There's plenty of robbers hanging around in the mountains, them that would kill a gent first, so's they could rob him safely afterward. There was plenty of that kind of hold-up men. And I was afraid for a while that one of 'em might have got Slow Bill, took his gold, and left his body in the rocks.

"Then I took a turn up the valley, but, though I went clean up and over the edge of the divide, there wasn't no sign of Slow Bill for me to find. And then I come back to Truro and went to work and just waited for Slow Bill. But Slow Bill didn't come. No, sir, I couldn't believe but that he'd come back with that money. But he didn't come.

141

"And finally, when the spring come, I knowed that I'd been a fool because I'd trusted my partner. I made up my mind that I couldn't wait no longer to make my last big killing. I just had to get home and marry my girl."

"Well, sir, I made the fastest trip across the continent that you ever heard tell of, but my train got in just a month too late. She didn't have no folks. Her ma and pa had died when she was little. She was living away off in the country on the ranch of her uncle, and he was a little old shrimp of a dried-up man about eighty, not caring nothing what she did, or where she went. All he could tell me was that she'd had trouble with him one day, and that the next day he seen her drive off in the rig of a gent he'd never seen before. After that he never heard from her ag'in. But he knowed that she hadn't gone off with any of the young gents in that neighborhood that she'd growed up with. He knowed that she was gone to some place far off, where nobody could trace her. Well, that was the last that I ever heard of her."

"My soul," murmured young Jim Legrange.

His father made a faint sound in his throat to call the attention of his son toward him, but young Jim could do nothing but stare in horror and pity at Jack Rooney.

"It's like something out of a book," he told his host. "It's too rotten and sad to be true."

"True? Look at me! Look at me, Legrange! The truth of such things as I been talking about is wrote into a gent's face. Do I look like I suffered them things?"

"Yes, yes!" gasped Legrange. "It's almost as though I were standing by you when you heard that she . . ."

"But that wasn't all," said Jack Rooney. "The finish of that little story comes when you get here to the house, and you stand and look up to that picture, and I can see from the doorway behind you that you're mighty moved by what you see."

"Jim!" broke in his father suddenly. "Are you letting Rooney sweep you off your feet?"

"No, Dad, no," said the son. And he nodded reassuringly to his father. He even reached out a hand slightly toward him. But these actions were involuntary. His whole heart was dwelling upon the narrative of the miner.

"Well," said Jack Rooney, "that was close to the time when you told me that Slow Bill was your father. And I had seen that my rope was floating down right over his head, and that he'd soon be in my hands. But the final blow was when you showed me the locket, because when I seen those two pictures I knowed that the hound that had robbed me of the money that was mine was the hound that had also gone to my back trail and robbed me of more than money, because he'd married the girl that I loved."

# Chapter Eleven
## *"Feet of Clay"*

Young Legrange came out of his chair like a soldier at a bugle note, facing his father. And Jack Rooney glared in the same direction, his lips twitching with the intensity of his hate. But Slow Bill never rose to an emergency of guns more gallantly than he faced this crisis. His color did not alter. The calm of his demeanor was as steady as a rock, and his eye was able to roam casually back and forth from one face to another.

"Dad!" cried young Jim.

"Good God," murmured the father, "do you mean to say that you are putting any stock in such stuff as this?"

He staggered the conviction which had been formed in the mind of the son, if he could not quite erase it at once.

"What answer in the world is there to such things as he has been saying?" asked young Jim.

"A very simple one . . . so simple that I hesitate to tell it. When I went up the cañon, I found the place to which our violent friend here had referred. I found the place where his precious pocket of gold had been. But someone else had found it before me. I found three men gutting the hole in the bottom of the creek. They had seen poor Jack Rooney at the place and had gone to examine. By the time I reached the spot, the work was done. The gold was gone!"

"A lie!" shouted Jack Rooney. "I saw that hole of the workings, days later when it had partly filled up. And that work couldn't have been done in three hours, which was all the time between when I first found the stuff and when you got up to it. No three men working three hours could have dug what I seen. They couldn't have dug the stuff out and washed it so quick!"

The rancher made a gesture of resignation. "Of course," he said,

144

"there seems to be nothing for you to do, Jim, but to balance his word against mine. I say that three strong men, working with all their might for three hours and panning out rich gold, are turned into giants. That's how they accomplished more work than you thought possible."

"Partner," said Rooney to the son, "I can see in your eye that you're believing me. Bill, what was the names of them three men that you're talking about?"

"I asked 'em their names," said the rancher at once. "They told 'em to me. Damned, if they haven't slipped out of my mind."

"Nothing slips out of your mind," answered Rooney.

And young Legrange involuntarily nodded his assent to a statement that he had seen verified a hundred times in his life with his father. That strong brain gripped the smallest details of affairs that touched him and never misplaced the information which he secured.

The rancher saw that he had lost ground. He started to make up for it instantly. And more and more he realized that he was backed against a wall, fighting for something dearer than his life.

"That's nonsense, Jack," he said without bitterness. "Three fellows I'd never seen before tell me their names. I'm a thousand times more interested in what they are doing than in their names. And yet you expect me to remember little things such as this? Of course, all I could see or think was that they were sweeping out of the sand the little fortune that might have belonged to you and to me."

"Bill, you was seen to be working for three days up the creek at that place!"

"Not at that place, but a little below it. After they'd scooped out the pocket, I was ashamed to turn back and tell you in town that we'd missed our greatest chance. I remembered that you were lying there, sick. I couldn't come back to you with talk like that. So I hunted up and down the creek for more color. A couple of hundred yards below the place where you found the stuff, I did find color."

"Ah," cried Rooney scornfully, "and that was where you made the ten thousand you took down from the mines?"

The rancher flashed at his son a single glance that might have meant anything, but which was in reality merely smothered rage when he saw that facts divulged by young Jim were now being used to undermine his own statements.

"I didn't find anything more than the color. I worked for two days trying to cut down to good stuff, but I got nothing except sweat for my pains."

"Then how did you get the coin?" asked Rooney.

And it could be seen that he was both curious as well as painfully eager. He was like one who wields a whip with both hands, and yet who looks on with an almost childish air of detachment at the object he is tormenting.

"I'll tell you all that. When I failed at the mine, I was about to go back to you. Then I remembered that you'd been waiting there for three days without word from me. You'd be making sure that I had cleaned up the pot of gold. It was heartbreaking to go back to you and tell you that I had failed. I hadn't the heart for it. I decided that I'd take a desperate fling to make big money out of little.

"I cut for New Truro up the cañon . . . you remember that wild-cat camp? There I tackled roulette. I had fifty dollars in gold to begin with. I made a thousand the first night . . . and lost it all the second. But the next morning we discovered that there had been a brake on that wheel, and that the crooked gambler that ran it had skipped out of camp. I went on his trail. I found him and beat him within an inch of his life. But I was ten days on his trail before I caught up with him.

"And after ten days could I go back again to the camp and face you? I couldn't do it, Jack. I was demoralized. I even feared that you'd accuse me of having gutted the hole and blown the money. I kept gambling. I drifted across the continent, from one town to another, playing for big stakes one day and little ones the next. If ever I made a big strike, I swore that I'd go back to the mountains . . . back to you in Truro, and I'd split my winnings with you.

"Then came my day. It was in Louisville, and the cards walked into my hand, as though they had been trained. I walked out twelve thousand dollars richer than I had gone into that house, and, as I went, I swore that I'd never play for money again. And I've kept that oath. No one has ever seen me wager a cent since that minute.

"I was first for starting straight for Truro and telling you the good news. Then, thinking of you, I remembered that the girl you loved and were engaged to, so you'd told me, lived very close to Louisville. So I started for her town. And when I got there, almost the first thing I saw was Miriam herself. But she didn't seem to be grieving particularly about your absence, Jack. She was sauntering down the street, laughing and joking with two young fellows . . . one on either side of her.

"I followed them on to her house. There I introduced myself as a man who had known you in the mountains. I made up my mind that, if she inquired about you cordially . . . if she so much as changed color, I'd be loyal to you, Jack. But she didn't. She looked me straight in the eye, as if she barely knew you, and she didn't keep the talk on you for two minutes.

"That settled me. I confess I'd fallen in love with her picture. Who would not? After that, seeing that she had lost all interest in you, it was only fair for me to paddle my own canoe, and so I did. I went to see her again. I talked for myself. And before long she decided to leave home and come along with me.

"That's all there is to the mysterious story you've made so black for me, Jack. And now, Jim, does it look as if I had cheated him?"

He turned carelessly to the son, as though perfectly certain that the reply could only be in the negative. And Jim the younger began to nod.

"Wait," cut in Jack Rooney. "Think it over, youngster. Would I have spent thirty years of my life on a false alarm? And can you believe that wild story about cleaning up twelve thousand dollars in one evening in Louisville?"

Young Jim cast an eye of wild appeal at his father. The older man had set his teeth hard so that the muscles stood out at the base of his jaw. It might have been a desperate effort to keep up his nerve, or else it might have been a passion of overtaxed temper. Young Jim could only pray that it was the latter, rather than the former.

"What stakes did you start with that night?" snapped Jack Rooney suddenly.

Alas for the small stone on which the giant stumbles. Jim Legrange was suddenly thrown off balance. He hesitated.

"Ten . . . ten dollars," he said. And, feeling that that slight pause had undone him, color washed across his face.

"Dad!" cried young Jim in an agony.

The color died in the face of his father. He grew as pale as death, and his eyes glazed forth hollowly, soberly at his son. There was a wild appeal in them.

"But," said young Jim, feeling his way grimly from word to

147

word, "then this man here . . . Jack Rooney might have married Mother, and not you."

Both of the older men winced. Neither of them, somehow, had felt the thing so vitally.

"Jack Rooney was in love with Mother. And . . . it was his gold that started your fortune. Is that right, Dad?"

And he threw out both of his hands to his father in his appeal.

Jim Legrange could not answer, but upon his forehead the great drops of moisture stood out, as though it were mid-afternoon in the summer of the year.

"It's all stolen," said young Jim, as his arms fell back heavily to his side. "The ranch is stolen . . . you stole my mother from . . . from your best friend, and you've let me grow up to worship . . . a thief!"

And he turned and ran from the room, stumbled heavily against the jamb of the door, and then hurried down the hall and out into the night.

# *Chapter Twelve*
## *"Epilogue"*

Jack Rooney tilted back his head. He did not laugh. There was in him, coursing wildly through all of his body, an emotion too exquisite to be termed mirth. It was rather a supreme delight that made his brain spin. And it seemed to him that for thirty years of waiting he was repaid all in an instant.

Then he looked down again, not at the face of his enemy, but at his fallen head and at the hand that was drooping down toward the floor. That hand arrested his attention—opened the flood gates of memory—and Jack Rooney was suddenly transported into the past.

Jack Rooney was living again in the old days. He saw himself caught in a desperate brawl in which he had been cornered by half a dozen ruffians. Suddenly a great fist had struck from behind him, across his shoulder, and it landed in the face of one of his assailants and smashed the man to the ground. That had been the hand of Slow Bill. Where was it now? And where was the man against whom he had aimed this deadly stroke? The heart of Jack Rooney shrank.

He turned to his old partner and laid his hand on Legrange's shoulder. "Bill, we're even now. Let's bury the past and watch young Jim carry on."

# *The Rock of Kiever*

"The Rock of Kiever" first appeared in Street & Smith's *Western Story Magazine* (1/19/24) under the byline Max Brand. Its hero, Charlie Stayn, who is a Texas Ranger, represents somewhat of a departure for Frederick Faust whose characters generally operate outside the law—good badmen and bad good men. Similarly, the story's concern with drug smuggling is also somewhat unusual. What is not unusual is the partnership that has formed between Stayn and Joe Toomby, a young man whom the latter had found and taken under his wing on his way out of Alaska. Either man is willing to die for the other.

# Chapter One
## *"Toomby's Exploit"*

When the three rangers reached the top of the hills, so that they could look down into the valley below them, they halted and drew together, very much as they would have done had they been approaching great danger, yet the outlook was peaceful in the extreme. There was nothing to cause the slightest foreboding except to people unfamiliar with the desert. To them, there was nothing alarming about the long sweep of the dull-red plain, the gray of the hills beyond, the Spanish daggers reared like ugly scarecrows everywhere, the mesquite, like low-rolling smoke, lingering in the hollows of the hills and in patches across the level. To a stranger, all of these details were things of despair, for there seemed nothing in sight that could support life. It was a gray country, from which the joy had been scorched by the daily travels of a million suns, burning the land dry, and then dead, and after that, parching and crumbling death itself.

This was the seeming of the land to the stranger, but it was not like this to the three rangers. They saw beneath them wood for fuel and water for drink, for they knew where the spring rose almost to the surface of the sands. Where there was water and wood, there was sure to be animal life, and, where so much as a rabbit ran, man could be supported.

In a word every one of the three was a man who would not have feared to cross the greatest of the deserts that lie between the Rockies and the Sierras, if he were given a rifle and a little salt to carry with him. They were adapted to their life by instinct and by natural selection. Under their wide hats, they had keen faces with cheeks so hollowed that the jaws and the eyes were given greater prominence. They had lean, strongly corded necks. Their flannel shirts hung loose around bodies from which all fat had long since burned away. Their faces were brown as the faces of mulattos, except where the leather hatbands had sweated the foreheads white.

In short, they were like the country in which they lived, with all of the non-essentials parched away and only the necessary strength of the body remaining. If their faces were keen as the faces of foxes, their wits were still sharper. They were unwearying men. The horses between their knees—tough mustangs though these were—had given way under the hard labors of that day and were trembling with weakness as they braced their legs apart and hung their heads on reaching the top of the hill. In the meantime, they overlooked the fact that after long absence they were nearing home; for the camp beneath them was home, and the men in that camp, or some of them at least, were old and tried brothers in arms.

There was a fourth man in the party, but he was not a member of it—a gaunt, swarthy-faced fellow, whom the rangers were taking back to their camp as a prisoner. He sat his horse with a dejected air, his limbs being so shackled as to make it possible for him to maintain his position in the saddle, but not to urge his mount to any great effort of speed. The vigilant guard that the three rangers kept over this captive showed that they considered him important to their mission.

Of the three rangers, two were privates. They gave their opinions first in voices so low that the rabbit that had flattened itself at the roots of the little mesquite bush nearby could hear only a rumbling murmur with its trembling ears. Then the sergeant replied that it was too much for any of them to undertake, that they could not explain matters to poor Charlie Stayn. The captain himself would have to do that. With this decision they made themselves content, but obviously it was one which taxed them. They straightaway rode down the hills with frowns on their foreheads and lips compressed—the faces of men very resolute because they were not a little afraid.

They debouched on to the rolling plain beneath. The hoofs of the mustangs raised little pinches of red dust cloud that floated softly up against the blue of the evening sky. New noises began to move across the desert to their ears, eager to catch the sounds because of their welcome familiarity. How very far they carried! First, was the small, clear ringing of a bugle blown in the camp before them. Then, after silence, they heard a horse neigh. Then another silence.

"That's the captain's roan," said Private Harry Vestry. "I could tell that old fool's calling to the end of the earth. Damn his old Roman nose, for a pitching, no-account rascal!"

"He *did* pitch with you," murmured Sergeant Pete Story.

They went on still farther. An owl dropped off the top of a stump and sailed across the field on unflapping wings, scooting just above the surface of the ground and sounding a deep, booming, melancholy note. Then, out of the gathering twilight before them, a voice sounded. Very shrill laughter will carry farther than a scream. This voice cut deep into the desert.

"It's Sam!" snarled Chris Montain, jingling his spurs viciously. "Darned if he ain't still laughin'. I left him laughin', and I'll come back an' find him laughin' still. Damn such a man, I say!"

The others sighed, as if Sam were, indeed, a cross which they all had to bear, in common.

"But he's a good ranger," put in the sergeant, as if duty bound.

"Confound his rangin'," said Montain, and they all cantered their tired horses forward, as though to escape from a disagreeable thought.

They came upon the camp, looking like an old, familiar face to them. Their horses, even, seemed to know, and began to whinny. The captain's roan answered. The other mounts began a babel of confused greeting. Then the men of the camp woke up with a roar, and into this scene of confusion the little party rode. There were thirty rangers in camp under the captain, and the thirty made noise enough for five score.

What handshaking, shouting of endearing nicknames, enormous curses of pleasure, showers of questions! Then Harry Vestry edged close to the sergeant. A huge man was coming upon them with a roar like the bellowing of a bull. He tossed big men and strong men out of his path as though they had been children. This formidable giant was indicated by Vestry to the sergeant.

"There's Charlie Stayn now," said the private. "You meet him first. You do the talking, Sergeant."

The sergeant groaned. "Why should all the dirty work come to me? Go meet him yourself!"

Harry Vestry, however, had discreetly dodged from view and

buried himself in a cluster of friends, answering questions as well as he could. The sergeant cast a despairing eye upon the huge fellow who was coming upon him so fast. He made a vain effort to get to the captain, but he was too late. Stayn gripped him by the shoulder, turned him around, and then shook him heartily by the hand.

"I'm mighty glad to see you back, Sergeant," said the big man. "And where's Joe? Where's my old pal, Joe?"

The sergeant coughed. "Special detail," he replied, and started on.

"Special what?" cried Charlie Stayn. "Special detail? Who's assigned to the job with him?"

"This is a one-man job," said the sergeant, beginning to sweat.

"It sounds mighty funny to me," declared Charlie Stayn. "I never heard of a one-man assignment before! Look here, Sergeant. . . ."

The sergeant, however, had managed to wriggle away. He called over his shoulder an indistinguishable something. Then he vanished into the captain's tent.

Captain John Naseby was a man of almost infinite discretion. He had watched his men riding in with the greatest satisfaction. Now, as the sergeant came toward him, the haste of the latter made him aware that something extraordinary had happened. Perhaps it was great good news. It could hardly be very terrible news, since three of the four men who had been sent on the mission had returned with the sergeant, and had brought a prisoner with them.

So, as the sergeant came hastily toward him, the captain hardly waited to return his salute before he swung Sergeant Peter Story inside his little tent and dropped the flap, which no member of the troop would dare to lift again until so bidden by the well-known voice.

"Now, Story," said the captain, the moment they were alone, "what is it all about?"

"Bad luck," groaned the sergeant, and stamped his foot as he said it. "The worst sort of bad luck!"

"Well," said the captain, "you can't always win, Story. You've been on top so many times, you've got to expect to be the underdog now and then. You didn't get any wind of 'em at all, I suppose?"

"Wind of the dope smugglers. Sure. I opened up the whole dirty game."

"Story! By heaven, that's magnificent! I think there may be a

156

lieutenancy in this work for you. You located the ringleaders . . . You know who has been receiving the stuff?"

"And who's been carrying it, and where they've been buying it in Mexico, and what ships have been landing it from China and Japan, and where the money is that's behind all the ins and outs of the whole game."

"Story, that's glorious. It's a thousand times better than I dared to hope that you could do. I only expected to get the names of a few leaders. Tell me quickly . . . just a few broad details, and then we'll have the whole yarn, when we can sit down over a cup of coffee . . . and maybe something a bit stronger . . . tonight. There *is* a lieutenancy in this for you, Story."

"There's nothing in it for me," said the sergeant gloomily.

"What's wrong, man? Has your girl turned you down?"

"I've lost a man who's worth ten times more than what we've done on this job."

The captain frowned, and, then, as an idea struck him, he cried out: "Not Joe Toomby, Sergeant?"

The other nodded.

As for the captain, he struck one hand into the other, hunted for words, found none, and then muttered, as though apprehensive of being overheard: "What will Charlie Stayn do when he hears?"

"Heaven only knows!" said the poor sergeant. He sat down on a stool uninvited and began to turn his hat in his hands.

"Buck up, man," said the captain at last. "He's a violent fellow, but he can't blame it on you. He must know that it was simply in the line of duty and business that poor Joe was taken. But how did Charlie seem to take the news when you told him?"

"I didn't tell him."

"But when he asked about Joe?"

"I said that I'd detailed Joe on special work."

"The devil!"

"I couldn't face him, Captain. Damned if my nerve didn't fade right out of me."

"Who *is* to tell him, then?"

"Captain, it's up to you, it looks like to me."

The captain set his teeth. "I suppose it is," he admitted at last. "I suppose I'll have to tell Charlie what has happened. But I'll hold this against you, Sergeant, as long as you live, unless you step out and face Stayn yourself."

The sergeant winced. This was even sterner justice than he had dreaded. He rose and seemed about to leave the tent to execute the last suggestion, to the great relief of the captain, but, at the last moment, with his hand upon the very flap of the tent, he weakened and drew back.

"He and Toomby were like brothers for all these years," he said. "I can't face him and tell him what's happened, Captain. I can't do it."

The captain swore with much violence. "Can he blame you?" he kept repeating.

"He'll lose his head," said the sergeant. "And if he does, I'll lose my life. That's the long and short of it. I'd have to tell him at the point of a gun, and even then he'd find some way of digging my heart out before my news was five seconds old."

"You want me to take that chance, eh?" said the captain sourly.

"It's a lot smaller chance with you," said the sergeant. "He'll know that you ain't to blame, because you didn't detail Joe for the work."

"I sent him along with you, and kept Stayn with me here. There was enough of a storm raised about that at the time, as you may remember, and, after you were gone, for ten days Stayn sulked and went about looking for trouble."

"What brought him out of it?" asked the sergeant.

"I don't mind telling you that it was a ticklish moment for me," said the captain. "I threatened him with dismissal, and he simply said that he wished that I would because, when he was out of the service, the first thing he wanted to do was to tell me what he thought of me."

"All that because Toomby and him was separated. What'll happen when he hears the whole truth? Captain, I always said that Stayn would wind up as a killer."

The captain changed color, but he was a very brave man after all, and, having faced a thousand dangerous predicaments before, he was ready to confront one more peril. He asked now for an explanation of how the tragedy had occurred.

The sergeant explained that they had been following a trail through the Kiever Mountains, and finally they had come in sight of the party they wanted to examine in the valley beneath them. There were a dozen well-armed men in that party, however, and it had seemed obvious that four men could not approach secretly enough to surprise the band, whereas if they attempted open battle, the odds of three to one were sure to vanquish the rangers, for the others were known men.

Joe Toomby then offered to ride down by himself and attempt to sneak into the party, where he would try to take enough stuff to prove that the little troop was bringing opium into the United States. There had been a conference of the whole party upon this point, and the result was that they had agreed that, though it was a very dangerous attempt, Toomby could make the effort if he freely chose to take the danger upon his shoulders on his own sole responsibility. The other three would stand as close by as possible, so that they could effectively cover his retreat, if he should be forced to fly in haste, as was not unlikely, and this proved to be exactly the case.

The daring ranger went down to the camp, stole among the sleeping men after he had tapped the sentinel on the head, and finally succeeded in getting one of the packages of opium into his hands. Thereupon, he started to escape, but at that moment one of the horses neighed, wakened a sleeper who saw the stranger among them, and instantly the whole party was on its feet, shooting.

The ranger had no time to get back to his own mount, but he sprang upon the back of the nearest horse that was tethered on a long rope to graze during the night. Being a consummate and most daring horseman, he managed to make his escape from the first fire of the smugglers. But before he could get under way or to any distance, two or three caught up rifles and delivered a deadly volley. He reached his companions—whose rifle fire checked the pursuit—a dead man, to all intents and purposes. They found afterward that no fewer then seven bullets had plowed through and through his body, at least three of which would in time have proved mortal by themselves. Yet, in spite of this terrible condition, Joe Toomby had acted the part of a man of the most reckless and resolute courage to the last moment of his existence.

He had propped himself against a rock, drained a canteen of water and whiskey mixed, allowed them to bandage his wounds to stop the bleeding, and rolled himself a cigarette of perfect manufacture. There he sat, having his last smoke and apparently enjoying every whiff of it.

He chatted with his companions. He freely took all the blame for his reckless adventure upon his own shoulders. He even foresaw that his old bunkie and boon companion, Charlie Stayn, would be furious with grief and rage when he learned how his friend had been allowed to walk into the face of odds. In order to prevent any further trouble, he had called for paper and pencil to write a note to his fellow ranger. At that very moment, however, death overtook him. He might have survived the other wounds for some time, but a bullet, singularly enough from a Twenty-Two caliber rifle, had penetrated his body beneath the heart, and he died of this wound just as he was about to put the pencil upon the paper.

His death was far from wasted, however. Not only did the sergeant now have direct evidence in his hands in the shape of the package of opium that the dead man had brought away from the sleeping camp, but the knowledge that evidence was now held against them forced one of the smugglers to weaken a few days later. He rode into the ranger camp, where the three were busy heaping stones above the grave of Joe Toomby. He gave himself up, turned state's evidence, and furnished the sergeant with such an immense mass of details that the latter had seen that this was a case which called for the attention of the captain himself. So he had returned in haste to the main camp, taking his prisoner with him.

# Chapter Two
## "Stayn Hears the News"

There was little gaiety in the ranger camp within five minutes after the arrival of the party. The news had gone the rounds in a whisper, passing lightning swift, as whispers always do, from one to another. So it came, finally, to the last man of the camp. They all knew, with the exception of Charlie Stayn.

That hearty fellow clung eagerly to the members of the newly returned party. He was full of questions. He poured them forth, pressing hard to secure more information about that strange special detail on which his best friend and old companion had been sent. Ordinarily, rangers were sent in couples—at least when they were riding through a country where there was a great deal of danger—and, since it was known that Toomby had been commissioned to ride into the Kiever Mountains, it was felt that it was exceedingly odd that he should have been sent alone.

The questions of Stayn were answered, after a fashion, but after a fashion that was increasingly poor. Men could not meet his eyes. Poor Vestry and Montain gnawed their lips and prayed that the sergeant might come out of the captain's tent; but the sergeant did not come, and still the fires blazed, and the coffee was boiled, and the tin cups filled, and the cigarettes lighted. But the talk fell more and more away as all eyes centered upon the great, shaggy head of Charlie Stayn.

He had one of those faces that, even in youth, appear somewhat battered and grim, as though life had worn upon them with special friction. In profile, his clear-cut features were extremely handsome, but in the full face, when his habitual frown was more noticeable and his lips were seen to be nearly always compressed, his savagery outbalanced all other attributes of his face. He had the look of one of tremendous passions. There were veins upon his throat and his forehead which started into blue prominence if he were excited. His neck was the round neck of a very strong man. If he stooped over, the great rolling muscles across his shoulders made knots and bulges that were noticeable even through his shirt and coat. He had a thick, round wrist, also, and one of those deceptive forearms that begins small but swells to formidable bulk of intertwisting tendons and cords and linked chains of muscle near the elbow.

He was not nearly so large as he seemed. He might be an inch or two above six feet; he was certainly a pound or so under two hundredweight. Yet he impressed everyone as being much more. Most of all, it lay in the great size of his head, crowned with shaggy yellow hair that could not be controlled with comb or brush. That head made him seem like a lion among men; he had the lion's wrinkled and fiercely thoughtful brow, too, and the lion's large, round, yellow eyes.

Such was Charlie Stayn. But his mere physical presence was the smallest part of him. There were more stories about him than about all the other men in the company of rangers put together. He was a scant twenty-four years of age. He looked at least ten years older, and he had packed into his brief existence enough excitement and achievement, of one kind or another, to fill a dozen lives. He was one who began young. At fifteen he struck a cowpuncher with his fist, breaking the man's jaw, and suddenly discovered his own strength. At sixteen he began to run amuck. At seventeen he put his furious energies into a trip to Alaska and three years of wild labor and wild money-making and wild spending there. He came back when he was twenty with the lion-look already in his face, a great deal of experience, no money, and Joe Toomby.

Toomby was a big man also. He was almost as strong, almost as good as Stayn, almost as reckless of his life, almost as dreadful in a fight. But Toomby laughed when he fought, whereas Stayn only showed his white teeth and glared with his yellow eyes. Toomby was merciful, gentle to the conquered, a lover of mirth and good cheer, and worshipped by the rangers, every man. He tempered the silence of Stayn. He won that silent fellow into conversation. Stayn was observed to smile and chat in the company of his friend, and they stood by each other in every peril. Each had saved the other's life half a dozen times. Each followed the other like a shadow. For two years they had prospected through the mountains after they came south from Alaska. Then Toomby had persuaded Stayn to enlist in the rangers to serve under Captain John Naseby. Toomby himself had explained matters to the captain: "There's a certain amount of fighting in Charlie Stayn that's got to be brought out. If he don't do it on the side of the law, he'll do it against the law. Take him in. I'll come in with him. I'll take charge of him and see that he keeps his hands off the other boys. All they have to do is to leave him alone. And remember, Captain, that if you get him, you get a man that's as good as twenty!"

The captain had taken a reckless chance, for the black fame of Stayn was whispered far and wide through the mountains. He enlisted the pair and found, in fact, that the power of his company was doubled at once. On every difficult mission he included the two young giants, and they never failed. They were as patient as grizzlies, as cunning as foxes, as courageous as only brave men can be. They had never been separated saving upon this single and disastrous occasion.

It had been devised as subtle punishment. Charlie Stayn, hard held, as a rule, by his respect for the captain and the wise advice of his friend, had broken loose at the expense of a few strong-handed miners who had obstructed him with foolish remarks in the streets of the town a few weeks before. Charlie Stayn used no weapon save his hands only, but he left a great human wreckage behind him, and, though he could have been severely punished by the law, the captain managed to bring him off safely. The separation from Toomby was the device to punish him, and it had worked like a charm.

Very proud, very haughty, totally self-dependent, yet Stayn was vulnerable in this one point. He accepted the justice of what was done; he behaved with commendable gentleness during all the days while Toomby was away, and he only showed signs of roughness when the party had actually returned. Then he found his questions evaded, his friend missing, many eyes fixed upon him with mysterious meaning; and now he sat on a slicker spread on the ground near the fire, with one knee supported by his clasped hands, staring at the fire, his face as dark as thunder.

This continued for ten minutes. Then Harry Vestry went by. A great arm shot out. Harry was stricken to the ground and found a hand at his throat. Above him he saw the contorted face and the leonine eyes of Stayn.

"Vestry," said the big man, "I got to have the truth. Understand? I *got* to have it."

Vestry was trembling so that he could hardly speak. He rolled his eyes, but he could see no comrade coming to his assistance. It was as if he had been seized by a lion, indeed.

"It wasn't *my* fault," he said. "I didn't send him. I never wanted him to go. It wasn't my fault, Stayn. You can't blame me!"

"For what?" asked Stayn.

"Toomby's . . ."

"Speak out!"

But Vestry was dumb with terror. Presently Stayn threw him away and stood up. He looked slowly about him, his yellow eyes lingering on every face, as though prepared to mark out a prey. He saw nothing to his mind, however, and went straight to the tent of the captain where he encountered the sergeant on the verge of coming out. The latter shrank, grew pale, and then hastily moved on, saying that the captain had something to say to him.

There was a little signboard put up by the captain so that he could post his orders concerning the camp at that place. Upon it Stayn rested his elbow for a moment. Then with gathered strength he entered the tent.

"Do you come into your captain's tent without knocking, Stayn?" said Naseby in his sternest manner.

For answer, and in place of any salute, or even removing his hat, the ranger tugged his sombrero lower above his eyes. "Where's Toomby?" he said.

"Stayn," said the captain, "I warn you that I will not be trifled with, and if . . ."

Stayn made a slow gesture through the air, as though he were wiping out the captaincy of the other and all distinctions whatever. When his gesture was ended, they were simply man and man, face to face. "Where's Toomby?" he said again.

"Stayn, there is good luck and bad luck in the world. . . ."

"Where's Toomby?" asked the giant, coming a little nearer to John Naseby.

"Stayn, show yourself a man . . . a calm, sensible, reasoning man and not a wild brute. Toomby has done his duty."

"And died," said the big man in a deep and hollow voice.

"Died," said the captain sadly, and all the time eyeing the other with a cold apprehension of what might happen next.

But nothing happened. The fury of Stayn, which had threatened to grow into a raging passion the instant he heard the sad truth, now evaporated to nothingness. He looked about him, as one who saw only half of what was near at hand. He seemed partly blinded, partly bewildered.

"I got to go," he said finally, muttering.

The captain found his dread turning rapidly into pity. "Go where, Stayn?" he asked.

"Don't ask," said Stayn, the ominous shade appearing for a moment again in his face. "Don't ask me. You took Toomby away where I couldn't take care of him no more. You got to answer for that. But now I got to answer to his mother for what I done. She give him to me and told me that, unless I watched him careful, he'd come to harm. Well, I got to tell her that I didn't watch good enough."

"I'll arrange it at once, Stayn," said the captain. "I'll arrange for you to have leave. . . ."

"You'll arrange?" echoed Stayn. "Man, d'you think that I'll stay here to wait for arranging? D'you think that I'll stay here to serve under you another day? I'd see you in blazes first!" He strode to the flap.

"Stayn," called the commander, "if you desert, it's like deserting an army in the field. You'd never do that!"

"I hear you talk," said the big man, "but what you say don't mean nothing. I'm going to see his mother. Then I'm going to get the dogs that pulled him down. No one man ever killed him. There was more than one. I'm going to get 'em all!"

He strode through the flap. He looked about him for a moment. Then he started for his horse. The captain, in the meantime, struck a little gong which hung in his tent. He struck it twice, and it brought two rangers instantly to him.

"Go, arrest Stayn," he commanded sternly. "Go at once and arrest Stayn and bring him back to me."

The rangers looked from one to another.

"Take as many more with you as you need," said the captain. "But I want that man, and I want him quickly!"

# Chapter Three
## "The Passport To Kiever"

They went to get Stayn with guns in their hands and dread in their hearts, but Stayn was not to be taken. He was away among the hills before the rangers had straightened out their horses after him. Having shaken off their first rush of pursuit, he dismounted, loosened his girths, for it appeared to him that he had brought up the cinches a little too close on his horse, and then, remounting, went ahead in leisurely fashion, for he knew that, having failed to take him with the first rush, the rangers would probably go back to the camp, arrange a hunting party with care, and then strike off after him, caring nothing for a wasted hour or two in the beginning of a trail. But Stayn had not served under Captain Naseby this last year for nothing. He knew that the captain never failed, and he knew that, in the end, no matter how long the rangers might have to stick by a trail, they always won out. He was beginning a game, therefore, in which he knew that he must lose in the end, but between this beginning and the end many things might happen. For the sake of what lay in between, he was determined to push on steadily. Toomby lay dead in the Kiever Mountains, and Toomby he was bound to avenge.

He did not ride west and north for the Kiever range, however, but cut off rather to the north and east. For two days he kept up a steady journey. Then he came to a village in the foothills of the Rockies. He waited for night. Then he tethered his horse and went down to the town. It was a warm, heavy night. All the doors and windows were open; shafts of light and many voices issued. He passed through clouds of unseen, choking dust, raised by children at play as they raced up and down the street with wolfish energy. He heard the needle-sharp wail of babies, the wrangling of a man and his wife, the rattle of tins and pans in the kitchens.

166

All of this, Stayn told himself, was the significance of life in a huddled group among men. They were all like this. They came together as sheep come, for shelter and for the mysterious comfort of numbers. But the numbers of the flock do not keep it from slaughter, and the foolish herding of men make them neither wiser nor braver. They die in the end, just the same. They are only more miserable than those who lead solitary lives because their years are made miserable by the nearness of their fellow humans, so that the crying of one infant starts another wailing and the wrangling of one family teaches the ill habit to a neighboring couple. Wherefore, Stayn, as he went down the street, despised and almost pitied these townsfolk.

He came to a little house set back from the street more deeply than the majority and distinguished by a rose garden planted before it. The garden was newly watered; the ground was still drinking with a light and whispering sound; and the scents of flowers and of the wet earth mixed heavily in the hot air. It was an atmosphere like that of a greenhouse, a tropical humidity. On the porch of the house was a figure in white. It rose with a crisp rustling when big Stayn came near.

"Missus Toomby?" he said.

The old woman's voice answered quietly: "Yes."

"Do you know me?"

"Yes, Mister Stayn."

"I've come with bad news for you."

"I know what it is."

"They've given you word of it?"

"Oh, yes! Captain Naseby sent to me at once."

"Missus Toomby, I broke my word to you . . . I didn't stay with him."

"Mister Stayn," said the little old lady, "let's not talk any more about it. God puts us on earth and takes us away when He wishes. Who are we to question Him?"

Such an attitude amazed and baffled Stayn. He knew that the little woman worshipped her big son and had devoted her life to his happiness, which was what made her even temper now so amazing.

"They put us apart," said Stayn, "or this would never have happened. Never!"

"Hush!" said the mother. "You mustn't talk of it any more. I've shut the door on that, don't you see? You mustn't open it again for me to make me sad. I shall go to his grave every spring and take some of these flowers."

She walked down the path toward the gate, leading Stayn along.

"He planted that Virginia creeper at the corner of the house," she said. "He used to dig the whole garden for me every spring and every fall. There was no one like my boy for that. He put the blade of the spade straight down into the ground and turned the topsoil straight under. After he stopped working in the garden, it never did so well. When he was younger, he was a very good help to me, you see. All that row of white roses . . . do you see them under the shadow of the wall? . . . were planted by Joe, dear boy. Well, Mister Stayn, you see that I have my boy about me all the time, and every morning, when I look out into the garden, I can remember him so well that even the song he used to sing, when he was working here, comes back into my mind."

At the little creaking gate, Stayn told her good bye and went off down the street again. His mind had been opened to a new idea. New ideas rarely came to him. He had decided what the world was and what he wanted to do with it when he was fifteen years old. He had never changed his opinion in the years that followed. But now a thought entered his head and grew slowly. There was something in Mrs. Toomby of quiet strength that, he felt, had dwarfed his own physical powers. Her will was the will of a giant. Her submission to fate seemed to Stayn more awful and wonderful than the stormiest defiance of it.

However, there was too much need of action in the immediate future to permit him to waste much time in the consideration of the old lady's character. Yonder in the Kiever Mountains poor Toomby lay dead and buried under a heap of rocks.

It was a long journey and not completed without many difficulties. The rangers had lost his trail, picked it up again near the home of Mrs. Toomby, and then swung almost due west at his heels as he rode toward the Kiever Mountains. They were a party of four. He found that out by dropping back along his own trail and hunting the hunters. The party was led by the same man who had commanded when Toomby had ridden forth. It was Pete Story, the best head and the coolest hand, next to Captain Naseby himself, in the entire troop. He had with him three picked men, the very best that the rangers could furnish, now that Stayn and Toomby were no longer of their number.

Stayn was pleased to see these warriors trotting down his trail, equipped for war. It was the custom to send out one man to capture one man in ordinary country; two men rode to apprehend a very dangerous criminal, perhaps; three departed under extraordinary conditions. Stayn had never yet known them to send four men to pursue a single fugitive. It was a quiet tribute to his powers, and he could not help feeling a little stir of vanity.

That day he made a detour to the south and led the rangers after him. Then, when he crossed the Kiever River and brought them hotly over it behind him, he doubled straight back like a fox, left his hunters a trail problem that would make them rack their brains for an hour or two, hit the river a few miles to the north, crossed it once more, and now rode on a straight line for the Kiever Mountains.

It was not a very complicated maneuver. What threw off the rangers, apparently, was that they expected him to rush ravening and straight upon his quarry, like a wild bull. They did not expect him to use any craft, but felt that he was sure to strike ahead for his goal, bearing down whatever lay in between. They did not know Stayn, as he would prove to them before they had been long upon his trail. He gained a whole day by this last maneuver, and now he headed away to do his real work.

As for the clues which must guide him when the time for acting came, he felt that they might not be so hard to unravel. He knew that his party lived in the Kiever Mountains and were, in fact, Kiever men—that is to say, they were of the tough Scotch-Irish blood that lived and thrived among the mountains, hunting, ranging cows over what other men would have considered a desert, mining with shrewd heads and hands of iron, working the few bits of lumber in their domain. They were a queer people, made stranger because they had lived two whole generations among these ranges of sharp-sided mountains, so that their peculiarities were hardened in them. They became a new type. They were famous throughout the West, and were, indeed, beginning to be known throughout the land. Travelers happened into these harsh, sun-dried, storm-swept regions and came out to write stories and articles about the "Kiever Men" and the "Men of Kiever." People in the West said of a man: "He's a Kiever." Just as they would have said: "He's a Smith." They were like a recognized family.

Their reputation was by no means savory. The land they inhabited was a land of rocks and sand. They raised only enough cows, and particularly sheep, to keep them employed. Their mining, lumbering, and such endeavors were futile pursuits. They were as active as swarming ants that cannot find enough to make the winter supplies. The Kiever men were all good workers and hard workers. The trouble was that they would not go into the employ of other people. They wished to work for and with one another. Moreover, they had a deep, almost a foolish, attachment for their range of mountains and for the uninhabitable deserts which extended upon either side of it.

Here they were, then, with a country that they dearly loved, but which could not support them. The obvious result was that they spread out here and there on little plundering expeditions to make matters better for themselves and their families. Sometimes they dipped on to the richer ranges that surrounded their own deserts and scooped up horses and cows in small numbers. Sometimes they dipped to the south toward Mexico and either raided savagely across the river or else brought smuggled goods across the line.

They were helped to immunity in these incursions by their own craft and daring commingled, but most of all by their horses, for, in the course of their stay in the desert and the mountains, they had improved greatly the fine animals which they brought with them. The Arabian horse developed in an arid country; its endurance was created to match the long distances and time without water, with small provisions. The men of Kiever, bringing with them to the West a strain that was almost the pure Thoroughbred, hardened and condensed the good qualities of that line. They produced a horse that had the bone and the intelligence and the courage and magnificent spirit of the Thoroughbred, but other qualities were compromised. They sacrificed a little size in order to secure handiness among the rocks and the twisting defiles of the Kiever range. They gave up a little speed for the sake of shorter legs. They gave up a little more speed for the sake of greater endurance. The result was that any Thoroughbred could have caught them in a dash, but they could have killed any Thoroughbred in a campaign through the rough mountains, or over the loose, shifting, burning sands of the desert. They could live on fare that would have been starvation to a Thoroughbred.

There was this quality also among the Kiever men and their possessions: they did not grow in numbers. Their men married late in life, because they were generally well past thirty before they had acquired enough property to set up a home. After marriage, they had small families of one, two, and hardly ever more than three children. The race never increased in population. They simply became more and more perfectly adapted to their surroundings. They had blue eyes and shining black hair. Their bodies were light in flesh and strong in muscle. They had starved faces, and their habitual expression was something between wistfulness and hungry ferocity. It is very odd to speak of facial expression of a whole people, but the Kievers had become developed to so perfect a type that it was possible with them. They were all tall; they were all graceful; they were all like cats in speed of movement and lightness of step; they were all aloof from strangers, true to one another, of few words whether in joy or rage, devoted to their country, and above all to the tall and ragged mountain whose name had been grafted upon them—Kiever Mountain—in the center of the range.

Such were the people among whom Stayn now prepared to adventure. He reached the verge of their country, with the Kiever range shooting straight up into the sky. There among the cliffs and the defiles of the foothills, he waited and rested and prepared himself for the work to come. To ride straight in among them would be the height of folly. He must have something that would serve him as a passport among the Kiever men. He made up his mind almost at once what that passport should be, for the Kiever men hated the Texas Rangers.

That formidable band of the warriors of the law had just begun to establish relations with the men of Kiever. It might be said that there had been clashes on the frontiers, and either party respected the other most heartily. The rangers were amazed to come in contact with a whole people who could ride like centaurs and shoot like so many reincarnations of Wild Bill.

The sturdy men of Kiever were equally amazed to find a body of enforcers of the law who never left a trail, who could not be disheartened and baffled like ordinary posses, but who clung to every cause and fought it to the last, and who were formidable not because of numbers, but because of the magic of discipline. They came to dread these rangers. But they could never dread the rangers so much as the rangers dreaded the Kiever men. The very mention of the name was anathema among the band.

So it was that Stayn selected his passport to win him favor among the men of Kiever. He did to the party of four rangers just what his bunkie and dear friend, Toomby, had done to the men of Kiever. That is to say, he invaded their quarters at night. It was made simpler than he could have hoped.

While the other rangers slept, the sergeant himself walked up and down through the night in the deepest thought. He had worn out his men; his horses were staggering ghosts of their old selves. In short, he had been too ardent in this pursuit. He had been too confidently eager to secure the person of Stayn. He had always hated the big man, and the big man had hated him. It was the sergeant who had suggested to the captain this means of punishing Stayn by separating him from Toomby. It was the sergeant who had envied Stayn's growing name and fame. Stayn knew all these things. He had stalked that camp of the four rangers this night, and now it was an easy thing to come straight upon the sergeant while that honest but somewhat overkeen officer of the law walked back and forth, blind with preoccupation. Stayn rose out of the ground behind him, struck him down, bound and gagged him, and brought him away without a sound. Then he left the sergeant securely tied in a safe place, and captured on the open range a gentle old mare of the Kiever blood. He placed the poor sergeant upon her and tied his legs beneath the belly of the mare. Upon the back of the sergeant he pinned a piece of paper with these large characters inscribed upon it: **I am looking for Stayn.**

That done, he turned the mare loose and, as he knew she would do, she started away at a gentle trot, headed for her master's home.

# Chapter Four
## "The Town of Kiever"

At the breaking of day, the old mare jogged into the town of Kiever. Early as it was, the inhabitants were already up and stirring. When the first man saw the bound figure on the back of the horse, his shout called out the rest. They flocked around the poor sergeant, laughing, cheering, whooping. They read the placard on the back of the victim and roared with mirth. It was the very cream of a good joke, this trick played upon a member of the rangers. They could appreciate it the more because the heavy hand of that organization was beginning to fall more and more heavily upon their ranks.

They pretended to have difficulty in untying the ropes which bound Pete Story, and, when he, raving and raging, commanded them to cut the ropes and get him down to the ground, they reproved him gently and assured him that, with their thrifty habits, they could not endure the thought of spoiling such a perfectly good rope as this. At length, when the whole population of Kiever had assembled to look and to laugh, they loosed the sergeant and allowed him to slip to the ground.

He looked about him, his face blackened with rage and shame. He was a high-strung man, was Pete Story, and, in his fury, he knew that, if he spoke, he would weep with his passion. Tears did not keep him from fighting, but they would even more disgrace him on this occasion. Therefore, he said not a word, though his blazing eyes were eloquent. What he wanted to tell them was that the man who had performed this trick upon him was coming to exact from them vengeance for the killing of Toomby, but his fury silenced him.

They loaned him a horse. They showed him every attention, smiling as they did it. They treated him as they might have treated a woman, and Story, being a hundred-percent man, gnashed his teeth and endured. Then, on the borrowed horse, he rode furiously back to the pass where he had left his three companions. He found them gone. They were looking desperately through the hills to find his trail, but a trail that began on foot and ended on horseback was too much even for their sagacity. It was two days later before they finally happened to meet their sergeant.

In the meantime, the news had gone everywhere through the mountains. The story that was told was a simple one. Stayn, a former ranger, had left the ranks and struck away for freedom. When four rangers pursued him, he had dropped behind, taken the leader of the rangers prisoner, and, instead of harming the man, had made a fool of him. It was a jest so exactly to the taste of the Kiever men that they were kept in high spirits indefinitely by the recounting of it. In the retelling, it lost nothing. The description of the poor sergeant on the back of the mare with his placard attached became a Homeric thing.

The formidable champion who had accomplished this feat was now lurking in their own mountains, and straightway they set about finding him. Nothing could hide him from the men of Kiever in the Kiever Mountains. In twenty-four hours, a group of six hunters found him. He was sitting beside a campfire that he had kindled in open defiance of the rangers, as though he felt that even with a fire to guide them, they could never find him.

He was sipping his coffee out of a tin cup, sitting cross-legged on the ground, and, when they arrived within the circle of the firelight, he showed not the slightest perturbation. He merely waved a hand to them and invited them to join him in his supper.

He stood up to kindle the fire and slice more bacon, and the men of Kiever considered his stature and admired it. They dismounted one by one. They entreated him not to waste his bacon. They had already eaten their suppers and the small appetites that they had with them could be very simply satisfied. With that, they took up a piece of the pone that he had cooked. They broke it into six small pieces. One of the Kiever men took from a pouch at his cartridge belt a pinch of salt and sprinkled a grain or two upon each of the pieces of bread, after which they ate their portions with a certain solemnity of manner.

Just what it was, Stayn did not understand, but he was uneasy, guessing that by this ceremony they were admitting him to their friendship and hospitality as the Arab who cannot harm a host whose bread and salt he has tasted. And this when he had come to find the murderers of Toomby.

Presently they lighted cigarettes and sat down around the fire after one had mounted his horse and ridden quickly away until he reached a high point nearby. There he sat in his saddle motionless, dimly outlined against the stars.

"Where has your friend gone?" asked Stayn.

"He'll keep a smart lookout," the Kiever man answered. "Finish your coffee and then we can talk."

So Stayn finished his coffee, lighted his own smoke, and waited for information. It was not long in coming. The eldest among the party now cleared his throat and made a little informal speech in which he informed Stayn that the people of Kiever understood that he was in danger from the rangers, that they had no great reason for liking the rangers themselves, and that they were willing to do what they could to shelter the fugitive from the justice which would otherwise overwhelm him. In a word, since they felt that every enemy to the rangers was a friend to them, they freely offered the right hand of good-fellowship to Stayn. They invited him to come to their homes. They bade him choose what provisions he wished from among the supplies that they carried, each man having a small pack behind his saddle.

To these things Stayn listened with profound amazement; for, though he had lived his life in the West where hospitality is a virtue as important as honesty in other lands, yet he had never come in contact with open-heartedness and open-handedness to compare with that of these men of Kiever. So he hesitated, turning his thoughts slowly to and fro in his dark mind.

The conclusion he came to was something in the following nature: *If I stay with these good-natured people and accept their kindness until I have discovered the men who murdered poor Joe Toomby, then I'll be a hound. But if I don't accept what they offer to me, and, if I try to support myself with my own efforts, dodge the rangers on the one hand and avoid the Kieverites on the other, I shall never be able to revenge Toomby, or even to save myself.*

This train of reasoning was sufficient to resolve him at once. He determined to make the most of their offers, and use them to

175

unravel the threads of the mystery of the killing of Toomby. However, he began by protesting: "This here is all mighty kind," he said, "but it'll make a crop of trouble for you-all."

"You tell him, Stillwater," said one of the younger men.

The person thus singled out now came to the front. He was older than the two others. His hair was streaked with gray at the sides of his head. His cheeks were more pinched and his brow deeper than the others, but his eye was as bright.

"First of all, stranger," he said, "why did you send the sergeant to us?"

"I thought you might be in need of a laugh," said Stayn.

"We figure that it was for more of a reason than that," answered Stillwater. "Who you might be, stranger, we dunno, except by your clothes we guess you're a ranger that has deserted his command. There's hell popping in front of you, then, and you've come to us to get our help. Is that right?"

Put so bluntly, Stayn could not but assent.

"All right," said the other. "Are we friends, then? Do you fight for us just as we fight for you?" He extended his hand.

It was hard for Stayn to close with this proffered alliance, but he saw nothing else left for him to do. So, with a sigh, he shook hands with Stillwater and the others. He had no sooner done so, than the men of Kiever uttered a deep shout of satisfaction. They murmured to one another as though in congratulation. They called in their watcher from the hill and told him the good news: "Here's another man for Kiever!"

"Better one real man," said Stillwater, "than a hundred half-men!"

They started back across the hills, for Stayn told them that he did not care to lie out among the hills. He had no fear of immediate pursuit by the rangers. What he wanted to do was to enjoy one comfortable night in a bed, because there were apt to be many days of hard living among the mountains in the times following. So they started in for the village, the more readily because, as they confessed to him, the entire village was anxious to see the man who had dared to insult those formidable and ever dreaded Texas Rangers.

They confessed, moreover, that they had been watching him and his pursuers ever since he first came within the edges of their territory. They had marked his tactics. They had admired his boldness.

They had even been close enough to see him turn back and stalk the rangers on the evening of that night during which he had captured the sergeant. They had actually crept close up and observed him fall upon the absent-minded sergeant, crush that poor fellow to earth, and carry him away through the darkness. They had followed. They had seen him catch the old mare and tie the sergeant upon her back. It was not purely instinct that had driven the mare into the village. It was, above all, because certain figures stalked behind her and herded her in the correct direction.

"Friends," said Stayn with much frankness, "I'm neither deaf nor blind. How the devil could you have come close enough to watch me, while I didn't hear even a whisper of you?"

At this, they merely smiled upon one another and returned him no answer.

In the meantime, they came in view of the town of Kiever. It looked rather like a fort than a town, at first. It was a tableland of a few acres at the foot of a lofty mountain, the little plateau itself being at least a hundred feet above the general level of the floor of that valley. The white walls of the little tableland looked like the walls of a fortress, and the houses of the village were lost behind a mass of trees. Kiever blossomed while the rest of the range was a burned desert.

Stayn found the reason when he had reached the town itself and penetrated with his newly found friends to its central part. Here there was a rude circular opening, perhaps of eight or ten acres. The town of Kiever comprised the irregularly scattered houses that fringed this opening. The central portion was a most closely cultivated vineyard, orchard, and vegetable plot. The soil was a sandy loam, enormously rich, and it was made fruitful by a great spring that welled up out of the ground in the center of this place. It was one of the many mysteries of the mountains. How it should have come to rise from the ground in this spot remained a mystery. Some asserted confidently that the entire rainfall on the whole surface of the Kiever range, concentrated in one spot, would not have been enough to keep this spring flowing half the year. Others explained it by saying that the spring must be fed with waters drawn from the distant mountains to the north which, in the winter, were thickly bedded down with snows. They reinforced this statement by pointing out that the water leaped up most boldly in the late spring of the year when the snows melted away. Then, they said, winding underground, through some channel, following a well-defined fault among the rocks, the water must flow south until, at the last, it came to the surface among the Kiever Mountains.

At any rate, here it was. The cold, pure waters were viewed every year by hundreds who rode in many miles. In fact, it only escaped being a tourist attraction for the reason that no railroad had ever penetrated the fastnesses of the Kiever range, but it made a lovely picture as it rolled out of the jaws of rock and washed across yellow sands, covering them with filtered blue shadows. It passed into a great reservoir that had been wrought out of the living rock at the cost of immense labor. From this reservoir the water was drawn off through sluice gates. It irrigated the acreage in the center of the village that was cultivated for the common good. It passed on through smaller canals and supplied each of the small plots of garden and orchard that belonged to the widely scattered houses of the town.

Finally, what was left tumbled down the north and south faces of the cliff and watered a few hundred acres on either side before the stream failed and sank entirely into the desert. From the well itself, one could look down on all sides and see the work of the water.

Sometimes, Stayn was told, the well shrank away to a mere pitiful whisper of water. Then the outlying farms beneath the cliffs burned up to a cinder. The alfalfa was cooked to the deepest roots through the beds of light sand. All was ruined, and this happened as often as once in five years, or sometimes once in three.

Still Kiever continued to flourish in a small way, never increasing in size, consisting always of just so many as could live by the agricultural produce that the spring made possible, and also of the handful of ranchers and miners and grazers who had retired from an active life and come to Kiever to enjoy the latter part of their lives in a season of mild-mannered quiet.

Such was the town into which big Charlie Stayn rode on this day. When he looked from the well over the little, squat-walled houses of adobe, each with its flower-brightening patio, its climbing vines, its silver-flowing canals, he felt that he had come into a sort of Biblical civilization, and the plateau itself rose like a head crowned with a misty wreath of green above the gray death of the desert beneath it.

# Chapter Five
## "Unwelcome Advice"

Stillwater took him to his own house. On the way, Stayn asked him how they had come into their feud with the rangers. He was told that the war had risen because a few of the men of Kiever had been guilty of occasional indiscretions. They had sallied forth from their mountains and committed certain small depredations in the plain. These raids called down the wrath of the rangers upon them. There had been pursuits. The rangers had sometimes taken a man of Kiever; sometimes the men of Kiever had shaken off the rangers and left them behind, perhaps with more than one casualty.

"It's dangerous work," commented Stayn. "One of these days, you might have the governor calling out the militia ag'in' you."

Stillwater smiled. "We'll never be found out," he said.

When he was asked for what reason, he explained simply enough. If a Kiever man was caught, he would have to be tried in the court at Kiever, which was also the county seat. If the case were carried to another court, all the witnesses brought from the Kiever Mountains would stick by one another and the prisoner to death. Their lies were uttered with a sort of holy, patriotic zeal.

This was not all. It was very difficult to attach the blame. Unless the criminals were actually recognized, and their faces known— which was hard, because of the great physical resemblance of most of the men of Kiever—their trails melted among the twisted valleys of the Kiever range, or else they were mixed up among the Kiever men who had not taken part in the raid. Stillwater was a sensible man, but this talk of his was hard to comprehend.

"But," said Stayn, "suppose that the people out yonder . . . north and south and east and west . . . are tired of being robbed. What then? Suppose that they call on the governor and march a few companies through the mountains?"

"We could vanish in the mountains, every one of us," said the Kiever chief. "We have cached away stores of food in a hundred hidden places. We have ammunition and guns laid up. We have everything we need. They would have to bring a hundred thousand men and form a cordon that would sweep this mountain range from end to end before they could find our hiding places. But we would not have to vanish . . . and the militia will never be sent. We do no killings. We take only what we really need . . . a few cattle and such things. Men must have meat to live by. Besides, we never plunder the poor. We take a few cows from ranches that can afford to lose them. Who can really blame us?"

"You never kill?" said Stayn.

"Not unless we're chased into the Kiever Mountains. Then we're on our own ground."

Here was a stranger doctrine than even Stayn had been prepared to hear. These odd fellows actually dared to consider themselves as a nation within a nation, keeping the government away the full length of their arm. Their poverty secured them from the intrusion of strangers; their remote position kept the government itself from exercising too close a vigilance over them. Neither was it the first time that such a thing had happened. The case of the Mormons was much to the point. They had made a people within a people.

They reached the house of Stillwater. While they were putting up their horses in the barn to the rear, Stayn broached the subject that was nearest to his heart.

"The last time the rangers came through," he said, "they got their medicine handed to them hot, eh?"

"They did," said Stillwater. "They lost the best man they got, excepting the one named Stayn."

To hear his own name was a shock to the big fellow. He lingered with his hands on the tie-strap of the cinch.

"Who's the man you mean?" he asked, without turning his head to his host.

"You been in the rangers, and you don't know?" asked Stillwater. "You don't know Stayn?" The amazement in his voice was as though he had asked: "You a collegian and yet do not know that the world is round?"

"Of course," said Stayn. "I know Stayn, but not the man who's next best, or was next best until your men put him out of the way?"

There was a grunt of surprise from Stillwater. "I thought that the whole company of rangers knew Toomby, Stayn's bunkie, was the next best fighter they had."

"Maybe he was," muttered Stayn. "So Toomby was the man you got?"

"You busted away from the company before they got the report?" asked Stillwater, still cold with suspicion, it seemed.

"Yup. Didn't hear a word about how things turned out in the trip to the Kiever Mountains."

"Well," said the other, growing more communicative, "Toomby was one of the gang, you know."

"Of course. I saw them ride out."

"You heard Stayn make trouble about it, then?"

"I did. They sent Toomby away to discipline Stayn. That was their way of doing it. The captain knew," he went on bitterly, "that, if Stayn was kept away from Toomby, it would make 'em both unhappy. He sent Toomby off by himself, and that's how Toomby happened to get killed, I suppose."

"Stayn couldn't have helped," said Stillwater. "Toomby come down on the camp all by himself. It was a pretty nervy thing to do. He stole what he wanted to get . . . the opium, you know . . . and then he was shot while he was riding away. He reached the other rangers, though, with his stuff. Now that they know we've been smuggling opium as well as having killed a ranger, I suppose that they'll be hot after us. Is that right?"

"They will," agreed Stayn, carrying his saddle to the wall and hanging it upon a peg.

He was more than ever surprised by the communicativeness of Stillwater. It was as though that shrewd and hardy mountaineer, having admitted the stranger to his hospitality, felt that nothing was to be feared from him.

"What d'you think that we ought to do?" asked the Kiever man.

"You want to know the facts of what you ought to do?"

"Of course."

"To get out with your skin sound and whole?"

"That's it."

"Find the men who shot Toomby and turn 'em over to justice."

There was an exclamation of surprise and dismay from Stillwater. "Give 'em up to be murdered?" he asked sharply.

"You asked me," said Stayn frankly. "I'm telling you. The rangers will never rest till they get the men that did the work. I know, because I've been one of them. They never fail. They get what they're sent to get. . . ."

"Why," broke in the other, "I could tell you ten cases where they haven't got what they wanted to get."

"When?"

"All inside the last three years."

"Three years is nothing to the rangers," said Stayn. "They'll stay by a trail for twenty years, and, in the end, they'll get their man."

He spoke gloomily, for such, he knew, would be his own fate. He had only the vague hope, growing momentarily more and more dim, that he might be able to make his peace for desertion and for disgracing the sergeant of his troop, by apprehending the murderer or murderers of poor Joe Toomby.

Stillwater had sighed in the deepest thought. He finally said: "What's got to come, will come. Besides, you may be mistaken this once. Anyway, it's pleasanter in the patio than it is out here. Come along in."

They went toward the house, and, on the way, Stillwater reminded him that he had not as yet given a name.

"Because," said Stayn, "a man like me that's on the run ain't apt to pass his name around any too free."

"You don't need to fear us," answered Stillwater. "We've broke bread and ate salt together. There'll be no Kiever man that will give you any trouble. There's only one man that we're looking for now."

"My name is Danby," said the ranger. "Who are you looking for?"

"Stayn, of course."

"Why for Stayn?"

"Well, we know about him. They say that he'll never rest until he has three lives to pay for Toomby's. Is that right?"

"It may be so," said Stayn, perspiring profusely. "If you have anyone here who knows him, you'd better send them out to lay for Stayn."

"Raid a rangers' camp?" asked the Kiever man mockingly.

"You wouldn't have to raid it. By what I know of Stayn, I guess that you wouldn't have to go far for him. When he knows that Toomby's dead, he'll break away and try to get at you, even if he has to ride alone."

## The Rock of Kiever

He had given away this much concerning himself because he felt that, the more frankly and the nearer the truth he spoke, the less apt they would be to suspect him.

In the meantime, they came to the patio, with Stillwater very gloomily brooding over the advice that his guest had given him. In the patio they found Mrs. Stillwater and her daughter working among the flowers, the wife with a hoe and the girl with a long-bladed trowel that, in her small, strong hands, cleaved deep into the moist loam at every thrust.

Stayn studied them curiously, while his host introduced him with a little humorous speech as the hero who had sent the sergeant of the rangers into Kiever that same morning. He saw that the Kiever women were the perfect type for the men—slender, graceful, with the same glossy black hair and the same direct blue eyes. They had the same voices—low and gentle—and they had even the same sun-browned hands. They had been busy all the day, no doubt, but here in the lamp-lit patio they were still working in the cool of the evening over their garden. In an instant they were employed on the comfort of their guest. Mrs. Stillwater went to prepare his room; Joan brought out food.

Stillwater and "Danby," in the meantime, took their ease in the little patio in comfortable chairs while Joan laid a small table, and Stayn, half-closing his eyes, felt the pleasantness of being cared for by a woman's hands—a new and strange thing for him.

He asked about the men of Kiever, partly from real interest, partly because he wished to listen rather to talk himself, and he heard how the first families had come in, the hardy strain of northern Ireland, rich with the blood of Scotch settlers. He heard how the colonists had made their city and grazed their herds. It was a story that came with more authority from the lips of his host because it was a Stillwater, his own ancestor, who had been the leading spirit and guide of the emigrants.

"He built this house," said Stillwater, "and he lifted that stone with his own hands. There's a prophecy about it, that he made after he moved it."

He pointed to a ragged gray monster of a stone in the midst of a flower bed. It seemed far beyond human powers to stir it.

183

# Chapter Six
## "Giant's Strength"

That big rock, the ranger regarded some time with awe, and feeling his own fingers hook and curl with emulation. He was fascinated. It seemed to him that he saw the form of a giant, tearing that boulder from its first bed, and dropping it here.

"How big was that Stillwater?" he asked at last.

"Six inches over six feet," said the other with pride, shaking his head at the mere consideration of such gigantic proportions for human flesh and bone. "And he weighed two and a half hundredweight. He could lift a hoss, I've heard it said by my father before me. He had great strength."

At once the dream of Stayn turned into reality. It *had* been a giant, worthy of a place beside Homer's Ajax the Greater.

"Why should he have moved it?" asked Stayn.

"They were digging the foundations for this house. They came on this rock and were working around it with picks and shovels. Then they began to pry at it with levers to budge it out of its place. One stick they used to start it burst. Then Stillwater jumped down into the trench and grabbed it. He pulled till it came up by the roots. He rolled it out of the trench. He got it and picked it up again and walked with it until something snapped in his back. It fell right there, and he fell on top of it. He never could walk after that day, and he died three months later. He made a prophecy about the man that was to move that stone. But nobody'll ever move it! Nobody!"

Stayn rose from his chair and stared. "From the looks of that flower garden," he said, "it don't look as though many folks have tried."

The man of Kiever turned and looked askance at him. "They've tried . . . many a man of them," he said sullenly. "For twenty years, men come and tried to stir it. Not Kiever men only, but other men all over heard about the Rock of Kiever, and come to try their hand at it. They never none of 'em could stir it! And since I was born, nobody has ever tried."

Now there ran back into the mind of Stayn something that he had half forgotten. That name of Kiever had always seemed familiar to him, and now he recalled that it was because, in his boyhood, he had heard old men talk about the Rock of Kiever, as being synonymous with huge, impossible weights for the hands of men.

"But," said his host sharply, "maybe you'd like to try?"

He ran his eyes over the body of Stayn with a new interest, as though regarding for the first time the full significance of that deep chest, those wide shoulders, and the mighty arms. The exclamation was like a keen spur prick to Stayn. He started, shook his head, and then instinctively took a step nearer to the stone.

"I dunno but that I might," he said thoughtfully. "It looks pretty big, but still, I might try. You wouldn't mind having some of your flowers spoiled?"

Stillwater shrugged his shoulders. He was frowning and had flushed deeply. He seemed to take it as a personal affront that anyone should think it even conceivable that human effort could budge the stone that had broken the back and the heart of his gigantic ancestor.

"The flowers don't matter," he said. "You do your best. The flowers can take care of themselves." He called: "Mother! Joan! Come down here!"

The girl was instantly in the patio. Her bright eyes seemed to Stayn like the eyes of a deer. She came aglow with excitement, so much emotion had been in the voice with which her father had summoned her.

"All here," said Stillwater, as his wife also came into the enclosure.

"It's hardly fair," protested Stayn, as this audience came before him. "It's hardly fair. I ain't been boasting, Stillwater," he continued. "I just said that I'd half a mind to take a try at the rock."

"Sure, sure," said Stillwater absently. Nevertheless, he went to the broad, low arch that was the entrance to the patio and raised his voice to a long, high-pitched wail: "Oh, Lufkin! Lufkin! Hey, Appleby!" He turned in another direction: "Jerney! McAuliffe!" Then he turned back to his guest and his family again.

"Why, Dad," said the girl, "what's wrong?"

He shrugged his shoulders eloquently again. "Nothing," he said, and deliberately took out his pipe and began to fill it.

As for Stayn, he heard voices answering and then coming closer, and he knew that he was about to be tested before a crowd. It angered him that he should be turned into a public show, but also he was made the keener to do his best. So he took off his coat and tossed it to one side. He rolled up his sleeves, to give clearance and free play to his elbow joints. He unbuttoned his collar, lest the strain of his effort should swell his throat and snap the buttons off. He tossed away his hat, and the lamplight that shone from the porch glinted and gleamed over his shaggy, tawny hair.

This was his condition when the others began to arrive. Four men had been called, but a dozen had answered and brought their chance guests of the evening with them. If the call were for four, it seemed probable that everyone within hearing would be welcome, so they had all come.

They flocked into the patio, chattering and as gay as so many magpies, and this was yet a new phase of the men of Kiever from the viewpoint of the ranger, for he had always heard of them and seen them as grave men, rarely speaking, using gestures almost more than words. So he gazed on them now with closest attention. They were like so many children, playful with one another. Then he heard his host say: "Here is Mister Danby, the man who played the game with the sergeant of the rangers this morning. . . ."

What a change came over the men of Kiever. They grew silent and grave as ever he had seen them. The women and some of the older children, who had come along with their parents, drew back behind the latter. One would have thought that Stayn was a public enemy.

"Danby has an idea," said Stillwater, with a pronounced sneer, "that he can move the Rock of Kiever. I thought that I'd call in you boys to see him try it!"

There was a murmur of wonder, of anger, and it seemed to Stayn, also, that he saw actual fear in the eyes of even the men before him, while the women, to the rear, shrank close to one another, as though for support.

It was baffling to him, but so much mystery began to be irritating. He said to his host gruffly: "You're putting the cart before the horse. I didn't say that I could lift that stone yonder. I said that I was willing to take a chance, and that was all. You got to repeat me right, Mister Stillwater!"

Stillwater merely shrugged his shoulders. "Whatever you said," he remarked, "there's the stone, and here you are, and here's a lot of us standing by to give you plenty of credit, if you can lift the stone. Step in, Mister Danby, and do your best."

As he said this, he smiled at the others, mutely inviting them to share in his spirit of derision. The rest, however, seemed to take this whole incident so seriously that smiles were far, indeed, from their minds.

"You brought Danby here," said one man sternly to the host of Stayn. "If trouble comes on Kiever because of him, who'll be to blame?"

This speech was followed by a murmur of stern applause. But Stayn shook his head again. He could not fathom these remarks. They were fatuous to a degree, in his estimation. How his single arm could work injury to this stout little village was beyond his comprehension. Even Mrs. Stillwater was in a trembling panic. There seemed, indeed, to be only one person present who was capable of remaining calm in this singular crisis, and this was Joan, the daughter. One strong young arm was passed around the shoulders of her mother. The other hand held the fingers of the older woman, and she watched Stayn with such a level, steady gaze that her blue eyes began to seem to him like one bright star when all the rest of the heavens grew dim.

In the meantime, here was this attempt of his awaiting his hand—this attempt upon which such a great deal depended. He had already prepared for the effort. Now, with his spirit swelling in anger and in pride, he advanced to the stone. He looked to Mrs. Stillwater and waved an apology to her. Then he planted his feet in the flower plot, his weight driving his boots into the soft sod well nigh up to the ankles, while there arose beneath him the faintly pungent odor of crushed green stems. He spread his feet apart so that he straddled the stone. He flexed his legs, so that he could be sure that all the muscles would work in harmonious accord from thighs to ankles. He worked his shoulders so that he could feel, slowly and surely, the play of all the solid and thickly padded masses of strength that lay across his back and deeply cushioned on the shoulder points. He bent down and up until he felt the presence of the most important engines of all—the two great ropes of sinew that ran up and down beside his spinal column.

He was now fit and ready. He stood up, took a deep, free breath like a strong, confident man, cast a thoughtful glance at the new moon that was beginning to prick a horn above the eastern trees, and then leaned to his labor.

He fumbled for only a moment, since he had already studied the rock carefully and knew at what angle he preferred to catch it. The stone was so rough that little keen projections bit into the palms of his hands and into his tough fingers, covered with leathery calluses. He heeded these incisions not at all. They were less than pin pricks, for the first upward heave of his body had not affected the stone any more than a wall is troubled by the blow of a child's fist.

He heard, running about the patio, a murmur of content, of ridicule. He looked up swiftly and savagely. He ran his glance across the contemptuous faces, and finally he rested his eyes upon the girl, Joan. She, at least, was neither angry, nor defiant, nor scornful. She was looking at him with a speaking tenderness of pity, as though she wished to run to him and touch his shoulder and tell him that it was in vain to struggle with such a burden, that the stone could never be budged, and that he was only shaming himself by the attempt.

With this glance upon him, he turned back to the rock. A smile sometimes is more powerful than the lash, and Joan's gentle look worked more upon Stayn than the cheering of the crowds could have done. He felt that swelling of the heart that comes to the very brave. He leaned again, took a new grip, and swayed to his effort.

The rock did not budge, but then it could be seen that the muscles of Stayn had not yet been used to their full power, for he was still increasing the might of his lift little by little. It could be noted, because his body was settling a vital inch or two deeper into the sod, as the pressure ground his narrow-soled boots through the soft garden muck.

Still the rock did not stir, and still this strange fellow found in the depths of his heart new mines of energy to be tapped and their riches brought forth. It was apparent now that he had reached almost the very utmost limit of his powers. His body was beginning to tremble from head to foot, and the strength of his vibration increased every moment.

Something parted—it was the stout flannel shirt that was torn apart down the back by the constant swelling of the muscles of the laborer. He seemed to have increased to twice his size. It was only the consciousness of his tremendous effort, of course, that gave him that seeming. But, as his neck swelled, and as the blood in it turned to a bright crimson and then to a purplish tone, the watchers leaned and gasped and held their breath. Some even dropped upon their knees in order that they might study the face of the strong man and strive to read there the sign of a coming defeat.

They saw a face, transformed and constricted by the strain. The eyes were starting from his head and covered with a film of blindness. Great veins thrust out upon his forehead. His lips were bloated. His teeth ground together. His nostrils spread for air like the nostrils of a racer, dying with its work, and the quickening, harsh gasp of his breathing became the only sound audible in the patio.

"In the name of heaven!" breathed the girl's voice. "Stop it! He's killing himself!"

It was Joan, and it seemed to Stayn that the sound of her voice went through and through him, and unnerved him. Pity for himself seized upon him. He wanted to stop, his muscles slackened, and he murmured: "Don't speak."

The words were an inarticulate mumble; all that could be distinguished was the deep groan of despair that made even the hardest of the men who watched the effort tremble in sympathy, for they could feel the pain of that complaint to the roots of their beings.

"He's done," muttered one. "He's reached the limit!"

"Look!" said another. "The rock's cut his hands! They're dripping blood, both of 'em."

"He's finished."

For the head of Stayn had snapped back, and that is the signal of defeat. He looked straight up into the heavens, though with eyes that saw not. There was nothing above for Stayn, except a trembling void of velvet blackness. He had no feeling in his hands. The pain of the cutting rock was forgotten. He only knew that there was one more effort that he could make, and that effort would either kill him or else lift the stone. Ah, how well he could understand how the giant had been broken in body and heart by the struggle with this brute, insensible mass of rock.

He called upon every resource of his being. It was a strange and foolish thing that a man should risk his life for the sake of budging a stone, but also it was a marvelous and heroic thing. Every person in the patio was trembling with the suspense, for what had seemed impossible at first, now seemed within the verge of the probable, because it was seen that Stayn was killing himself with his effort. A murmur of horror came from the onlookers as a trickle of blood ran down his nostrils.

Then his shoulders rose a little and there was a sound like a very faint, very muffled sighing. He shoulders quivered an inch or two higher. The sound grew more distinct.

"Lawd a'mighty!" shouted a man, his voice sharpened to the height of hysteria: "The Rock of Kiever is moving! Stop him!"

The boulder had, indeed, been stirred from the bed in which it had taken such a deep root. It was stirred, it was raised, and now the final effort of Stayn brought it clean from its place. He staggered two steps with it. Then the rock and the man fell together. But what the giant of the other generation had barely been able to accomplish had been done again now by a far smaller man. The giant had been broken by his labor; but Stayn, though he had dropped in a faint, was sound in bone and muscle. It was only that the last of his strength had run out of him, like water from a cup.

# Chapter Seven
## *"As Consciousness Dawned"*

As for the men of Kiever, they acted as though the blow that had fallen upon them had been even more crushing to the spirit than that which had prostrated Stayn. They stared mutely from one to the other. At length the oldest among them said soberly: "It's happened at last. Now, lads, there's big trouble headed for us and coming fast."

"Stillwater," cried another, "why in the name of heaven did you let him try it?"

"A man of his size?" said Stillwater in disgust. "How could I know that there was enough of the devil in him to make him strong enough to lift that rock? How would any of us have known? You all saw him start. You all had a chance to stop him then. But you thought he'd make a fool of himself, just as I thought. That was why I let him go ahead . . . and that was why *you* stood by and watched. Don't blame me for what's happened."

"How'll the trouble come?" asked one of the women.

"Perhaps not at all," said the quiet voice of Joan. "Who can tell? It was only a guess . . . there was nothing in it, no doubt. How *could* trouble come to us?"

"Go into the house, girl," said her father sternly. "This ain't a thing for womenfolk to talk about!"

She did not hear him. She was too busy working over the fallen body of Stayn. What happened to him after his great effort seemed of no importance to the other men who had watched what he had done. They stood about and continued their conference. But the girl now rose and touched the arms of two of them. She made them raise the limp form of Stayn and carry it into the house, and to the chamber that had been prepared by her mother for the guest. There she hovered over him, found his pulse hurried and feeble, his breath shallow and drawn irregularly, his body growing hot with a fever. What would come of it, she could not tell, but it seemed to her a miracle that this man, mighty as a lion in his appearance and in his powers of body, should have been wrecked by a single effort. Her mother came to her to watch and wonder. She, too, asked the same question and asked it aloud.

"Well," said Joan thoughtfully, "it shows just one thing . . . that his heart is too big even for his big body."

"Why, Joan," said the mother, "what a very queer thing to say."

"Hush!" said Joan.

It was the first time she had ever spoken in this imperious fashion to her mother, and the latter regarded her with surprise and then with a touch of alarm, for she saw Joan leaning over the unconscious ranger with a faint smile on her lips, as though she reveled in this battle to bring him back to his senses. It was more than the mere love of battle, however, that showed in the face of the girl, and the mother, wise in instincts, saw and understood. She parted her lips to speak, and then changed her mind and looked rather wildly about her, as though she hunted for someone to whom she could make an appeal.

There was no one there, of course, and she left the room hastily to find her husband and give him warning of the premonition that had come into her mind. When she reached the patio, however, she found that her husband was in the center of a most serious conference, and she could not draw him away.

The debate had turned, ever since the withdrawal of the body of Stayn, upon what danger could now be threatening the community, as though the lifting of the stone had torn up their domestic security by the roots. It was finally decided that the chief threat could only be from the rangers, one of whose men had been killed in the Kiever Mountains and another recently disgraced. That seemed certain.

"Send for the Tuckers," someone suggested.

So the Tuckers were sent for, and they arrived just as Mrs. Stillwater came back into the patio. They were outlanders to the rest of the assembly. The Tuckers had neither the faces, the eyes, the physical stature, nor the blood of the men of Kiever, for they were short, squat men with wide shoulders and long arms. They looked well enough on horseback, but they seemed almost deformed when they were afoot. They had come among the men of Kiever some ten years ago, being outcasts from some far distant clan. Their reception at first had been dubious enough, but they had lingered among the Kiever Mountains, taking scrupulous care not to infringe upon the rights of the men of Kiever themselves.

Their caution was simply due to the fact that this was their last refuge, and, if they were driven from these bald, rugged mountains, they would soon be hunted down by the hounds of the law on the open plains that surrounded the heights. So they had behaved themselves with the greatest caution until, luckily, they were able to rescue a Kiever boy who had wandered away from home, lost his horse, and was now perishing of thirst.

That rescue gave them a right upon the men of Kiever, and they had used it with such care that, from being admitted as friends and allies, they had eventually become the leaders of the mountaineers. It was under the direction of the Tuckers that the depredations were carried on through the neighboring regions. They were the guides and the leading spirits. They had married Kiever women. They had young families of children, though each of the two was a gray-haired man, for the Tuckers turned gray early in life. They were perhaps forty years old, but they had packed into that compass events enough to have crowded a dozen lives.

Now, when they came among the men of Kiever in the patio of the Stillwater house, they had the bearing of chiefs. The others gave way before them, yet, like good Westerners, they did not at once communicate the immediate news to the Tuckers.

They were bidden good evening; they were asked what was what?

"Nothin' much," said Bill Tucker, the elder of the two, "but we just heard that Stayn cut loose from the rangers and headed on for the Kiever Mountains. There's going to be trouble here, boys, for some of us. Unless," he added sardonically, "a little incident might happen to poor Stayn . . . which I sure hope not."

These kindly hopes caused broad smiles to appear upon the faces of the men of Kiever, at least those of the younger generation, for these were the ones who had grown most into the influence of the Tuckers. The more mature men merely frowned, for violence was not the way of the older generation.

The two brothers were now informed of the strange thing that

193

had just happened in the patio of the Stillwater house, and the huge boulder, one end gray with weathering and the other black with the garden mold, was shown lying on the ground.

They said not a word, but regarded this thing calmly. Then Sam Tucker laid hold of one end of the stone. He managed to tilt it. His brother took the other end. They were strong men, built after the fashion of those who can labor with ease. Their united strength was barely enough to make the boulder quiver. It could hardly have been started from its place. When they had made this trial, they stepped back, wiping their foreheads and looking significantly at each other.

"Who done it?" they asked.

"That ranger who tricked the sergeant and sent him into Kiever this morning," was the answer of Stillwater. "I found him and brought him home with me."

"What manner of looking man was he?" asked Sam Tucker.

"Looked bigger than he was . . . and he was bigger than he looked," was the puzzling answer of Stillwater.

When they asked for an explanation, he said that Danby, at first glance, seemed a giant, but upon comparison it was seen that he was barely above six feet in height, yet when he came into action, he proved a giant, indeed, for there was the boulder that he had ripped from its old bed in the earth. These things the Tuckers considered gravely for a time.

"It sounds pretty queer," they said. "We dunno but one man that could be apt to do such a thing."

"Who's that?" asked Stillwater. "Because there ain't been any man that I've seen or heard tell of that could have done what Danby just now done."

"Well," said Sam Tucker, "I've seen just one that might. Ten years back, I was riding down a trail in the mountains, and I come to a place where the trail pinched out and there wasn't enough room for my pinto to go along unless he plumb leaned into the side of the mountain. Then, around a corner, I met up with a kid riding a mule. I told him *he* ought to back up. He told me that his mule didn't know how to back. We had a talk and a ruction about it. Damned if that kid didn't charge at me and yell out that we'd both take our chances of going over the side. Well, I sent my pinto at the mule and they met head on. They both reared, and the pinto done it so quick that it slid me back over his tail. I missed my footing, stumbled, and slipped over the side.

"It was a plain precipice, mind you. There was only a chunk of brush sticking out from the side twenty feet down. I aimed to get a grip on that, but I was going down so fast when I reached that there place, that the branches of the bush just slipped through my hands and cut them to pieces, and I fell farther down.

"There was a ledge just below the bush. It was about three feet wide, but it shelved off fast. I hit there on the back of my head and shoulders and was knocked plumb out. When I come to, I was up to the top of the cliff again and lying on the trail like the whole thing had been a dream.

"It wasn't no dream, though, because there I was, and there was the kid. I'd say he was about fourteen years old. What he'd done was to climb down that cliff, got hold of me, tie me on to his back with his rope, an' then, damn me, if he didn't climb up that face of rock, sticking his fingers and his toes into cracks that a monkey would have been scared to try to hold on by. There he was, fourteen years old. Maybe he weighed a hundred and thirty pounds, because he was pretty big for his age. I weighed about a hundred and eighty pounds . . . make it ten more for my clothes. Well, he packed near two hundred pounds on his back right up the face of that cliff where it would have scared a fly to walk by itself, let alone carrying somebody else.

"Where did he get that strength? It wasn't his size . . . it wasn't hard muscles, because the muscles of a kid are soft and flabby, compared with a man's. Well, I aim to guess that it's because the strongest men have got their muscles *plus* a lot of nerve strength. When that kid got me to the trail, he wilted like a rag. I had to work over him an hour before he come to. Then he was shaking so he couldn't walk. I had to back my pinto off the ledge. Then I come back, and I had to tie the kid on the mule and lead him off down the trail. I dunno what become of him . . . I dunno even his name, because I had my own reasons for wanting to travel fast that day. But if that kid had growed up to be ten years older, maybe *he* could have tore up the Kiever Rock!"

It was a strange narration, but it was listened to with impatience by the men of Kiever. They had a problem before them; they wanted a solution; they did not care to listen to the long-winded yarns of even a Tucker. They told him, in short, that they were in trouble. Danger, according to the old prophecy, now threatened the town of Kiever. What could be done?

"We'll have to look at the gent who done this thing," said Sam Tucker curtly. "Come along, Bill."

Accordingly, they went to the room where Stayn lay stretched.

"They're going batty because of the talk of that other old blockhead before he kicked out," said Sam to Bill. "We'll have to work up some bunk to feed 'em. We got to add to our reputation out of this."

"That's easy talk, but hard to do," responded Bill. "They're excited . . . they'll be apt to run amuck if we don't watch ourselves. We been losing ground with 'em, Sam."

"I know it . . . because we bumped off that ranger. They don't believe in shooting to kill. Since we shot Toomby, they figure that they don't want us among them so bad. The fools!"

With that comment, they came into the room where Joan was still working feverishly over the big man and had so far succeeded that his eyelids were beginning to quiver and lift, showing the filmed, blind eyes beneath.

Instantly there was a low, excited shout from Sam. He ran to the bed and brushed the girl away from it.

"What's wrong?" asked his brother eagerly.

"By the eternal!" gasped Sam.

"Well?"

"It's him!"

"Who?"

"It's him, I tell you. It's the kid! Ten years can't fool me. That face of his I could pick out of a million. It's got the same pucker between the eyes and the same jaw. It's him! No wonder he lifted the rock! Now look at this!"

Joan had rolled up the sleeves of the dazed man so that she could bathe him with water and fight his fever. Sam Tucker raised one of those limp arms. It was a mass of twisted, corded muscles, like a bundle of sinews.

"It's the kid that carried me up on his back to the trail, just like you heard me saying. I guessed it! There ain't two men in the world, maybe, that could have done both them things."

"I've got *another* guess," said Bill Tucker darkly. "Lemme at him." He leaned over the wakening Stayn. "What's your name, partner?" he asked softly.

"It's Danby," said the girl, who had been fluttering about the bed, anxious to continue her ministrations, and eager to be rid of the two men.

"Shut up!" commanded Bill harshly. "I'm running this little party for a minute." He leaned again above the other. "Your name, partner?"

There was a confused murmur.

"What did he say?" asked Sam Tucker, not quite sure what his brother might have in his mind, but excited by the manifest suspense under which Bill was laboring.

"Nothing yet. Keep back and don't talk. I'll get it out of him . . . just as he comes to." Again he whispered: "I'm your friend, old son. Speak out. Tell me your name? What's your real name, partner?"

The lips of Stayn, still swollen and thick with the blood that had rushed to his head during that immense strain at the rock, now quivered and parted. "Stayn!" he muttered. "My name's Stayn. Who wants to know?"

Drawing a gasping breath, he opened his eyes wide. They were still dazed, but his brain was plainly clearing fast. The answer had brought a snarl from Bill Tucker, but now he caught his brother by the shoulder and hurried him from the room. At the door he paused and shook a finger at the girl.

"Keep your mouth shut, Joan!" he commanded, and dragged Sam with him down the corridor outside and beyond her view.

As for Joan, she swayed where she stood as the meaning of that name gradually came home to her understanding.

# Chapter Eight
## "Joan's Prayer"

In the hall outside, the Tuckers held swift consultation as they walked along.

"Will you hold out for him, now that you know Stayn is the kid who saved you ten years back?" asked Bill.

"Listen," said Sam. "Am I a plain squarehead? Hold out for him? Don't I know that Stayn will get the two of us, if we don't get him? The thing to do is to finish him quick. If the girl hadn't been in the room. . . ."

"Lay off that talk," commanded the other brother. "We got to work through the Kieverites. We got to show them that Stayn is a crook and a man-killer. He came here under a different name, didn't he? That's what we got to work on."

So they came out into the patio and confronted the others. The great tidings came out at once. The man who had lifted the Rock of Kiever was, in reality, that professed enemy of the tribe, Stayn, the ranger. He had come there seeking the slayers of his bunkie, and, under the assumed name of Danby, he was planning to trick the men of Kiever into giving him the information he wanted. It was the boldness of a very brave man, but it was also the boldness of an implacable enemy. They must get rid of him at once.

There could not be long argument about this. There was a deep murmur of indignation from the others, when they learned that he who had accepted their hospitality was the ranger of whom they were now in dread. Stillwater himself was the most violent of all. He wanted action at once, and he even proposed that they give the ranger a one-minute start and then ride forth to hunt him down like a fox.

"He is a very sick man, dear," said Mrs. Stillwater. "Besides, how do you know that he intended to harm us all? He only wished

198

to find out the names of those who had killed his friend. Can you blame him for that?"

At this point, she turned upon the eyes of the Tuckers—eyes which were by no means friendly.

One of the older men said gloomily: "I saw from the first that no good could ever come out of killings. I say it now. We ain't going to have no luck while we work with guns. And the smuggling trip will be ruin to us in the end."

He was not the only person among the clan of Kiever who had the same opinion. In their estimation, it was better to live on scant food and dress in poor clothes, than to take part in the marauding expeditions which had been made the fashion among them by the leadership of the Tucker brothers.

But the consensus of opinion was that Stayn, having come upon them with a bloody purpose—and such they could not doubt was the motive that had brought him to the Kiever Mountains—could not be allowed to depart with his life to threaten them hereafter. It was decided that Sam Tucker and Stillwater himself should go to the big man and apprise him that he was a prisoner.

In the meantime, however, Joan had been busy with her invalid. She had been roused to the depths of her soul by what she had seen and heard this day. She had seen the Rock of Kiever lifted and moved by the hands of a single man, and one who was not a giant. She had seen the lifter stricken down by the very greatness of his effort, and, now, when she had cherished him back to consciousness and felt that marvelous joy of the life-giver, as though the touch of her hands had restored him, she heard him confess with the very utterance of his name that he was a sworn enemy to her people.

He was that Stayn of whom so many wild reports had come, even into the heart of the Kiever Mountains—reports of ferocity, savage energy, terrible malice. Men said that he killed for the pleasure of killing, like a beast of prey. There had been tales of slaughters performed by his naked hands.

So she shrank from the big man on the bed, while he stared back at her, bewildered.

"What is it?" he asked her at length. "What's happened . . . and who are you?"

"Hush," said the girl. "I have to think."

"Ah, yes," said Stayn. "It's Joan. Now I remember. Now I remember."

It was strange that a slayer of men could have the smile of a boy, she thought. Neither was he as old as his reputation, or as the leonine expression of his features might have led her to guess. Now he was crushed by the great effort he had made. His thick arms lay helpless beside him, his great hands were turned palm upward, and his fingers trembled. It seemed to Joan a very terrible thing that there should be lodged in any man strength so awful that the full use of it might destroy him. So, in a step, she went from fear and horror to pity.

"Do you know what you have done?" she said.

"Well, I lifted a rock they said I couldn't lift. What else?"

"You have brought misfortune on the people of Kiever."

"How?"

"There was an old saying . . . that Stillwater who lifted the rock before you was the man who said it."

"Was he as wise as he was strong?" asked Stayn.

It seemed to Joan that she felt his eyes wandering over her face constantly, that only a small part of his attention was given to her words. There was a faint smile on his face which she had seen before when men, exhausted by the labors of a long and weary summer day, felt the rising of the cool night wind against their faces. It embarrassed her. It almost made her forget the stern things that she had to tell him.

"He was very wise," she said in answer. "He laid down the laws that we have lived by . . . until lately." And she frowned.

"What broke his laws?"

"The coming of two strangers," said the girl darkly.

"What two?"

She shrugged her shoulders, still gloomy with thought, for she had heard her father say that the Tuckers would ruin them sooner or later. She could not help breaking out now. "Dad says that we'll go down some day, because we've kept the Tuckers with us."

He turned his eyes up, considering that name as though it were dimly familiar to him.

"But the thing that the first Stillwater said about the rock was . . . so long as it lay in the place where he left it, the luck of the Kievers would be good . . . but that, when it was moved by the strength of a single man, we would fall into misfortune."

There was the mystery laid bare. He could well understand now, the mingling of rage and scorn with real fear as the people of Kiever stood about and watched him. He could understand why there had been a dread like the dread of death in their faces as they watched him tugging mightily at the rock.

"If I'd known," he said, "I never would have touched it. Will you believe that?"

She did not answer.

"Besides," he said, "there's nothing in such talk. How could there be?"

She had gone from the bed as though to control an emotion that was too strong for her, and, glancing out the window, she saw the men of her tribe gathered in close consultation. It startled and alarmed her. When they spoke, they gestured toward the window of her room, so that it was plain they talked of the big man who was now under her care. She saw Sam Tucker grasp the butt of his revolver as he made some declaration. So she whirled toward the bed again.

"You've given them your name," she said. "And now there's danger hanging over you."

"What name?"

"Stayn!"

At that, he lifted himself upon his weak, shaking arms. "They know that name?"

"The Tuckers got it from you while you were coming back to your senses . . . ."

"Then it means . . . !"

He finished that exclamation by attempting to leap from the bed, but his overstrained muscles refused to respond. He had less than a child's strength remaining, and he had the bulk of a heavy man to lift. He managed to throw himself from the bed, but then his knees buckled under his weight, and he dropped to the floor with a groan at his weakness.

The girl uttered a faint cry of pity. She had seen him so lately doing what scarcely any two other men could have done. Now he was like one benumbed. He strove to push himself up, but, if his arms were weak, his legs seemed quite unstrung. He must flee, for in another moment they would be coming to take him. He must flee. But how could he manage it? No doubt in a few hours the strain would pass from his limbs, and he would be almost himself again. But, in the meantime, they would have overtaken him and struck him down.

He must be helped on the first steps of his journey to safety, since he could not take them by himself. She slipped her arm about him, taking all the weight that she could endure upon her shoulder, and so she helped him. He came to his feet with a staggering lurch that nearly cast them both down. Then he stood wavering, moaning with rage and despair.

"It's no use," said the giant. "I can't manage. I couldn't even saddle a hoss."

"Are you going to give up?" she demanded fiercely.

She caught him by the arm and shook him as a teacher might have shaken a child. Then she said through her teeth: "Lean on me. Trust me. I'll help you through. Merciful heaven, give me strength to save him."

# Chapter Nine
## "Among the Hills"

Once when she was a little child, kneeling over a tangle of dead grass in the fall of the year, watching the stir of small life as only a child will watch it, she had seen an ant carrying off to the common storerooms, no doubt, the carcass of a bumblebee. It was only a small ant, and the bee was a monster of its kind, with hair on its body, stiff bristles, that dug into the ground like so many shares of a plow and checked the poor ant at every step or so of that laborious progress.

That was not all, for the body wedged against stalks of grass here and there. Sometimes the ant would bend them aside enough to squeeze through with her precious quarry. Sometimes she had to drag the monster down a twisting avenue, made rough and wild with the projected roots of grass, until she could find a new and open road through the mass of standing straw. But still she toiled ahead, pausing only to consider a problem, but never to doubt or to give up her labors.

As Joan led the big man out of the house, she was reminded of that ant, for, though Stayn struggled desperately to bear his own weight, his legs were nerveless. They shook and failed beneath him, and she heard him gasp and draw in breaths that were almost sobs. She dared not look at his face. All the while, her arm was still around him, and one of his huge arms lay lax and limp across her shoulders.

Once he stumbled over a small hillock, and his weight dragged them both down. It was heart-breaking labor to get him to his feet, but, when that was managed, he had not gone ten steps with her before he collapsed for no reason whatever, except that the nerves of his legs refused to obey him. Flexed as they had been in the lifting of the great rock, that immense strain had crushed all sensibil-

203

ity out of them. He was brought to an erect posture with even greater labor this time, but, thereafter, he seemed to manage better. The agony of shame at having to lean upon the meager strength of the girl affected him. It sent a thrill of false life through his body. He was almost bearing his own weight when he came to the barn.

There she made him sit on the barley bin at one end of the line of stalls. She herself ran into the corral, and with wondering eyes he watched her rope snare in quick succession two big horses—both grays and very apparently blood brothers. She led these animals into the barn. Then she took down his heavy saddle and swung it with an effort upon the back of the better of the two horses. She took a second saddle and placed it upon the other.

"What is it?" asked Stayn. "If I need two horses in a long hunt, do you think that I can become a horse thief and take your father's stock?"

"Your own horse is tired," she told him calmly, shifting the lantern to another wooden peg against the wall. "Besides, it isn't good enough to stand up against the Kiever horses . . . they're the best suited for these mountains. They'll save you."

"But why two saddles?"

"Do you think I could let you ride alone?"

"Child, child!" cried Stayn. "You ain't figuring on coming along with me?"

"Yes."

"In this night?"

"Is there any difference between night and day?"

"Joan, when God had finished everything else and got His hand all practiced, He made the best thing last . . . and that was a good woman."

She did not even hear him. She was too busy cinching up the saddles, and scolding the larger of the two horses, which was intended for the use of Stayn, for the big animal kept puffing out its stomach, until at last she dug her knee into its ribs and drew the cinch home, and that painful pressure made the brute submit.

Now all was ready, and none too soon. They heard a muffled shouting from the house. Then, through one of the barn windows, Stayn saw lanterns swinging back and forth across the garden.

"Quick!" said the girl, continuing in command of the situation. "Get on your knees on the barley box."

The gray horse danced sidewise from the big man, but finally she managed to persuade him to stand nearer, and Stayn fell rather than climbed into the saddle. He took the reins, but they were almost dropped by his quivering fingertips. The girl, however, had whipped into her own saddle like a flash, and she rode out of the barn in the lead.

"Don't worry," she whispered back to Stayn. "Let Tom come on. He'll stay just beside my Jerry, here. Can you manage to keep your balance in the saddle?"

"I'll manage some way."

Voices began to trail toward them. One man with a lantern ran out to the barn, and the light as he swung his lantern flashed upon them. He raised his shout at once. It was answered by a score of throats.

"They're coming!" groaned Stayn. "And if we gallop the horses, I can never keep my seat."

"There's no need to gallop yet," she said, fighting for hope. "You may be more yourself when the need comes."

They had reached the edge of the mesa. Now they wound along the easy trail at its side into the plain below. Stayn could never have sat the saddle even at the mild dog-trot at which they were journeying, only that the girl swung in close beside him. Her hand was beneath his armpit. Her shoulder was against his ribs, supporting him as she swayed far out in her saddle. She even abandoned her own reins and, managing her own horse with her voice and the sway of her body only, she took the reins of big Tom and guided him down to the level going, with Stayn lurching heavily in the saddle.

After that, she turned sharply to the left, and they jogged on, hugging the foot of the mesa. Speed could not save them until Stayn could sit his saddle and manage his own horse. But the grip in his knees was coming back to him little by little, and his hands on the pommel of the saddle were taking a firmer hold as those wrecked nerves in his great body began to respond to the demands he put upon them.

They had not covered a hundred yards when half a dozen horsemen shot down the winding road and plunged straight ahead into the darkness, yelling as they went. They had not dreamed but that the fugitives would go straight on to put a greater and greater distance between them and the town of Kiever.

**205**

But other hunting parties were following.

"We have to gallop," said the girl to Stayn. "Can you manage it?"

"Yes," he said, certain that he would topple at the first long stride.

"Put your weight back in the saddle," she said, talking as if he were a child. "Sit as though you were in a chair. Tom has an easy gait. I trained him myself. Steady, Tom! Get up, boy!"

At her soft call, the good horse swung away in a lope that was, indeed, as gentle as the sway of a rocking chair, and Stayn found that he could still hold his place, though reeling perilously now and again.

They kept on, and with every moment he felt his control over himself returning. Still, it was a strange and terrible feeling to be robbed of all of his power. The slender girl was stronger, for the nonce. She could have hurled him from his seat and left him crushed by his own weight on the ground.

A group of fierce riders swarmed into the mouth of a cañon. Straight on in their rear the girl pursued her course. When Stayn protested, she explained briefly that, wherever else the men of Kiever might search, they would never look to their rear to find their quarry. For three miles she held up that narrow valley. Then she turned aside among the hills.

As they labored up the slopes, they saw three armed men flee across the skyline above them, riding along the crest of the hills, but these, like all the others, urged hotly forward. The men from Kiever had outdone themselves in their eagerness, and, as a result, they swept out in a widening semicircle, the rim of which must grow thinner and thinner.

On the crest of the hills, when the fugitives halted the horses to give them breath after their climb, Stayn said to the girl: "I'm back to my old self. I can manage this trick without any more help. Now go back to Kiever to your father. Tell him that I'll send in the money for his horse, or else send back the horse itself. He has my own nag in the meantime. Tell him, too, that I didn't plan anything against him, not even if he had had a hand in killing Toomby. But I knew that he didn't . . . he ain't the kind to shoot a man in the back, and I had to find out who had done that dirty work. Tell him that. As for you, Joan . . ."

She cut him short, saying—"Hush."—in a most peremptory

fashion, and then she took his hand, not in friendship, but much as a doctor might have done to discover the rate and the strength of the pulse, saving that she held his fingers only. He fought hard to keep his control, but, in spite of himself, his fingers quivered. Then she dropped his hand, and it struck heavily, lifelessly, against his thigh.

"Nonsense," said Joan. "I'll see you through this. Besides, the worst of it is not over. This is only the night. When the day comes, they'll have a thousand times better chance of seeing us."

"I'll not go a step farther with you, Joan," said Stayn desperately. "Heaven knows I've done many wrong things in my life, but I've never yet compromised a woman. . . ."

For reply, she reached forward, drew the reins from his nerveless hand, and then rode on, leading his horse beside her own, while big Charlie Stayn groaned, but admitted his helplessness.

# Chapter Ten
## "The Rear Attack"

He could not argue against her after that. When he pleaded with her to go back, she simply shook her head, and so they worked on until the gray of the dawn came. They stopped then, simply because the tired horses were beginning to stumble over the rough going, and every stumble threatened to throw Stayn from his seat.

Joan built a small fire. The small pack behind her saddle furnished a tin and some tea. She brewed him a strong cup and, as he lay in the sands with his back and shoulders resting against a slanting rock, she helped him to drink it, for his shaking hands could not manage it. She had to feed him as a helpless infant is fed, but she went about it very gravely, sitting cross-legged beside him. She would test the heat of the tea by touching the cup against her lip, and then she tilted it at his mouth so that he could drink. Stayn, groaning with the shame of his weakness, wondered at something in her that made her seem very old—as old, compared to him, as the hills themselves were, compared with the young sagebrush that grew upon them.

It was most of all marvelous to him that, seeing him reduced to such an empty shell of manhood, she did not smile. Neither was there anything foolishly tender, but she went about her work with a sort of scientific precision, as though she were a nurse and hired for such tasks.

A nervous sweat started out on Stayn's face. She took out a handkerchief and wiped the moisture away. She gave him half of a thick slab of hardtack and another cup of tea.

When that odd meal had ended, his strength was so far returned to him, that he was able to climb to his feet without her assistance. That achievement gave him such a false hope that he cried out to her that their worries were ended.

"It's coming back to me!" shouted Stayn, and waved his hat like a happy boy.

The hand he put in the pommel of the saddle was firm and strong. He lifted his foot to the stirrup, but at that moment the big gray sidled away. Stayn blundered after it, hopping on one foot, stumbled, and collapsed upon the ground. All that his false strength availed him now was to enable him to push himself back into a sitting posture.

"I was a fool," he confessed to the girl. "But this is the end. I'll never be myself again. Leave me here, Joan. It's no use. I'd rather let them finish me today than go on half living. Something went out of me when I lifted that rock, something that will never come back."

She did not even bother to reply until, with the help of all her strength, he was brought to a standing posture once more. Then she said, as he leaned against big Tom, his head bowed and the horse sniffing curiously at him: "I've heard of what Charlie Stayn has been, but, if I hadn't heard, I *would* leave you here. For the sake of shame, will you make no effort?"

Shame, indeed, sent the hot blood into his face. He drew in a breath. Then he answered: "I *am* shamed, Joan. But what's happened to me? I'm like a wet rag. My own weight's too much for me."

"You've done by yourself what three men could hardly have done," she answered. "But one day of rest would bring you back to your old self. Now there's nothing left to you but courage. Is that going to fail you, too?"

It was a new thought for Stayn, and he turned it soberly in his mind while he addressed himself to the labor of regaining the saddle. When he sat in it again, and watched the girl whip easily into her own saddle, he had reached a conclusion.

Half of that dashing, reckless bravery for which he had always been distinguished must have grown out of the sheer power of his body which made him confident that, in any danger, he needed no weapon, save his hands, if he could get at an enemy with them. But now that this reliance was stolen from him, what could he do? How would he respond to a crisis? Already it had taken the sting of a taunt from a girl's tongue to bring him to himself. What further shame awaited him? So, shaken in spirit, as he was weak in body, he allowed his horse to trail along behind Joan on her mount. He hardly cared now, he told himself, how this adventure ended. Then a spirit of fatalism awakened in him. His luck had died when his bunkie died, and the bullets that had killed poor Joe Toomby had prepared the way for the slaughter of Stayn.

It seemed as though she had read his mind, for suddenly she halted her horse and called to him: "Look! Look! Isn't that a world worth living in?"

He stared gloomily about him. The sun was not yet up, but it had flooded the east with rose and drawn a wide band of color around the horizon. The cañons were thick with blue mist; their heads were crowned with pale fire; a cool wind blew out of the sunrise into their faces. Indeed, it was a world worth living in, and all the more worthwhile because he knew that here and there among those naked mountains the men of Kiever were hunting for him. He turned to the girl with a faint smile.

"I've been acting like a child," he said. "But from now on, you'll see that I'm different."

Not until then did he know that a weight had been resting upon her, but now, as her brow cleared and her smile answered him, he understood.

In the mid-morning they rested their horses again and ate the remainder of the hardtack that was in her pack. By this time, the strength of Stayn had returned a little into his body. The deadly tremor was passing from him, and, above all, that unstrung, unnerved feeling that had been eating away his heart was growing less. Still he was only a fraction of that man who had been the most formidable unit in that company of Texas Rangers. As the girl had said, he had poured forth from himself the last atom of his strength. Perhaps, indeed, he would never again have all the power that had once been his, just as one nerve-wrecking, heart-breaking race will sometimes take the edge from the speed of the Thoroughbred. He realized that. He must find something in life better than a long series of battles with other men. Perhaps the answer was riding here beside him. He looked on Joan as he had never before looked upon a woman. There was no answer in her face. If it was lighted, it was with the beauty of the mountains. All she had given to him had been, perhaps, through the sheerest charity, and what she had done seemed to him so big that all his life, contrasted with it, was nothing.

They mounted and rode on again. It was nearly noon before they received any intimation that danger was still thick around them. They had descended from the highlands since the prime of the morning, and now they were riding along one of those narrow valleys which split the Kiever Mountains across and across as a chopping block is furrowed by the edge of the axe.

It was Stayn who saw the danger first—the wink of the sun on steel in the midst of a grove of stunted trees a few hundred yards away. He swerved his mount to the side and into the mouth of a cañon that fed into the bottom of the main valley, down which they had been holding their course. As they passed behind the edge of the rock wall, Stayn, looking back, saw two horsemen trot into view.

The girl was as white with fear as though it were her life that was endangered.

"Do you think they saw us?" she breathed to her companion.

"I don't know," he said through his teeth. "But we must ride hard."

He set the example and loosened his rein, the tired horse responding instantly with a strong gallop that roused the echoes and sent them pealing back from the faces of the cliffs on either hand. They turned an elbow corner of the valley, and there they saw that they were surely trapped, for, a little distance away, the cañon ended in an abrupt wall. There was no exit that way. It was a blind pass into which they had journeyed.

There was not even more than one shelter from the eyes of the hunters, and that was an immense boulder that stood in the very center of the valley, ample enough to shelter them both from view. For that they rode, and took their places behind it. Through a crevice in the ragged top, they could look through and command a view of the elbow turn around which they had just come. But would the hunters appear?

They waited, it seemed, endless minutes; perhaps excitement multiplied the interval. But just as the girl whispered—"They've not seen us. They've gone by."—a horseman swung into view and another came up beside him.

Of all the men of the Kiever Mountains, fate could not have sent two shrewder or hardier enemies, for here had come Sam and Bill Tucker in person, hunting together on the trail which equally concerned them both.

211

They reined in their horses at the turn, as though they were by no means certain of their quarry. Perhaps they had seen only a glint of something that seemed to be disappearing into the mouth of the cañon, but now the view of the blocking wall, the empty valley, and the silence assured them that there was nothing here. They were reining their horses about again, when one of their mounts, tossing its head as though protesting against this change of direction, whinnied sharply.

"Catch the nose of Jerry," whispered Stayn to the girl, and, stooping over the neck of Tom, he slid his hand over the trembling nostrils of that good horse just in time to shut off a reply to the neigh. But Jerry, as the girl reached in imitation of her companion, tossed his head to the side, and in an instant his answering challenge rang as piercingly as a trumpet down the pass.

The moan of the girl's despair was like the prophecy of death to Stayn. He saw, through the crevice, the two brothers wheeling about again. Then, with yells of exultation, they charged straight down at the rock.

Oh, to have had them charge even in this same mad fashion in the old days, when his strength was upon him! But now, as he drew the rifle forth from its case, his hands trembled so that it nearly slipped down into the sands. He laid it in the crevice. He took no time to aim, for with those shaking hands he knew that he could never hit a mark. He must only hope that the threat would be enough to turn the charge. He pulled the trigger, and the rifle clanged.

The ball flew wide, as he knew it would, but perhaps the advancing riders heard the distant singing of the bullet and thought it nearer than the fact. At any rate, they brought their horses to sliding halts with shrill yells of anger and wheeled quickly away, one to either side like wild Indians.

They rode until they were a good distance away. Then they joined one another for a brief consultation. But almost at once they decided what must be done. Sam Tucker remained with both the horses, finding shelter from any rifle shots which might fly that way by dropping behind a convenient rock. In that place, he effectually blocked the exit from the cañon, and his brother, if he chose, could ride back to find more of the men of Kiever, and so crush the fugitive with mere numbers.

But such lingering measures were not to the taste of these men of determined action. Bill Tucker was presently seen climbing up the steep wall of the valley with his rifle slung across his shoulders, and now it was plain what the plan of campaign was to be. He would simply gain the top of the cliff, circle around it until he was commanding the rear of the rock, and from that position shoot down Stayn or else drive him forth from the shelter, when he would become an easy prey to the other brother who waited in the throat of the cañon. Only one thing might check him, and that was a long-distance rifle shot to drop him from the side of the cliff.

Stayn picked up his rifle again and fired. The shot went wild, and Tucker, half wheeling about, was seen to wave his hand defiantly. However evil the man might be, he had courage in plenty for his portion. Again Stayn strove to draw his bead, but though his practiced eye instantly caught his target in the center of the circular sight, yet the tremor of his hands and body kept the target jumping in and out of the deadly circle. He could only pull the trigger and trust to chance. So he fired again, and again the climber waved defiance. Stayn turned with a groan and let the rifle drop from his hands. Even his marksman's skill had deserted him.

As he turned, he saw Joan, white of face but with a firmly set jaw, leveling her own rifle through the crevice and drawing her bead with a steady hand that would not fail. He caught the barrel of the gun and drew it back. She struggled furiously.

"Let me have it!" she pleaded. "Don't you see that it's your last chance?"

Only a shred of his old strength remained to him, but that shred was now to make him master of the weapon. She could not budge it from his grip.

"Do you think that I could let you do such a thing on my account?" he asked her firmly.

"Oh, don't you see?" she answered. "If there ever was a cruel man and a bad man in the world, it is he!"

"Still," said Stayn, "he's a man. . . . and, besides, it's too late now."

Tucker had gained the top of the cliff at that moment. He waved his hand again and began to advance along the edge. Stayn gazed curiously up to him. In another minute the fellow would be at an angle that would command the rear of the rock, and, when that

213

time came, Stayn knew he must ride forth and face Sam Tucker at the cañon's turning. Certainly he could not wait there and let the brother open fire with bullets which might strike down the girl.

As he sat the saddle, watching the fatal progress of Tucker to the commanding position, he found one great cause for rejoicing. His body had ceased to tremble. The ecstasy of that danger had turned him to steel. Neither was there the slightest faltering in soul. He was about to die, and a deep thankfulness welled up in him that he was about to die as a brave man should, without flinching. He wished for only one thing, and that was some right word to speak to the girl. For her courage had deserted her at last, and, clinging suddenly to him, she burst into tears.

# Chapter Eleven
## "Naseby's Justice"

Captain John Naseby, as has been seen, was a man who acted upon the spur of the moment, but he was by no means incapable of second thought. On the spur of the moment, he had sent the sergeant and his three followers upon the trail of the recalcitrant private, Charlie Stayn. On second thought, he wished that he had ridden upon that dangerous duty himself. He had no sooner made up his mind on that point than he determined to sally forth at once. Therefore, he had an interview with his lieutenant, gave him necessary instructions concerning several matters, reports on which were due to come in at any time now, and then, selecting two old and tried campaigners, rode forth upon his best horse.

He had taken only two men with him. It was not that he underestimated the work that lay before them. He knew that he was riding into hostile territory, when he invaded the precincts of the Kiever Mountains. He knew, above all, that when Charlie Stayn was cornered, he would fight in a manner above the capacity of any two normal men. But the captain felt that much had to be sacrificed to speed. He had chosen the three best horses in the entire outfit, horses with fine, racy lines that bespoke the generous mixture of Thoroughbred upon the mustang base, which gave them endurance and meanness at the same time.

The two men he took with him were only privates, but they had served for ten years apiece. They were by no means brilliant fighters, but they were steady as rocks. They were not dazzling marksmen at a target, but they could shoot at a man with nerves as steady as those of any college rifleman intent on winning his letter. These were qualities which, after much experience, the captain was inclined to prize among the ardors of a manhunt far above the flashiness of the professional killer.

On the whole he was well satisfied with his outfit as the party jogged out of the camp, not in haste, but conscious that the race is no more to the fleet of foot than it is to the hasty in judgment, when one has to do with sundry scores of miles of desert traveling.

He plodded on and on, until he reached the Kiever Mountains. There his little party camped for that night—without a fire. Not that anyone, in that particular section of the sun-blasted mountains, was likely to be out spying upon them or stealing close to make inquiries about that fire, but the captain was not a man to take chances. He camped, then, without a fire, but, nevertheless, he did not avoid the precaution of maintaining a watch also. He let one of his men take the first watch. He himself sat up through that bitter, sleepy time in the middle of the night when the brain grows numb with weariness and the minutes turn into dreary hours. His second follower kept the final watch and lighted a small fire in the light of the dawn.

Over this flame they cooked their coffee. After that, they climbed into the saddle and rode for four hours without exchanging a word with one another. The captain himself was an Indian on the trail. He loved it and its work with the most passionate devotion. He could read its strange characters as other men read and enjoy a book. He could tell the age of the print of a horse's hoof, and the direction toward which the circling of the buzzard pointed before he had watched its first round completed; he could tell a thousand little features that the eye of the average man could not follow. Accordingly, he liked silence and a chance to use his eyes when he was on the trail. His two followers were of the same ilk.

It was well toward the heel of the morning when Jim Renney, riding in the lead, lifted his hand above his shoulder, the signal for a halt. Instantly three pairs of field glasses were focused down the trail. Then they received an order from the captain that sent them whirling behind a number of great rocks. From this shelter, each man standing at the head of his horse to prevent it from neighing, the captain himself, as lookout, beheld two squat-bodied, savage-faced riders go by, hastening onward with eyes so intent upon some forward trail that they paid no attention to the few and scattering signs that the rangers had left upon the hard rocks over which they had been riding for the last half mile.

The eye of the captain brightened and sharpened, as the eye of a miser might have done, had he seen two loads of unguarded treasure drift by him. He waited until they were well past. Then he brought his two followers together.

"Men," he said, "did you see the pair that went by? Did you recognize 'em?"

They had not, so he went on: "From this minute, we have a new trail. Stayn never existed, so far as we are concerned, from this instant. Afterward, we'll take him up where we've left off. But the two you've just seen are a brace of the hardest man-killers that ever saddled a horse in the West. Those are the Tucker brothers. They disappeared ten years ago. We've heard rumors that they were among the Kieverites, but we hardly believed it, because the men of Kiever don't take in strangers. Now I've seen with my own eyes, and I know that the rumor is true, and I know, lads, that if we get the pair of them, we'll collect enough in rewards to give us a happy holiday."

So they started on the new trail. The captain went first. Just far enough behind to keep him in sight came his two men. They followed on until, at noon, or thereabouts, the captain held up a hand, and they came hastily up with him.

"This way," he said, pointing to a cañon mouth. "They've gone in here, and, unless I've forgotten the Kiever Mountains, this is a blind pass. Leave your horses here. We'll finish this on foot. A man's rifle is steadier when his feet are on the ground."

They advanced with the greatest caution, their rifles ready, stealing along in single file close to the right-hand wall of the valley, and so they heard the crackling of the rifles. It stopped them for a consultation. At first, they thought that the two brothers might have retired to this place to settle some old dispute, but the captain doubted that. Not that they were too tender-hearted to murder each other, but each knew his need of the other. Accordingly, the rangers started on again, and reaching the elbow-turn of the cañon, they came in view of the strange picture.

Just before them, crouched behind a low-lying boulder with his rifle resting on the top of it, was one Tucker. The other was hastily circling the top of the cliff. The captain saw the stratagem at once.

"They've rounded up someone behind that rock," he said. "Now they're ready to cut him down from the front or the rear. There's Bill ready for action. . . ."

The man on the cliff had paused and raised his rifle. At the same moment, a rider on a great gray horse broke from behind the rock in the center of the cañon and came toward the turn.

"Stayn!" cried the captain.

At his voice, Sam Tucker turned from his shelter, with an oath. He hesitated only an instant, then the sight of that hated uniform of the rangers determined him. He swung his rifle toward them, pitched it to his shoulder, and curled his finger around the trigger. But the shot was never fired. A bullet from the captain's gun crashed through his brain, and Sam Tucker quivered and lay still. His brother on the heights made up his mind instantly, turned, and disappeared from view.

It left the captain with only Stayn himself to confront, and the problem of facing him seemed simple enough. For he reeled in the saddle as he rode, his hands clutched the pommel, and the horse galloped wildly, with a free rein. That was not all the wonder. A girl now darted out from behind the rock on a second gray horse and sped after Stayn, shouting in a shrill voice to him.

"By all the powers . . . ," began the captain. "A woman . . . and Stayn!"

They saw the girl overtake the ex-ranger. They saw her point to the rangers at the mouth of the pass, but Stayn shook his head and held doggedly straight ahead. His horse proceeded at a soft dog-trot. The girl followed close, eyeing the rangers with terror.

"Shall I take him?" asked one of the men of his captain. "He's wounded."

"Stand fast," said John Naseby. "Unless I'm a fool, without eyes, that's a new Stayn we're looking at. There's less lion in him, and more man. Don't touch your gun, if you hope to have a good word from me!"

So Stayn came up to his old commander, and raised his hand in a clumsy salute. It was then that Naseby so astonished his men that they gaped upon him, for he turned his back upon the fugitive ranger and deliberately took out the makings of a cigarette. Moreover, he calmly rolled it, while Stayn jogged by with a stunned look in his eye, and the girl scurried past at his side, watching the rangers as though they were a dreadful pestilence.

"In the name of heaven, Captain!" cried Jim Renney. "You ain't going to let him get out scot-free?"

"Man, man!" exclaimed the captain impatiently. "Remember

that poor Stayn lost his bunkie only the other day. Now will you have his future wife lose Stayn?"

So Stayn was never taken. The captain himself secured his honorable discharge from the rangers. The captain himself stood up at the wedding of Stayn, and the name of the first child of that union was John Naseby Stayn.

As for Kiever, the ill-fortune which had been prophesied by the first Stillwater did not fall for two long years, but at the end of that time the spring went suddenly dry and never again gave up its flow of water. There was not a man among those of Kiever who did not swear that the calamity was caused by the moving of the Rock of Kiever by the strength of a single pair of hands.

**Max Brand**® is the best known pen name of Frederick Faust, creator of Dr Kildare™, Destry, and many other fictional characters popular with readers and viewers worldwide. Faust wrote for a variety of audiences in many genres. His enormous output totalling approximately thirty million words or the equivalent of 530 ordinary books, covered nearly every field: crime, fantasy, historical romance, espionage, Westerns, science fiction, adventure, animal stories, love, war, and fashionable society, big business and big medicine. Eighty motion pictures have been based on his work along with many radio and television programs. For good measure he also published four volumes of poetry. Perhaps no other author has reached more people in more different ways.

Born in Seattle in 1892, orphaned early, Faust grew up in the rural San Joaquin Valley of California. At Berkeley he became a student rebel and one-man literary movement, contributing prodigiously to all campus publications. Denied a degree because of unconventional conduct, he embarked on a series of adventures culminating in New York City where, after a period of near starvation, he received simultaneous recognition as a serious poet and successful popular-prose writer. Later, he traveled widely, making his home in New York, then in Florence, and finally in Los Angeles.

Once the United States entered the Second World War, Faust abandoned his lucrative writing career and his work as a screenwriter to serve as a war correspondent with the infantry in Italy, despite his fifty-one years and a bad heart. He was killed during a night attack on a hilltop village held by the German army. New books based on magazine serials or unpublished manuscripts continue to appear. Alive and dead he has averaged a new one every four months for seventy-five years. In the U.S. alone nine publishers issue his work, plus many more in foreign countries. Yet, only recently have the full dimensions of this extraordinarily versatile and prolific writer come to be recognized and his stature as a protean literary figure in the 20th Century acknowledged. His popularity continues to grow throughout the world.